HEPH

L.B. Dunbar writing as

elda lore

HADES
elda lore
L.B. Dunbar writing as

This is a work of fiction. Names, characters, businesses, places, events and incidents are either the products of the author's imagination or used in a fictitious manner. Any resemblance to actual persons, living or dead, or actual events is purely coincidental.

Cover Design – Amy Queau, QDesigns
Edit – Kiezha Ferrell, Librum Artis Editorial Services

OTHER WORK BY elda lore

Modern Descendants
Hades (#1)
Solis (#2)
Heph (#3)
Triton (#4) – coming Fall 2017

Heph

HEPH

"What the hell?"

The first arrow whizzed past the windshield at enough speed I questioned the object. I dismissed it for a low hanging twig. The second one was unmistakably recognizable. The long shaft with a narrow head hit the driver side window and was repelled. A flimsy piece of wood was no match for my 2016 Camaro, but when I heard the *thud-thud-thud* of a flattening tire, I reconsidered that thought.

It was hard enough to find the entrance to Hestia's property: Turn right at the large boulder, head south three miles. Search for the gravel road. At the curved tree, enter a barely visible, two-tire path leading into the thick forest. The evening light of the northwest made it harder to see under thick foliage. A puncture to the tire would result in finding the rest of the drive in total darkness.

A puncture, that's what had to have caused the flat.

I stopped the car and exited to find a thin shaft sticking out of my front tire. A tender tug with my thick hands and the stick came clean, but the damage was done.

"Kids," I cursed, believing wayward children were using the forest as their playground. A sharp poke to my back made me think otherwise.

"Turn around. Slowly." The voice was distinctly female, feminine and sweet, but sharp like the point of the arrowhead and quivering like the release from a bow. Whoever she was, she wanted to sound tough. Turning as she directed, I came chest-to-face with a diminutive woman. Her head hardly reached my shoulders, her frame almost as slim as the arrow pointed at my lower region.

"Don't move."

Considering where she had her weapon aimed, I didn't plan to cross her, although the differences in our stature were almost comical. I stood over six-four and twice her width, maybe three times. A large man by nature, my only curse was a limp from a metal leg hidden under my jeans and an ugly, scarred face. Yet, even though she had a weapon trained on me, I had an inexplicable desire to draw her close to me, soothe the wounds I suspected, and protect her.

My hands lifted slowly in surrender. Under a cap that covered her hair and with a scarf over her mouth, the next thing to pierce me were eyes the cobalt of rare sea glass. Smoky blue, but brilliant, they roamed the expanse of my body. My breath caught in my chest, and I choked on the very air I needed to breathe. Her eyes opened wider as she stared back at me, and a moment passed where I felt as if she recognized me. My heart thumped in my chest, like an eager pet welcoming home its master. In those thirty seconds, I sensed a familiarity with her, and a thrill rippled through me. But her eyes squinted, and the recognition passed.

"oh rrrr ew?" she muttered through the scarf. Still frozen in the awkward position of her arrow at my zipper and my hands in the air, I didn't fully understand her, but her attention exhilarated me. Instantly, I was turned on, harder than I should be with a weapon aimed at a vital part of me. My hand lowered, thinking only to remove the scarf from her cheeks, but she flinched sharply to her right, and it gave me the entrance I needed. *Snap* went the arrow aimed at my dick. I grinned slowly, holding up the two halves, sliced by my finger like a broken pencil, she blinked at me. My heart fell to my feet like Icarus falling from the sky. A thud reverberated inside me, and I was certain it was audible in the silence of the woods. She inhaled sharply. Had I frightened her? Her ocean blue eyes widened.

"I didn't mean to frighten you," I offered. Instantly, she straightened. Eyes narrowing, she took a large step back. I wanted to smile. She was so much tinier than me, but her attitude stood taller than the trees surrounding us. Using the bow as her next weapon, she leveled the tip to my chest, but her eyes were the armament that captured me, captivating me with secrets hidden deep within their smoky visage. Did she feel the warm vibe between us heating to a frenzied inferno? My body vibrated with need and I took a cautious step toward her.

"Stay back," she snapped, abruptly removing the pale, lavender-colored cloth covering her mouth and revealing lips in a deep, magenta-purple, accentuating her eyes. The tip of a pink tongue swiped over them, enhancing the sheen. My mouth watered, thirsty for a sample of such a rich color, doubtful that one drink would satisfy me. My curiosity piqued at the juicy plum flavor I imagined, yet I set aside thoughts of seduction with a need to reassure her she was safe with me.

"Look," I spoke, my gruff voice rippling around us in the enclosure of tightly packed trees. "You do realize you're the one who shot my car, so don't suddenly look afraid of me."

"I'm not frightened." Her spine snapped straight. Her bravado impressed me. Hell, even the harsh sound of her voice excited me. *Stop it, Heph*, I cursed myself. *I could not be interested*, I argued, not after the number of times I'd been recently burned by women. I was here to forget the temptation of the fairer sex, not forge my way through another one. *Oh, the irony, given where I was headed.*

"Look, maybe you can tell me why you shot my car or why you are traipsing around these woods?"

"You're trespassing. Go back from where you came." My eyes narrowed. Frustration built as I turned my head left and right, sensing the impending darkness, knowing where the narrow path ahead could lead. It was an isolated locale. No other inhabitants lived near Hestia's Home, my destination, and that was its purpose: to be hidden and harbor those it housed. After all that had happened to me, I needed the seclusion it offered to regroup and reevaluate my life. Knowing who owned these grounds, her claim startled me.

"Do you know Hestia?" It was the only explanation for her accusation.

"Do you?" she snarked, with bow still trained at my chest, as if she could hurt me.

"I do." I had to smile a little, and folded my arms, accentuating my size. She reminded me of my sister, Veva. Feisty and terse, Veva could sting like a bee but also could soothe like honey.

"How?" The non-threatening weaponry at my chest trembled at the recognition that we shared Hestia in common.

"How do you?" I replied, not letting this little mouse have the upper hand. Her eyes pinched again, the expression telling me—no, *warning me*—it was none of my business. Her name, her history, and her friendship were not for me, but the need to protect her filled me again. I knew why women came to Hestia's Home and her silence told me many things. Taking another quick scan of our surroundings, I realized the darkness grew deeper under our covering. I wouldn't be able to see to fix the flat unless my huntress helped me.

"Okay, little spark, if that's how you want to be, maybe you could help me with the tire, and we could get to Hestia's?" I stated, slowly relishing the challenge she presented to me.

"Maybe you could just follow me?" She tilted her head, tipping the bow to suggest I could lead, as her prisoner.

"If that's how you want things to be," I chuckled, my lips curving to tease her before I spun for the diminishing path, but not before I noticed her stiffen again.

"Women," I muttered, recalling in quick flashes all that had happened lately, stalling to observe the soothing change in scenery with a wandering gaze. My eyebrows rose in surprise when she poked my back with her damn bow. The crunch of heavy leaves and snapping twigs under foot gave warning to any wildlife. A giant and his captor mouse proceeded through the browning foliage of the wooded northwest. Although many leaves remained green, fall was settling in slowly, and the colors changed subtly to yellows and oranges.

"Men," hissed behind me and a sharp pinch to my lower back reminded me of my warden. Unafraid of her, I plowed forward.

"I hope all the parts to my car remain in the morning," I teased. "These woods suddenly seem dangerous," I added, a spooky tone to my voice, but concerned for my tyrant. How often did she wonder alone within these trees? Was she safe here?

"I think your precious vehicle will be safe *enough*," she replied as if reading my thoughts. I liked the idea we could be that in tune with one another.

Too soon, the house appeared as if by magic, plopped down in a large, circular ring of cypress and pine, serving as centurions of protection. The homestead stood two stories high, framed in white with a plethora of windows on each floor and a large covered porch gracing the front. A huge barn to the side, several yards from the home, housed the small factory where Hestia taught her trade, and where I'd learned to control fire myself, as a child. A billowy cloud of white puffed out the large chimney, which meant the fires inside stoked hot. The house had the same effect, only small plumes rose from the three stalks, forming wispy trails as they reached for the sky.

The air was chilly this far north, and I was thankful for my lined flannel shirt and cap. The warmth inside the house beckoned me further. A prodding at my back reminded me to keep walking. When I turned for the side door, I surprised the peanut behind me, but she'd soon learn I was as familiar with this home as she was. Opening the door, not waiting for an invitation, I found Hestia in a position I often did: stoking the flames in an old-fashioned stone hearth, complete with copper pots on one side and a large black kettle on the other. The stomp of my feet signaled for her attention, and she turned quickly. Her blazing smile welcomed me, and for the first time in months, I relaxed.

"Hephaestus, my darling!" she exclaimed as she approached, her tiny frame opening her arms to embrace me although I was twice the size of her. With white-blonde hair and weathered skin, she wasn't old, per se, but instead appeared buffered by time. The oldest of the three daughters of Titus: Hestia, Hera and Demi, she lived hidden away in the woods, versus the family farm in Nebraska.

"You're so late. I've been expecting you for hours." She pulled back from our embrace, holding onto my thick forearms.

"I was unavoidably detained." I arched a brow and looked over my shoulder, realizing I blocked the view of my captor. Stepping left, the fierce elf stood exposed, equal parts irritated and perplexed by the warm greeting.

"It seems I have captivated, I mean, become captive to this one." I nodded in the direction of the mouse, who was still covered by a scarf, hat and fingerless gloves. Removing the gloves first, delicate fingers wiggled with relief. The ends of her nails were short, with the look of grease under them. Intrigued, I stared, sensing her hands knew labor like mine. Next came her scarf, wound triple around her neck, revealing skin as pale as Grecian china. Finally, her cap slipped off her head and a tumble of cherry-rosebud hair fell past her shoulders. My heart leapt at the color, which matched her lips, and my chest rose and fell as I took in short breaths. Her blue eyes sparkled in the reflection of the flaming hearth, and I suddenly wanted to lay her down in front of it, mapping out each inch of white skin and slipping fingers through that vibrant color teeming off her head.

"I see you've met," Hestia said, breaking my stare. "She's a little spitfire, isn't she?" Hestia chuckled as her hand slipped over my elbow and her head rested on my bicep.

"A little spark of *something*," I replied roughly, my lips curving as I regarded the beauty before me, but my insides twisted at the unbidden attraction after my sudden break-up. I shook off that nagging sensation of recognition, when she opened her mouth to speak.

"My name is Phyre," she said, lifting her chin. "And I'm the whole flame."

PHYRE

The way he stared at me unnerved me, in an unsettling-yet-feel-good sort of way. His chocolate brown eyes were large circles on either side of a slightly crooked nose. Broken, I imagined, as I knew how to reset one, and understood the effects of one not set properly. His lower face was covered in heavy scruff, a perfect amount that was more than thick peach fuzz and less than grizzly bear. When he pulled off his cap the second he entered the house, the thick hair on his head nearly matched his face. Cut trim to his scalp, no bangs provided coverage of a heavy gash to the forehead, next to a long-healed scar.

It had been a long time since I found myself attracted to anyone, but a sense of recognition knocked on my closed heart. The instant he looked at me, the warmth of his eyes calmed me, and elevated me, at the same time. Emotions spiraling in opposite and contradictory directions, I felt centered and out of control all at once.

"What happened to you?" Hestia instantly fussed, turning this man to face her. Her aging hands rose to his face, while he had to bend at the waist to lower for her inspection. Mothering hen to any creature, I thought, as Hestia tenderly massaged over the wounds. I knew her touch. I'd experienced them myself upon arrival here.

"I got into a fight. With War."

I snorted. How ironic, I thought, but neither of the other two flinched at the name.

"What happened?" Hestia's voice softened, her hands now cupping either side of his face.

"Zeke happened." His voice grew deeper, rougher than the sultry, gruff sound exhibited outside. Rumbling through me, vibrating from my toes to ripple up my legs, it set off a long-suppressed eruption at my core. I questioned the sensation and cursed myself for such an immediate reaction to him.

"Who's Zeke?"

Turning to face me, Hestia and the man she called Hephaestus, stared at me as if they had forgotten I was in the room. I didn't like to be forgotten. Too often in the past, I had been, and the flame burned until someone noticed me. But that thought was not for these two.

"We can talk later, Heph," Hestia said, releasing his nickname, and ignoring my question.

Adara, my oldest sister by nature of Hestia's Home entered the breakfast room. Her eyes latched onto Heph and she stopped short. The cheeks of her caramel skin pinked. Her head high, her smile forced, she was a beauty, a goddess of fire, refreshed from a night near a blaze. Her eyes didn't waiver from Heph's nor did his leave her face. My heart pinched as they stared and I realized they shared a history. It felt as if someone stabbed me with scissors.

The smile on Adara's face brightened further, a genuine curve to a bow ready to shoot an arrow of love. Then it fell.

"Adara, you're the first to welcome Heph home. Well, the first after Phyre." Heph's eyes leapt from Adara's, to mine. His smile slowly melting as he noticed my frown. Something wasn't right. The air thickened heavier than the hearth smoke. Heph's eyes returned to Adara and a conversation ensued in which Hestia and I were intruders. I was ready to remove myself, struggling at the thought of walking away from him. A strange sense of knowing Heph filled me, which seemed impossible. I came here a year ago, shortly after he left. In the long journey it took to get here, surely we had not met before, and yet I stood behind him, like a moth drawn to a flame, unable to resist the temptation of scorching heat.

"It appears that makes me second then, not first, for Hephaestus." Adara's eyes flicked away and a false, brittle smile formed on her angular, exotic face. Men would worship her, if we didn't live here. Adara did not wish for that fame. It appeared, however, that she did wish for Heph's heart. The observation caused the stabbing pain to my side deepen.

"I'll tell the others we have company." With those words, Adara excused herself and Heph's gazed followed her before he hung his head. Hestia frowned. She didn't like discord within her home.

"Phyre, my girl, you need to wash up." The woman who took me in, who I owed my new life, watched me with eyes that saw too much. "It's your night for dinner duty." My shoulders slumped. I hated dinner duty, but I could use the time to contemplate what had transpired. Who was Hephaestus? What was he to Adara? What were these strange feelings I had toward him?

The idea of dinner distracted me. I wasn't a very good cook. In fact, my first night of active participation, I burned everything, including the bottom of a pot where I boiled out all the water. Thankfully, I had a partner on the nights it was my responsibility. I'd often take over the set up and clean up while my surrogate sisters hovered over the stove and hid my incompetency. Hestia knew the truth, but she didn't call me out on it.

"We each have a talent," she told me. "A gift. Your journey in life is to discover it. Then nurture it and never let it go."

I didn't believe her at first. I'd come a long way since then, with all gratitude due to Hestia.

"And Heph, as long as you are here, you work as well." Hestia smacked his chest playfully and the crooked smile he gave her sent my center beating like a brass drum. Heph turned those giant swirls of chocolatey goo on me, and I heated further. Certain my skin was a bright pink, I turned and stomped toward the kitchen.

The true kitchen was off this smaller entrance space, housing a rectangular table and space for work. Breakfast and lunch were served here. Dinner was mandatory, served in the more formal dining room on the opposite side of the main kitchen. I started setting the table with a clatter and a clank of silverware and plates, my thoughts racing with questions about Adara and Heph. I set one platter down so hard it spun.

"What's gotten into you?" Ember asked me, entering the dining room in search of a large serving plate in the sideboard cabinet. Another sister through Hestia's Home, her vibrant orange, curlicue hair hung over her brown eyes and she swiped back the rippling bangs.

"Nothing," I barked, setting a second plate down with a flimsy spin and watching it sputter like a dime.

"Huh. Well, did you see who's here?" The remaining plates vibrated in my hand.

"I don't know who you are talking about," I lied.

"Come here." She motioned for me to set down the last of the dishes and follow her. For some reason, I felt like a woman walking through flames. Somehow, I knew who she meant, even though I didn't know him. Entering the hardly used, front living room, I noticed a gathering of my sisters between two windows. Not sisters by blood, but by location and history, the women giggled and sighed around the large, eight-mullioned windows. We stood in unison with only single names, unique-colored hair, and large eyes on a delicious man.

"Isn't he lovely?" Flame, a pixie of a girl with bright blonde hair streaked with light blue framing her face, sighed.

"Mmm...mmm...mmm..." hummed Seraphine, her arms crossed over her chest as she admired the view through the window. Her head tilted, highlighting her signature bangs, too long and jet black with bright blue streaks, hiding her eyes.

"Are you ready for him, Adara?" Adara brushed back her stick-straight, charcoal locks, letting them cascade off her shoulders like a seductive sketch. Her dark eyes were alight; I'd never seen her so piqued.

"He isn't here for me." Her voice trembled with sorrow and hope. She wanted the specimen outside the window, and inside me my blood boiled. I didn't like the feeling. I recognized the sensation, but I would never take such jealousy out on my sisters. I loved these women, and they loved me.

Ember hadn't commented, and I felt her eyes weighing on me. I refused to look at her as my eyes remained attracted to the bonfire of a man throwing off heat as he swung an ax and chopped wood near the studio barn. His back arched, his muscles carved, he lifted his arms and lowered them with a sickening *thwack* on the log before him. His muscular back rippled and rolled as he struggled only briefly in removing the ax for a second hammering.

"Good gods above, what are we staring at?" Ashin stood behind me, a giggle in her voice. I didn't have to turn around to see Adara's true sister. She was just as beautiful as the elder version of her, with a gray-black cast to her long locks.

"Him." My voice quaked; I couldn't draw my eyes from the giant of a man standing in the middle of the yard, shirtless, sweating, and splitting wood.

"He came back," she whispered behind me. "For you." Ashin turned to her sister, and my heart ached unquestionably at the thought. A familiarity with him burned deep inside me, calling out for me to recognize him. But I didn't and I couldn't. Men were not for me, no matter how appealing the one before me. I recalled the scar on his forehead. The gash next to it. As much as he piqued my interest, I would not be the cause of another mark on him.

"What happened?" Hestia's infamous question, sprang to my mind in regards to Heph. It was a question that haunted all of us here. What happened to bring us here, to a home for women ranging in age from eighteen to twenty-eight. Huddling and giggling as we ogled a man out the window, one would never imagine the horrors of our pasts.

"All right, ladies, I think we've had our fill." Ember clapped her hands like a mother hen, and Flame giggled.

"Can you ever have your fill of a man like that?" Seraphine breathed, stepping back from the window. Her eyes met Adara's and a silent conversation ensued. I couldn't pull my eyes from his back, and I hated that I wanted to rub my hands over that broad expanse. I sensed each girl exiting the space, and yet I remained. The smell of dinner wafted into the room, but thoughts of Heph tempted my senses, moistening my mouth for something more delicious.

"What about you Phyre? Could you get your fill of him?" Ember's question startled me, her eyes on me instead of the showcase outside.

"You know I stay away from men." My voice softened. "I wouldn't know how to please one like him." I turned to face her probing dark eyes.

"Plus, I'd only end up hurting him." My voice lowered. Even if I could handle a man's touch, which I didn't think I could, I'd only hurt him with mine. She nodded somberly smoothing a sympathetic hand down my arm.

"You never know, honey. That was a long time ago." Pausing a beat, she added, "With a man like that…" Seeing the pain in my features, she softened her tone. "Don't fret, Phyre. It could happen."

I nodded, but my head seemed drawn back to the window. My eyes narrowed as I stared.

"Dinner's almost ready," she added, and I tipped my chin to acknowledge what she said, but I watched the muscular display before me. My heart raced at the exertion of his body. He moved like a machine, smooth and structured. One wrist was covered in a band of thick leather. The delicious thought of him removing that band and snapping it at me sparked my imagination, and rejuvenated the heavy beat between my thighs. As if he heard my thoughts, he stopped working, his head held high like an animal, listening for a barely perceptible sound. He twisted his neck left to right and then swung at the waist to face the house. I leapt behind the curtain, hoping he didn't catch me. Risking a peek around the velvety fabric, I saw him standing with his hands on his hips, chest heaving, facing the house. His skin was mouthwatering smooth, golden tan and unmarked, glistening with sweat in the dim glow of evening. My lower abdomen fluttered like a candle flame in the wind, and heat spread through my body, warming my insides. My hands balled into fists, as I shook off the desire to climb such a structure as him.

HEPH

Phyre was the newest addition to Hestia's gaggle of women, and the most irresistible of them all, I could admit. Adara and Ashin had been the first to arrive, wandering aimlessly through the woods. A third sister accompanied them, but had returned to civilization. Seraphine arrived one day, telling Hestia she heard the home could help her. Startled at the possibility, Hestia offered Seraphine refuge. Ember followed shortly after that. They found Flame, only roughly sixteen at the time, battered, broken, but not beaten. She did not accept defeat. Flickering back to life, she earned her name. This new one, though, I couldn't get a read on. I didn't understand women.

Surprisingly, I surrounded myself with them. The daughters of Hestia's Home were different; they understood me. Hestia understood me, and that's all that mattered. A surrogate mother, she recognized in me things I hardly saw in myself. She showed me patience and kindness when others did not. She provided me with a gift when I felt I had none. She didn't allow men to stay for extended periods at her home, but she welcomed my visits every few years.

At the moment, time stood still as I sensed her staring at me. Phyre. The name didn't fit the stature of her body. Little spark seemed more appropriate, as she prickled over my skin when she looked at me. They had all been there, gawking at my body through the window. I couldn't help but hear their giggling. At times, it was hard to remember they weren't laughing *at* me. I was a big man, with a limp, and a scar, and a misshaped nose. But it was more than all of them watching. It was the fact that *she* watched me. She wasn't fast enough to slip behind the curtain, and I noticed her fingers wrapped around the curtain's edge, imagining them holding onto me. Her presence lingered where she thought I couldn't see her. Her hair wouldn't let her fade into the background, and I envisioned it teeming down, curtaining me as she rode over me. That vibrant color made my mouth water. She'd taste like wine,

I decided, and I wanted to get drunk on her. In some ways, I already was, and I racked my slow brain to recall how I knew her. The hint of her lingered deep in the recesses of my heavy head and meager mind. I wasn't bright. Not enough, anyway. In fact, that's part of the reason my mother rejected me. That, and the bitterness necessary to spite my father, but I refused to let thoughts of them cloud my attempts to recognize the girl.

I needed the energy release exerted in breaking down the logs before I could sit at a table of women, chattering and giggling, and eyes wandering. But more than that was the problem of Adara. She'd be wondering what happened to me. Why I didn't return like I promised. Why I didn't take her with me like I vowed. Hestia would remind me I owed her girls nothing. They were here to get healthy and whole on their own. The thought concerned me. What had happened to my little spark to draw her to Hestia's hearth? What danger frightened her and what evil lurked inside her refusing to allow her to see she was beautiful?

"Dinner," Hestia called from the side door.

"I need to shower," I yelled back as I swiped my flannel and thin Henley from the leaf-covered lawn.

"Too late."

"I stink," I laughed, low.

"We'll survive. I've smelt worse." Her blue eyes glittered under a mop of white-blonde hair. If Persephone, my sister's best friend, could grow old, she'd look like her aunt one day. Regal, stately, although dressed in jeans and a flannel like a mini-lumberjack-wannabe.

"I'm so happy to see you," she offered as I slipped my long-sleeved Henley over my head before I reached the door. Her tone softened, as did her eyes, which searched me for the reason behind my surprise visit. She hadn't overreacted at my unannounced entrance. She welcomed me like she always did and then instantly sensed I was here only because I needed her comfort. The warmth of her home to remind me I was loved despite all the rejection I'd received.

"Can I help?" I asked the orange-haired Ember as she plated large pieces of chicken onto a serving dish.

"Could you carry that, please?"

The women here could fend for themselves after Hestia repaired them. One pleasure I took in their skill was their culinary expertise.

"Smells delicious."

"Mmmm…so are you," Seraphine said as she entered the swing door to the kitchen. I blushed deep almost dropping the tray. Her flirting undid me and she knew she flustered me. I didn't understand flirtation. I went in for the kill, dove deep, and then walked away. Words were not my strength. I'd tried them and failed. Subtle expressions and touches not my thing, either. I didn't have a thing when it came to women. I entered, released, and withdrew.

"Seraphine," Hestia mocked with false concern. The matronly ruler of this stead understood Seraphine's teasing nature. I didn't intend to act on any flirtations. I'd already built a little fire in that direction when it came to Adara. A fire I needed to extinguish.

"He knows I'm teasing. I set you a spot next to Adara." She winked. Secrets ran deep *among* these women, but spilled like an overflowing cup *between* them. I didn't need to know their pasts to understand their pain, but years of sisterhood lessened their hurt and built a new wall of protection for one another. Seraphine would remind me often of my history with Adara, if I refused to address it. Avoidance was easier for me. Silence was better. The truth could cut deep.

I followed the women into the long dining room. The table set like a Thanksgiving feast despite the mid-week, September evening. I loved the lavish display, but the aroma tempted me to eclipse it. My mouth watered at the flavors seeping into the air, and then my eyes caught hers. A new desire for taste filled me, and I hungered like I'd never eaten before.

"Heph, sit here." Seraphine tapped on the back of a chair near the head of the table to the right of Hestia and next to Adara. I pulled out Adara's chair, and she sat. All eyes were on me. I hadn't had time to properly greet each of the women, yet they accepted me back into the fold. Questions fired at me before I took my seat.

"Heph, how are you?"

"What's new?"

"How's Solis?" A question asked with a raised tone of interest.

"Where have you been?"

The last one seemed to suck the air out of the inquisition and the table fell awkwardly quiet. The little spark half way down the table didn't seem to mind the chatter. She only swung her head left to right in wonder.

"Okay. Enough of the firing squad. Let the man eat and then we can chat." Hestia set her hands together for grace.

"Fathers of the sky and mothers of this earth, thank you for the bounty provided at this table. Thank you for the heat of home, the love of family, and the life of fire. We eat in gratitude this day with the return of our prodigal son." Her eyes shifted to me and she winked. "Amen."

A muttering of amens coursed around the table, and the clatter of spoons in bowls and trays passed refilled the room.

As I turned to offer Adara mashed potatoes, a silent thank you crossed her pretty mouth. Those lips once brushed mine, and she was sweet. But I sensed Phyre's lips would be sweeter. Adara's dark eyes dropped as our hands touched when the dish passed to her. Yes, the flames of love marked me, once upon a time, but no spark remained. Love was a circle, not a one-sided line, and Adara had never crossed that line. She was only a marking on a compass in my search for something I had yet to find. My true north still awaited me. On that note, compelling laughter that crackled like a campfire, sending out sparks and lighting the darkness, drew my attention to the end of the table where a cherry-colored head was thrown back in delight.

"Did you have safe travels getting here?" Seraphine kicked me under the table, and my attention turned to her at the question. To her surprise, she hit my metal leg, and only the vibration rippled up to the flesh part of me.

"Shit," she muttered under her breath. "I'm sorry." Her eyes didn't look at me as she stabbed food with her fork.

"Someone shot at my tire." I dangled a roll in my hand, keeping my eyes forward but feeling the weight of sea glass eyes down the way. A brush against my thigh, and I noted Adara's hand rested there. I shifted my leg, releasing her touch before the inquisitive firing squad began again.

"What?"

"No!"

"Are you okay?"

The overwhelmed gasps and questions of concern were fired at me.

"It was an ar…" My eyes locked on Phyre, but a subtle shake of my huntress' head, and I let the word fall. My brow pinched wondering why she didn't want the truth said. Her head began to hang and her eyes focused on her plate.

"It was nothing," I deflected. "I'm fine. Actually, I think it might have been some wayward kids playing." I didn't want Phyre to feel bad about what she'd done. I only teased her hoping to draw her into conversation. The solemn look on her face proved I had the opposite effect.

"It's late in the season for camping," Hestia spoke. "I haven't noticed any random tents in the area." Like a mother goose, she protected her goslings with a daily sweep of the trees. Rogue campers were warned they were set up on private property and were gently escorted to the main road.

"Oh, well, maybe it just sounded like a shot."

"Hunters?" Flame's voice hitched, and a hand covered her quivering lip. At eighteen, she had a tiny frame of delicate bones, making her appear even younger. The horrified expression on her face made her eyes look wider as they filled with liquid.

"No," I tried to back-pedal. "It just sounded like it." The lie dug me deeper, but the grateful look on Phyre's face kept me digging.

"We'll check it out in the morning," Hestia gave the girls a reassuring look while she patted my hand. "For now, we're thankful you are safe."

My head hung at the false truth. I didn't wish to frighten them. No hunters walked here. No campers trailed the land. No past could find them. My eyes shifted to Phyre, sad that hers dropped. She was so confident as she held her bow and arrow earlier, but suddenly seemed self-conscious. Avoiding me, she twirled her fork over her plate without touching any food. Dinner discussion resumed, and I ate, letting the renewed chatter comfort me as my thoughts wandered. Phyre didn't want to admit it was her, even to ease the minds of her sisters, and I wouldn't expose what she'd done: no harm, no foul. But curiosity ate at me. *What was her story?*

Dinner concluded after a final course of apple pie. Full to discomfort and suddenly sleepy, the stench of me caught up to my senses. Standing abruptly, I thanked Hestia for dinner and began to clear my place.

"Leave it," she fussed. "Tonight, you're our guest. Tomorrow, you have kitchen duty," she teased and her blue eyes lit up when she looked at me. I loved this woman for her motherly ways. She did her best with me, considering I wasn't her son. She actually had no children of her own. The girls were her family, blood not defining them.

"I need a shower," I reminded her.

"I wondered what that smell was," Seraphine joked across the table. I shook my head, and my eyes fell to Adara. Thoughts of a shower reminded me of her curvy body pressed against mine. It wasn't supposed to happen. They were off limits to me, but somehow, she'd found her way to my room over a year ago. I no longer wished to remember. I didn't want to entertain Adara again. I'd already sent her the wrong message. I suffered the pain of mixed signals myself from her. Then Lovie. Callie. So many mistakes.

If I were my brother Solis, I'd whisper something seductive to Phyre, leading her from the table with no questions asked. I'd have my way with her against the wall just outside this room and then step out to wash myself. But I wasn't Solis, and he wasn't like that any longer, not since he'd met my sister, Veva Matron.

"If you'll excuse me?" I dipped a deferential nod to the table and turned to leave.

"Where are you going?" The strangle to her tone was like glass shattering at the window. It cracked and scattered, and the room grew silent. "Is he staying here? In the house?"

"Phyre," Hestia addressed her. "Of course not, honey. You know I don't allow men to stay in my home. Heph is aware of the rules and makes a room for himself above the studio."

Wide, bottle blue eyes stared at me, questioning her own outburst and holding me hostage. The room remained quiet.

"You have nothing to fear from Heph, Phyre. You're safe with him." Adara said, but I couldn't read if her intent was reassurance or sarcasm.

My shoulders fell at the realization that Phyre's question came not from a curiosity at my leaving, but in fear that I'd stay. My heart ricocheted through my body like a ping-pong ball. I didn't want her to be frightened of me. Instead, I sensed I should be afraid of her.

PHYRE

I hated the quiver inside me blowing like a flame, warming me each time his eyes looked at me. I hated that I liked it when I should not have. My mouth got away from me, and I cursed myself for my outburst. I revealed too much when it came to him. The answer to my unwarranted question shouldn't have mattered to me, but like a moth afraid a flame would extinguish before it reached the heat, I had a sense of losing Heph as he stood and excused himself from dinner. The twist of his body, the dip of his head, seemed so final, and I panicked. My level of fascination with him frightened me, even though I was perfectly safe. Yet with him here, I sensed a danger of a different sort.

Hestia asked me to take clean linens to the studio shortly after the dishes were cleared. I think this was her way of reassuring me that Heph was not attached to the house, and I could trust the distance placed between him and us, the girls. I couldn't admit to her that I didn't trust myself. I didn't fear his nearness. I feared his exit. Riddled with confusion, I stomped across the darkened yard, walking the path to the large barn door spotlighted by the security light. I fumbled with the stack of sheets, blankets and towels that Hestia had provided for our guest. Climbing the stairs to the offset loft, I didn't tread lightly, and my feet stomped up each step. It was rare that I entered the space. Two apartment rooms existed upstairs, but we were near-to-never with outside visitors. I'd been here a year, and I couldn't recall the last man to grace our property other than deliveries of groceries and mail.

When I got to the first door, I paused, using my elbow to knock in an effort to balance my pile. When no answer came, I pressed awkwardly again. Banging my elbow hard enough, the door slid open.

"Hello?" I called out. The slip of hallway space provided ample lighting to the darker entry, and I used my foot to press the door further.

"Heph?" The sound of water running drew my attention. The space was no more than a living room with a kitchenette area. A door to the back hid the bedroom, but it stood wide open. I stepped forward, a strange pull tugging me toward the forbidden space. The bed stood covered in a thick duvet of rustic-barn door-red. Hestia didn't keep sheets underneath, preferring to make it fresh. A bag on the floor near the door sat open and spilling forth with clothing. *How did that get here?* He must have gone back to his vehicle. He hadn't carried a thing when he walked from the car. Jeans. Flannels. A pair of boxer briefs underwear –in red–peeked out from the case. Thoughts of his broad back, chopping wood earlier, exposed over the red waistband made my body tremble. The linens tumbled out of my hands on the bed. My eyes fixated on the Christmas color. I swallowed hard, and then heard the clatter of something dropped in the shower.

That magnetic force of a moth to a flame drew me toward the open bathroom door, inviting me forward as steam poured out the space. I walked slowly, breathing deeply, clenching my fingers so my short nails bit into my palms. *What are you doing?* I screamed at myself, but my will pulled me on. As I reached the open doorframe, my eyes could not look away. Encased in a box of steam, the glass structure did nothing to conceal the specimen inside. Large, toned muscles, rivaling that of David, the glorious statue, stood inside the shower. A grunt filled the space, echoing over the glass walls and reaching out for me, encircling me, and pressing me forward as if by a guiding hand. The thought forced my eyes to drift and notice the placement of his own hand. His hips rocked subtly forward, his profile reinforcing the artistic sculpture of his being. A free hand pressed flat on the steamy glass, his palm facing me. Slipping in his efforts as his body rolled forward, the slithering of soap slapping over the thundering sound of water, a gruff moan left his lips.

I braced my hands on either side of the doorjamb, unable to look away from the performance before me. I ached to fulfill his needs. My center pulsed, imagining the heat of his hard length filling me. I shouldn't have watched, but *gods forgive me*, I could not look away. He was glorious as he pleasured himself, and my eyes would not release me. The ache clenched, pulsing a rapid rhythm on its own to match the slipping motion of his hand. A warm, shivery sensation trickled down my thighs and crawled up my lower belly. My hips thrust forward once as I fought for control. His arm worked faster, the free hand cascading down the glass, struggling for purchase. My pulse raced at my throat, and my fingers gripped the door frame. I encouraged the ache, matching the rhythm between my thighs with the strokes of his fist.

When he finally released a heavy grunt, his free hand banged once against the glass. Caught in the fantasy, a frustrated moan escaped me. Both hands instantly released the wood frame, covering one over the other against my mouth too late to suppress my response. One final jerk of his hand on himself and his head hung as he sighed in satisfaction, "My little spark."

With that, I ran.

HEPH

I heard a bang and pressed open the shower door. Not bothering to turn off the spray, I called out. "Hello?"

A scrambling over the floor and a second bang followed. Not thinking of my nakedness, I walked out of the running shower and crossed to the open bathroom door. On the floor, my clothes lay scattered around my case. I charged the short distance to the front room, noticing the main door still in a state of swinging forward and back. Someone had been in here. In two large steps, I crossed the living space, and yanked at the wood barrier. The hall remained dark, but feet scrambling down the stairs clued me to the retreat of someone.

"Hey!" I yelled, naked and uninhibited, from the top of the stairs. A swish of cherry-rosebud hair slipped from my view as the staircase only partially revealed the working studio below. A light flicked off, and the lower floor went black. My brow pinched, and I spun back for my rooms. Crossing the threshold, I closed and locked the door without thought. I'd never had to worry about anything when I stayed here before. I had nothing to hide. But the newest member of Hestia's girls was an utter mystery to me, and I didn't trust myself with thoughts of her, as proven by my shower.

Stalking back to the bedroom, taking note of the scattered clothing, I also noticed a disheveled pile of bedding and thick towels. My shoulders dropped. Whoever was here—and I had a good hint as to whom—had brought me necessities. That same someone was the cause of my trekking back to my car in the dark and retrieving my bag for fresh clothing. I'd slept in the same dregs for a week, once upon a time, but I didn't wish to repeat the experience. Daily showering was necessary, clean clothes a must.

When you worked with fire and metal as I did, the warmth of a refreshing shower soothed away the heat and hard work of the day. As water trickled down my bare skin, I reached for one of the plush towels left behind and inhaled the scent of Hestia's home. A hint of something fruity lingered. Just along the edge of the terrycloth, a fragrant hint of peaches, plums and pears combined. Phyre.

"Just what I thought," I muttered. She'd be a virtual display of succulent sweets, and I hardened again. Then another thought occurred to me. *She wouldn't have*, I wondered, curious if she'd seen me. The toppled pile proved she'd gotten close enough. If she hadn't seen me, she'd heard me.

"My little spark is full of fire," I spoke to myself and drew the fresh towel to my nose again, inhaling deeply.

+ + +

After satisfying myself a second time, I showered again. Still on edge and knowing I couldn't sleep, I wandered back to the main house. I saw a light in the side window and I entered to find Hestia sitting in her usual spot, a rocking chair, staring into the embers of the withering hearth fire. She looked up at me as if she knew everything and I scratched the scruff on my neck sheepishly.

"Coffee?" she offered.

"Got anything stronger?" She smiled slowly, pointing to her coffee mug and then nodding to a glass container on the mantel. The whiskey was slightly warm, being so close to the fire, and I poured myself a generous dose into another ceramic cup on the table. Items lay out for the come-and-go-as-you-please presence of breakfast hours ahead in the next day. Hestia was a planner.

"Sit," she commanded softly, although she knew I would. I curled onto the floor, folding my good leg and letting the weight of the other rest over my ankle.

"How are you?" A troubled expression crossed her face. Her lips pressed upward and her brow wrinkled. Her soft blue eyes focused on my jean-covered knees.

I scrubbed my face with a thick hand before I spoke. "I'm tired."

"What did Zeke do?" Hestia asked, knowing my source of exhaustion.

"He forced an engagement."

With the answer, Hestia stopped rocking. The slipper covered foot crossed over her leg slid to the floor with a gentle thump. "He what?"

I exhaled, hanging my head.

"He betrothed me to Lovie, Aphrodite's daughter." Aphrodite was the daughter of one of my father's many lovers. As a promise to Aphrodite, he tried to give me her daughter, but Lovie hadn't chosen me. She wanted someone else.

"Why?" Hestia's startled eyes questioned me, softening as she spoke. I shrugged and took a sip of the warm alcohol.

"I guess he wanted to poke fun at the cripple," I mocked, looking down at my leg, hidden under my jeans.

"Don't talk about yourself like that," my surrogate mother admonished. When my own mother had rejected me, Hestia stepped in to raise me. "You know that isn't true."

"I know it's impossible for a beautiful woman to love an ugly man."

"Hephaestus," she warned, her face falling in sympathy to the many scars on my body, those marking my face and the metal leg under my jeans. I didn't like that look from her, of all people. She taught me not to pity myself, so pity from her was the last thing I wanted. "You know I believe beauty glows from within us, reaching outward to show others our worth," she added, ever the wise parent. I tipped up my mug, changing the course of the discussion.

"Even with that, I'm not a prize," I muttered. "I find it difficult to commit. With Zeke as my role model, it's no wonder why. He wants me to return and take Lovie back. I don't see the point." Lovie, sleek and lively, raven-haired and wild, her flirtatious personality didn't match my more somber one. Vibrant compared to my brooding, we were not a good match. But I couldn't deny I jumped at the suggestion—she was beautiful, and hope sprang that someone like her might still find something in me to love. How very wrong I was, when I found her on her knees with War.

My attempts to drown Lovie's rejection came at the expense of Callie. A sweet girl, larger and curvier, our body types matched, but our hearts didn't. She was eager to please, and taking her came without difficulty, but not without risk. She wanted me to pick her, and I couldn't. The idea of me marrying someone else heightened her interest in me for a month or two. She wanted to know what could attract the lovely Lovie. Little did she know, nothing I did had pleased Lovie. Everyone learned the truth when her affair with War was exposed.

I had left two women in my wake when I ran from Olympic Oil, my father's estate. Oh, irony, *again*, that I'd come here, surrounded with more of the female gender, to face another woman who I failed.

"That special woman is out there for you, Hephaestus." Hestia liked to say my full name. Rolling it off her tongue, it sounded motherly, lovingly spoken, and reminding me of another female heartache from my home.

"I met my mother."

Hestia's hand covered her mouth. She nodded once, exhaled slowly and smiled weakly.

"What did Hera have to say?"

"She wanted me to visit her farm. She'd like to get to know me."

Hestia's lips tightened. Estranged from a woman I'd only met once, Hestia disapproved of her younger sister's rejection of me.

"I see." The pause allowed for the unspoken question. *Would I go?*

"I told her I wasn't interested." I answered without being asked. "I think it's a little too late for a mother-son bonding experience."

"Heph…" Her voice was too weak to scold me.

"I mean, it's been, what, hundreds of years? I think there is a limit to how long a son can live with that kind of rejection."

"Damn her," Hestia growled into her coffee mug, taking a heavy pull of the alcohol hidden inside.

"I don't need her, Hestia. I have you." She smiled back at me, warming me with her tender eyes. As Hera was my true mother, making Hestia my aunt, we shared a bloodline. But family was more than blood,

30

as Hestia's Home proved daily, and Hestia was the woman I considered my mother.

"Maybe…"

I raised a hand to stop her. "No. I have nothing to say. She tried to apologize, reaffirming again it wasn't me. It was Zeke." My father, Zeke Cronus, and my mother had a lifelong love-hate relationship. In their love, they created me. In their hatred, my mother rejected me to spite him and his multiple affairs. I was the link between the daughters of Titus and the sons of Cronus. This did not win me favor among my other siblings. Silent and secluded, my brother Solis was the one to draw me out of my shell. He was my best friend, as well as my brother, and now the lover of my sister.

"I met Veva." My voice rose with pleasure at the thought, hoping to change the subject once again. "It's strange to finally acknowledge her as my sister."

"How did you find her?" Hestia's question spoke of fondness for one of her two nieces. As the daughter of Hera from another father, I knew of Veva's existence, but she never knew of me.

"She loves me," I laughed, trying to lighten the tone, but finding no irony in my words. Veva was very forthcoming in expressing how she felt. She told me she adored me, and that meant the world to me.

"And why would she not?" Hestia chuckled in return.

"Actually, she fell in love with Solis."

"Oh my, that must be a feisty tale." Her laughter carried and I smiled in response.

"It was certainly a long and winding road before they found true happiness."

"And what about Persephone? Did you meet her as well?" Hestia asked fondly.

"I did." My tone lowered. The beautiful blonde princess, filled with life despite heartache, had befriended me without question. Both she and Veva's attention encouraged me to take the risk and hope for the best with Lovie. If those two women could love me unconditionally, why couldn't Lovie? But in matters of the heart, I knew better. Friendship and sisterhood were not the same as a passionate, all-consuming love. My thoughts flicked to Phyre and my heart yearned with a need I never felt before.

"I see you have a new girl." I commented gingerly, hoping not to sound obvious in my interest.

"Phyre? She's been here a bit. You've just been away too long." One eyebrow rose, but no bite filled her words. "She's something special."

"A little spark," I chuckled, and we heard the clatter of a glass in the other room. Hestia raised a hand.

"Hello?"

No one answered, and Hestia tilted her head.

"Whoever is out there should be in bed." Her voice rang like the mother she was, teasing in warning to her errant toddler child. Only, whoever she spoke to was a grown woman. She shook her head, chuckling into her coffee mug.

"Girls," she muttered.

Yeah, girls, I thought.

PHYRE

Watching Heph had been the craziest thing I'd ever done. With his suitcase in my path, I stumbled over it, entangling my foot in those stupid, sexy, red boxers. So entangled, that the second I had them untwined from my foot, I ran with them in my hand. Not wanting to toss them aside, I slipped them in my puffy vest pocket. The material taunted me, calling out to me, to do something masochist like rub my hands over the super-soft cottony fabric or worse, run my nose over them. I forced myself to leave the room before I did the outrageous, which was turn back and face Heph.

My ankle throbbed as I hobbled back to the safety of the main house. After making my way to my room, I returned to the kitchen through the dark hallways. I wanted a large glass of water and some ibuprofen tablets, which Hestia kept by the kitchen sink. Maybe I needed ice, too, I thought, as I was about to open the freezer. Then I heard the gentle mutter of voices.

Nearing the doorway between the kitchen and the breakfast room, the rugged voice of Heph spoke of a variety of women. His engagement. His mother. His sister. Her friend. He hadn't mentioned if the engagement was over, only that it was troubling. My shoulders fell at his sense of inadequacy. I could say unequivocally that Heph was the most beautiful man I'd ever seen. His broad body, short beard and white teeth did things to me. At the mention of my name, and "a little spark," I had confirmation that I did things to him, too. Things I probably shouldn't do for him, because if I ever acted on the attraction, I could hurt him. Hurt him beyond repair.

When I fumbled the glass in my hand, sighing at the sound of his nickname in reference to me, I was almost busted.

"Whoever is in there should be in bed," Hestia called out, like I was a three-year-old sneaking down to see Santa on Christmas morning. After setting my Christmas tree on fire at the tender age of four, and burning my house to the ground, I no longer believed in Santa Claus. I preferred the lump of coal. It could burn. Sight unseen, I prepared to leave as Hestia chided me when I heard Hestia speak of Adara.

"Did you make her promises, Hephaestus?" The question rang with disapproval, but asked tenderly with concern for both parties.

"I don't think so."

"Heph?" she warned and I stepped closer to the doorway.

"Maybe I said things in the heat of passion."

"I didn't think I had to remind you that my girls are off limits to you."

I imagined Heph hanging his head, much like he did at dinner as he tried to dig out of the hole he made spinning a lie about his car tire. He hadn't turned me in for spearing his wheel, and I wondered why not.

"You don't."

"I love you, Hephaestus."

"I know." His typically rugged voice, softened, sounding sad and contrite. I couldn't fault Heph for an attraction to Adara, but while she was beautiful in an exotic sense, Heph was equally as remarkable in a roughed-up, steamy god replica. Adara's admiration of him made sense to me in a weird sort-of way. Blood boiled inside me and my breathing heightened.

"I didn't mean for anything to happen," he clarified as way of apology.

"I'm sure you didn't, but I see her looking at you. And I see you looking at Phyre."

I stood taller, my short breaths coming faster. Jealousy built and died, like the spark from flint on a rock.

He looked at me?

"Be careful there," Hestia warned. "She's fragile."

The hair on the nape of my neck rose. *Was she warning him against me or Adara?*

"She's a special girl, still discovering herself. She's still healing. I don't need you lighting up another heart here." Her chuckle softened the warning. "I won't let you play my girls."

I had to smile at the protectiveness Hestia took with us, but her caution bothered me. I wouldn't hurt him. Not intentionally, but that's what had happened in the past. I hadn't meant to burn down the tree or the house. I hadn't meant half the other things I couldn't control, but there was one night I would never beg forgiveness of.

"I don't think you have anything to worry about." With those words, I realized I'd misunderstood. While Heph consoled himself in the shower, possibly to me, possibly to someone else, the comment was clear. He wasn't really interested in me. Maybe he called every one *my little spark*. The boiling sensation heated within me, and I needed my own brand of oxygen before I did something I'd regret. Returning the glass to the sink, I hopped up the stairs as best I could without making noise. The hallway was lined with doors, one for each girl; Hestia's room was on the main floor.

Entering my room, I crossed to the window seat, opened the cushioned seat below and reached inside for my secret stash. Looking up and out the window, I noticed Heph enter the barn studio. Moments later, Adara followed, searching behind her for any witnesses. My chest burned inside like the flame I was about to strike. Lifting the window sash only enough to draw out the smoke, the match struck the flint strip, igniting into a tiny fire, and I breathed deep the sulfurous scent. It wasn't enough to squelch the envy, hot and heavy within my heart as I thought of Adara experiencing Heph in a way I wanted. I lit the candle and watched it burn, setting my hand over the flame in hopes to calm me, but the heat only ignited the turmoil inside my ribs. My heart melted with sadness that Adara would get back her man and I'd remain alone. Continuing the torture, my fingers drifted over the dancing flame, as the minutes ticked and I watched for Adara's return.

HEPH

I had just returned to my room when the doorknob jiggled. I recognized the signal. Opening the door, Adara stood at the threshold in a white night shift. My eyes drifted to the hint of dark circles behind the semi-sheer material. I looked away, knowing taking Adara would be a mistake. Her creamy, caramel skin tempted me once upon a time, but not any longer. My wounded pride was too raw from Lovie. My heart confused over Phyre.

"Come in," I offered, leery of her presence.

We stared at one another. I waved a hand for her to take a seat on the couch. Nodding in gratitude, she sat, her body awkward, her hands clenching the cushions on either side of her thighs. Memories drifted through my thoughts, but I refused to go back there. Looking at her no longer stirred desire, only regret. I had disappointed her with innocent promises. But she had disillusioned me, as well. *Beautiful women do not love ugly men*, Zeke said, and from Adara, I understood that truth. Exotic and erotic, sexual attraction fooled me into a spell disguised as love. She wanted to leave Hestia's Home. I was her ticket out.

"It's been a long time," she began, nervously smoothing down the length of her nightdress.

"It has." A year had passed since we last shared promises.

"I suppose things change." She smiled weakly, her dark eyes lowering, as if she knew my answer before I spoke.

"I'm sorry." Her face spun away as if I slapped her, and I stepped closer. Her hand rose to halt me.

"What happened?" That question would always haunt me. Maybe it was separation. Maybe it was time. Maybe it was the reality that I could not give her what she needed, or she couldn't fulfill my needs.

"I'm sorry I didn't return sooner."

She spun back to me. "Didn't you love me?"

"Did you love me?"

We both knew her answer. In the final night of passion, the words crafted in my mouth, and I presented them in silver to her. She had no response. When I told her I would marry her, her smile spread, but no reciprocal words matched mine. In that second, I knew. She wanted me to take her from here, but not because she wanted to be with me forever.

"There's so much I haven't done," she offered, changing the subject. I took the risk and sat next to her on the couch. My long legs stretched forward, and my hand rested behind her back.

"If you aren't happy here, leave. Tell Hestia and go."

"You know it's not that simple." I nodded as if I understood, but I did not.

"Why not?"

"Because of Ashin. And Eshne." Adara had taken on the role of mother to her two younger sisters. It left her without a childhood and freedom. Sensing Ashin would be safe with Hestia, Adara was ready to have a life. Her younger sister had already made the choice. Eshne left years ago.

"I think Hestia will let you do whatever you wish." I tried to reassure her with the touch of my hand on her lower back.

"You know I'm afraid to go alone. Afraid of what I could do. Afraid of getting caught."

"So you thought I would protect you."

A shaky hand rose and swiped through her stick-straight hair. It slipped slowly from her fingers like the flow of a flame.

"I'm sorry," she mumbled. She held her forehead in her hands. "I thought you loved me."

"I did. But you didn't love me, and I don't think that's fair."

Her head nodded and a tear slipped down her check. My thick hand covered her slim back and I rubbed up and down her spine.

"I tried. I did. I could see how much you loved me, but all I could think of was leaving. You made me feel things I didn't know I could feel. The physical safety. It gave me hope that I could get there." She turned to me, liquid slowly seeping from her eyes. "I'm so sorry I'm too late."

I tugged her to my broad chest. I understood her sense of entrapment. She loved Hestia, as I loved Zeke, my father, in my own way. I wanted to please him, as Adara wanted approval from Hestia. Adara did not want to disappoint. She didn't want to seem ungrateful. Leaving with me, as my wife, would be a better excuse than wanting to go alone. Without her love, I had no assurance she would stay with me, though. Maybe she thought it would grow over time, as I had thought with Lovie.

The physical connection of Adara in my arms reminded me of pleasant memories, but those thoughts were part of a false love story.

"I'm sorry, too. I'm sorry I wasn't enough for you." I'd said the same words to Lovie.

Her tears came faster, her chest heaving harder. My arm wrapped awkwardly around her, and I patted her shoulder. I cared about Adara and wanted to help her as a friend, but I wasn't good with tears. Comfort was not my thing, but I drew from her my own as I held her. Lovie's rejection stung, though not as hard as Adara's had. I still had feelings, even if I didn't have a decent face. Adara's apology brought about my own sorrow. Her face buried into my flannel and her arm slipped over my waist. She held me as hard as I held her, each hoping for relief from our aching hearts.

It was early morning when I walked Adara back to the house. In a second-floor window, I saw the flicker of a candle. Hestia preferred all fire remained in the hearths. The light flitted, and on a puff, blew out. An unseen face lingered in the filmy smoke. My heart raced at the thought that maybe Phyre watched me, and then I thought of Adara at the door. Phyre witnessed it all, and my heart faltered like a horse suddenly lame during a race. She would not understand the history of Adara, or the fact that Phyre sparked thoughts of the future.

PHYRE

Only a few short hours later, I found myself sitting in the breakfast room with little sleep and lots of coffee. Heph entered and quietly sat across from me. His eyes never met mine, and when Adara entered, I stood to leave. I didn't need to witness the love-birds silently mating, after spending all night envisioning Adara wrapped around him. My mind desperately wanted to erase the possibility after being haunted by visions of him in the shower. The nickname *my little spark* played in my head, on repeat, ridiculously wanting the words called to me.

"If you don't mind, I need to borrow Phyre for a bit this morning. As she, *found me*," Heph coughed addressing Hestia, "after my flat tire, perhaps she could guide me back on the trail and help me repair it." His words stalled me at the kitchen door. If Heph had carried his case to his room, in the dark no less, surely, he could find his own car in the morning light.

"I have work to do." I took another step for the kitchen when Hestia answered.

"I think that's a great idea. It will give Heph a chance to learn more about you." Forcing a smile on my face, I turned and nodded once to Hestia, not missing Adara's eyes shooting up to look at our mother-figure. She glanced at Heph for direction and then at me. A frozen smile returned to his face, agreeing with Hestia.

"If you think that best," I offered, trying to assure Adara with my eyes that I had no decision in this plan. She looked away, and then walked from the breakfast room in the opposite direction. I hated to admit it, but my heart pattered at the thought of being alone with Heph, like a deer trotting ignorantly through the woods.

I placed a hat on my head, zipped up my down-filled vest, and then followed after Heph in silence. We trudged through the forest, out of sight of the large house. The foliage canopy shaded us from the sun. The walk, ordinarily peaceful, filled with tension thicker than the trees. I didn't know how to make small talk, chattering like Ember or flirting like Seraphine. Not that I would flirt with Heph. He had business still with Adara. I didn't wish to intervene, though that stabbing thing returned to my heart as I watched the muscular backside of Heph walk before me. He knew how to wear a pair of jeans. The tight-fitting Henley and a short cap gave him the look of a lost lumberjack.

We reached his car, and Heph went straight for the trunk. The sports car looked masculine and mean, although not something I would expect him to drive. He was a big man, and a truck seemed more fitting, especially considering I knew he worked with heavy metal to make anything from sculptures to weaponry. One of his sculptures sat in the yard: the perpetual image of a flame in rusty iron served as a reminder of all our gifts and the blessing of fire. *Oh, the irony*, I thought, as I still wasn't certain I could control mine.

He still hadn't spoken as he set a jack under the front axle and pumped several times to raise the vehicle. He unscrewed the lug nuts and removed the tire. He rolled the ruined tire to the trunk and removed the smaller sized spare.

"I can pay for a new one," I finally offered, uncertain how I would explain to Hestia the need for money or the reason why I shot the tire in the first place. We didn't have money on our own. We worked collectively and each earned a share. Hestia banked the money for us.

"Don't worry about it." He lifted the shot tire without effort, and the vehicle shook a bit with the force of it in his trunk. He wheeled the new one forward and began replacing it.

"I'm not certain why I'm with you. You haven't asked me to do anything." My hands slid into my pockets and wrapped around something soft and comforting within.

"I thought about making you replace it, manually, but decided that wouldn't be very chivalrous of me."

"Chivalrous," I laughed. "That's a big word."

He huffed as he replaced the final lug nut and lowered the jack.

"For a simple man, right?" His exhale sharp with the finishing touch of his labor.

"What?"

"You think I'm stupid, don't you?"

"No," I snorted. "That's not what I meant." He stood so quickly that he startled me, and I fell back, stumbling over a twig at my feet. My hands slipped from my pockets, preparing for the impact of falling on my backside, but his hands gripped my pockets and yanked me forward. My breasts slammed into his chest, my face knocking into his pecs and giving me a whiff of his manly scent mixed with the balsam spruce around us. The fragrance dazed me, and my head rose slowly to face him.

"You're a genius actually," I muttered caught in the balsam-spruce-Heph haze. "I know you made that sculpture by the fire pit and I've seen other pieces you've designed around the place. Hestia also mentioned you make weaponry, like bows and arrows." I took a deep breath, which was a mistake, as I inhaled more of him. "I'd like to see more of your work one day.

"You would?" His surprise, surprised me. His dark eyes smoldered as he stared at me. He inspected my face as if he thought I was teasing him, when I wasn't. He was a master craftsman and I wanted to learn more about his trade. "Then why pick on me for a word like chivalrous?"

He truly wanted an answer and I breathed deep. "Because you seem like you know how to work the ladies." My head hung at the admission. I knew he'd been with Adara.

"Phyre, you're mistaken." His chocolate eyes widened, and then they softened. He looked at me like I was a precious metal. He bit his lower lip, tugging up a corner. Being this close to his face, I noticed another scar hidden under the heavy scruff at his chin, the gouge matching the one on his forehead, raised and bumpy.

Without realizing it, my hands rested on his biceps, larger than some of the tree trunks behind me. My heart raced under my clothing, and he took a deep breath, dragging my breasts up his chest. Without thought, my hands slipped upward, taking their time to feel the size of his shoulders. His hand slipped out of my pockets. One cupped my face, and the other held something in my peripheral vision. I turned sharply to see red material before me.

"Were you in my room?" His gruff voice rippled through me, as he teased me. I wanted to feel the strength of that tone over my body, vibrating against me, but my eyes closed in embarrassment as he held his boxers before me. The lie formed quickly.

"Those are mine."

He bit at his lip again, as they curled with pleasure.

"How strange. I have the exact same pair." He paused as his thumb on my cheek rubbed gently. "But mine have somehow gone missing." A subtle hum vibrated after the statement.

Quickly, I forced myself not to react. My eyes didn't leave his, all teasing chocolate with a hint of mischief.

"Maybe it was the campers who shot your tire?"

"I don't think so." His smile grew.

"Or hunters."

"Wrong answer, my huntress."

My heart leapt as he labelled me his.

"Well, you can keep them if you wish." I shrugged one shoulder, as if it meant nothing to me that he could take my pair, which were really his.

"Maybe you could just hold onto them for me. For safe keeping." He returned the sinful, red boxer briefs to my pocket. One hand still on my cheek, the other curled into my vest pocket, he tugged me against him, forcing an already existing connection. Our eyes stared.

"Are your lips naturally that color?" I bit my lip in response and the tip of his tongue peeked out for a stroll over the lower bow of his.

"Some men think it's beautiful," I snarked without steam. My breath rushed out warm and covered his mouth.

"You are beautiful." My insides melted like the slow drip of wax on the outside of a candle.

"And that hair," he added. Thick fingers curled around cherry-rosebud tendrils. "Is that natural as well?" He had to know the answer. Each of us had unusual color to our locks. I nodded without releasing his eyes.

"Do I know you?" His gruff voice lowered.

"I don't think so," I answered, *but I wish*, I screamed inside my head. Holding me against him, felt strange and right wrapped together. Safe and home filled with unnerving anxiety, like waiting to open a present when you just know something good is inside the box.

"You seem so familiar to me." His eyes narrowed and his thumb brushed my skin. He shifted up to my hair and traced over the long locks in their unusual color. "I would never forget hair this color." His eyes lowered slowly to my mouth. "Or lips that matched." His mouth leaned forward, and I swallowed with thirst to drink from his lips, but Adara flashed in my head, and I gently pressed on his shoulders.

"We should get back." My voice quivered as I spoke, despite wanting to sound strong, stand my ground, and resist him. He dropped his hold so quickly it was almost as if I imagined it happened. The brushes on my cheek lingered and the pain in my chest returned. I stepped back.

He began to walk to the other side of his car. I remained still, as if one with the leaves on the forest floor.

"We can drive," he said, holding the passenger side door open. Instantly my head swung to the back seat. My heart raced as I stared at the dark, empty space.

"I think I'll walk."

His brow pinched, and he stared at my face. The intensity forced me to look at the backseat again.

"I'll walk," I repeated. "I need some more air." He gently shut the door, crossing to the driver side.

"I'll walk with you. I can come back later to get the car." His eyes searched my face but he'd find no answers there. My secrets were buried deep, no longer burning a hole in me.

"That's okay. I'll be fine." I smiled too broadly, adding false cheer to my tone.

"It isn't safe." His voice grew deeper.

"I'm fine," I argued. Heph stopped before me. Closing my eyes, I took a deep breath, steeling myself to speak the next words. "I'd like to be alone for a few minutes." He stilled at my words, bit his lip again and nodded, allowing me my privacy, as I lied. Did he think I was rejecting him? It was quite the opposite. I wanted him, but I couldn't have him. Being in his arms brought to life how lonely I could feel at times, despite the affection of the girls. Heph felt like safety and security, but thoughts of my sister, Adara, willed me to step back. Heph stepped aside, waving a hand before him to proceed. My head hung, and my feet tread heavily as I walked away from him, feeling as if I had just run away from home. Only I knew what that felt like, and this felt nothing like the first time.

+ + +

"What are you making?"

The rugged tone at my ear startled me, and I flinched, swiping the hot material over the flame and melting the glass strip too much.

"Shit," I muttered, pushing back the safety goggles with my wrists.

"I'm sorry," Heph said. "What was it?"

Still holding the glass rod to sculpt beads and the hot mandrel needed to form the circular shape, I spun to face him, finding his presence too close. My breasts brushed over his too tight T-shirt and when I took a deep breath, the force dragged them up his chest. His hands came to my hips, and I lost all thought. *Had he asked me something?* Creamy chocolate stared back at me and I wanted to lick him to see if he tasted the same as those delicious eyes. Our stance reminded me of days ago when we stood by his car.

I shook my head briefly. *What was wrong with me?* A trickle of sweat riveted down my forehead toward my eye. With both hands still occupied, and my goggles perched on my hair, I couldn't help myself. A thick finger rose in my peripheral view and instinct kicked in. I flinched in the opposite direction and swung the fiery rod at him. A fierce motion halted the impact I anticipated, and I turned my head upward, still bent at the waist, ducking from the intent of his hand. My breaths came heavy, sharp and quick. My chest rose and fell rapidly, as my heart raced.

"Are you okay?" he asked me, staring down at the awkward position of my head nearly resting on his thigh.

"I…" I stood taller instantly. Attempting to step back, I bumped into the flamethrower behind me. Heph held my wrist, the hot rod in my hand raised in the air. The flamethrower at my back jostled and Heph reached around me to settle the machine and turn the dial to the off position. The movement brought him even closer to me, and my nose rubbed over his gray T-shirt, inhaling the manly scent of him. Heat and cedar clouded my senses. My lids closed, and my lips pressed forward to the soft material matching the cotton of his boxers hidden in my room. I don't know what came over me. We stood in this position for what felt like eternity. My mouth pressed over his heart, feeling the vibration through his shirt as it beat against my lips in a steady rhythm. I wanted to crawl inside him and wrap the sound around me. Our awkward embrace felt familiar and strangely comfortable. A cough to the side of us forced him to step back, and I licked my lips, savoring what I'd done and attempting to hide them in my embarrassment.

"Don't let me interrupt," Ember giggled, walking behind Heph and continuing on to her work station. My eyes closed and my head fell forward, which only brought my forehead back to Heph's chest as he remained close. The last one-hundred and twenty seconds rushed through my memory and I realized I tried to strike him with the heated mandrel. My head sprang upward.

"I'm so sorry," I whispered, embarrassed by kissing his shirt, resting on his chest and overreacting to his touch.

"What happened?" That infamous question coated me in warmth from his too-close breath. I couldn't tell him. I couldn't even hint at the damage I had done, or what had been done to me. I shimmied my shoulder and tried to arch my back away from him. The flamethrower jabbed my lower back, and he slid me to the side as if we danced. His large body still blocked me from making any other move to escape him.

"You startled me."

"I…I only wanted to wipe the sweat." His brows pinched, accentuating the scar on his head and the healing gash. A few things became clear. A fight. His lover with another man. He'd been defending someone when he incurred that cut.

"I...I forgot what I was doing." The answer wasn't enough of an explanation. How could I forget I held a hot instrument in my fist? The nature of my motion turned it into an instant weapon. "I...you can't touch me." His thick fingers released my wrist. His other hand removed from my waist. He stepped back with raised palms like he had when I held the arrow at his lower region. My eyes closed at the memory. *Oh my God, to think what I'd almost done to him.*

"Are you okay?"

And the correct answer always remained: "I'm fine."

"You don't look fine. You look pale."

My natural skin tone was white. Not peachy, not creamy, not nude, but china doll white. I couldn't get any paler. His hands lowered like he wished to cup my face. I recalled the pleasure of his touch on my cheek days before. In an effort to recall it late at night, I rubbed my fingers gently on the warm skin. My own touch did not replicate his.

"I..." he began.

"Please don't." I didn't trust myself. One of two things would happen: I'd burst into flames to hurt him or I'd overheat at the contact...and burst into flames with excitement. He wouldn't understand, and I couldn't explain. I was different.

A small part of me put faith in Heph's understanding that Hestia was unique herself, and if he had years of knowledge about her, he'd know that certain *things* were unexplainable. Hestia made me understand myself. I was unique, she lovingly told me. I, however, did not think I could explain it to Heph.

"I didn't mean anything." His rugged voice lowered, and his head hung in that submissive way. For a large man, his spirit spoke of tenderness. He did not wish to be unkind, and he hadn't been.

"I overreacted." The words raised his head.

"Why? Do I frighten you?" His brow pinched. "Because I'm big?" He took another step back. A thick finger circled his face. "Because of this?"

My mouth fell open, and I blinked at him.

"Are you...You can't be serious?"

"Yes." His lids blinked in response, surprise in his expression.

"Heph," I laughed nervously. "Surely you don't think your face frightens me?"

"It has, obviously."

"I think you're handsome." *What? How lame did that sound?*

"Handsome?" His brow crinkled and the gash cracked from the motion, the tender scab split open.

"Your…your head is bleeding," I said as distraction. I don't know why I stuttered. I don't know why I pointed with the mandrel still in my hand. Thick fingers rose and swiped at his forehead. Pulling them down for inspection, he saw the blood and excused himself. The instant he stepped away, my shoulders relaxed, and then they fell. I missed the heat of him, the scent and the comfort of his nearness. I spun to brace myself on the work station, letting the mangled glass rod and cooling mandrel fall on the hard surface.

"I'd say *get a room*, but that's not allowed," Ember teased behind me. "You okay, honey? That looked kind-of intimate."

"He's promised to Adara." My voice defended my sister, but rose harsher at the thought.

"I don't know about that. I think it was history. Past tense." Her hand came to my back and rubbed gently.

I spun to face my friend. Ember was closest in age to me and had learned to control her power. Her wild orange hair piled on her head and her special safety goggles covered her eyes, giving her the appearance of a mad scientist. I had to laugh, and my shaky hands came to her shoulders.

"Well, there is no present tense for me. I don't think I'll ever be able to be intimate with someone, especially not him." The nervous laughter turned to silly crocodile tears. Strangely, I wanted to be intimate with him, but I didn't know how without hurting him. And I didn't want to hurt Adara, if she still had feelings for him.

"Oh, sweetie, it will happen. Someday. You'll be whole again."

The problem was, with Heph standing so close to me, I already felt whole, and it frightened me.

HEPH

"What happened to Phyre to make her so edgy?" I demanded of Seraphine as she dabbed at the cut and applied two sterile strips.

"What happened to you?"

"I went to touch her face and she nearly stabbed me."

Seraphine tossed her head to the side, a motion to move her jet-black and bright blue bangs.

"Well, Hephie, maybe you shouldn't touch girls you hardly know." One eyebrow rose and twitched before she smiled in earnest at me. "You better be careful here. You've got two girls vying for your attention. Surely, someone's going to lose."

"Seraphine," I sighed, my shoulders falling in disbelief.

"Why don't you just ask her what happened? I'm sure she'll tell you." Seraphine inspected her work a final time.

"You know I'm not good with words. I can't just say, *what's wrong with you?*"

"Heph, of course not. That would be insensitive." On that note, she held the cleaning agent on a cotton ball against my head for a moment longer than necessary.

"Of course, I think you need to go with Plan A. Adara for the A, in case you don't understand."

"Ha," I snorted. "Why?"

"Because she…she's crushing on you hard, and you owe her."

"How do I owe her?" Did no one see how badly Adara wanted to leave? Wanted to branch out on her own? Hestia's Home wasn't a prison. The girls could go, but comfort kept them close. Could no one notice a member wanted to separate from the fold?

"You led her on. If you don't want her, you need to lead her off."

"What?" I chuckled, knowing Seraphine had it wrong, but I would not betray Adara. She had seduced me. Slipping into my room last night replicated the way she came to me in the past. The first time it happened, she startled me. I remember her sliding through the door, her back falling against it and the intensity in her eyes. She asked me to kiss her, and not willing to turn down a beautiful woman, I did.

"Oh, Hephie." Seraphine shook her head, and I wondered how women who had been removed from men for years had any more knowledge about relationships than me.

"Did you enjoy Adara last night?"

"How did you…" Irritation rose in my voice. I would not betray my night with Adara either. We had agreed. I would help her find the strength to talk with Hestia, but our sexual affair would not rekindle.

"There aren't many secrets here."

If what Seraphine implied was true, and she believed I'd slept with Adara last night, no wonder Phyre removed herself from me. No wonder she wanted to stab me. I had no tolerance for infidelity, and I didn't think any of these girls did either. In fact, I knew that's how Adara and Ashin ended up here. Ashin's husband tried to bed their younger sister Eshne, and Adara inflicted enough bodily harm that he'd never have a woman again.

"Nothing happened." I looked away, dismissing the discussion.

"That's what men always say." She patted my knee and stood from the stool where she sat.

+ + +

A few nights later, Phyre and I had dishes duty. While she washed, I dried, and we worked in awkward silence. Normally not a man of words, I couldn't take the quiet. With her hands plunged in the water, I came up behind her, but not too close.

"Tell me how I scared you the other day? What did I do, so I don't do it again?" I thought a lot about her response. Her eyes when they looked at the back seat of my car matched the horror in them when she went to stab me with the hot stick.

"You didn't do anything. It was all me." Her eyes remained on the dish in her hand, but her fingers circled the plate more than necessary.

"I don't want to frighten you."

"You don't," she said, handing me the dish to dry. I stepped closer. The faintest brush of her behind over the seam of my jeans ignited a flame as instant as the flamethrowers in the studio. I set the dish aside.

"It was nothing." She leaned forward to continue scrubbing dishes, forcing her ass back. I didn't move. The columns of my arms came to rest on the sink, pinning her before me.

"What's going on, then?" I muttered behind her ear, sensing my nearness disturbed her, but not in a negative way tonight.

"I'm washing dishes," she giggled, and those tiny sparks from a bonfire crackled before us.

"Can I ask you something?" She continued to circle the pan in her hand, rubbing around and round without any friction. Her face looked up and met my reflection in the black backdrop of the window over the sink.

"Were you watching me the other night?" I reached for a loose tendril of hair from her ponytail and wrapped the piece behind her ear. Through the reflection, I noticed her eyes closing.

"I…"

"Did you like what you saw?" I could not believe I was asking her this, but I had to know. It had been on my mind for days. Her eyes sprang open.

"It…" Her throat rolled. My mouth curled up as her lids fell closed again, as if recalling a memory. "It made me…I…I didn't expect…"

"Did you come?" The thought startled me. The question surprised her. The words echoed loudly in the otherwise empty kitchen.

"No," she snapped, but her eyes reflected in the window spoke the truth.

My hands circled her upper arms and dragged up to her shoulders. Massaging over them, I slipped down between her shoulder blades. I caressed in soothing swirls until I found the small of her back. My palms circled each side of her waist. My cheek lowered to scrape over hers and my lips pressed to her neck.

"Then you know, thinking of you, made me come, too."

My nose traced the curve of her ear, and my lips kissed the tip. Palms slipped to the flat of her stomach, and I pressed her back, letting her feel what she did to me against her backside. Her head tipped, exposing her neck to me, and I sucked at the spot where her jaw curled into her throat.

"I don't want to just think of you, though. I want to experience you. Every curve, every dip, every fold. All of you around all of me."

She exhaled and sagged against me. Instantly, she was in my arms, cradled to my chest, and I carried her out the back door, remaining dishes forgotten. Her arms looped around my neck and in a hushed tone, she told me to put her down. In the darkness between the house and the studio barn, I stalked on.

"I want you," I muttered, kissing under her ear.

"Heph, it doesn't work that way," she whispered though no one could hear her.

"Yes, it does." This was me. I spoke what I wanted when I wanted it.

"Not for me." Her hands slipped from my neck and pressed against my chest. I don't know where she thought she'd go. I held her firmly against me.

"Why?" Truthfully, I didn't understand.

"Because you slept with Adara a few nights ago."

I stopped. Releasing her legs, her feet fell to the earth with a thud.

"I did not have sex with Adara," I huffed.

"She came to your room."

"And she left it," I huffed again, rubbing a hand down my face. "When?"

Adara and I talked. There had been tears, and I held her. She fell asleep, and I let her rest in my arms, needing the connection to someone myself. I understood her loss. She couldn't have me because she couldn't give to me. And I couldn't have Lovie, because Lovie was never meant for me, honestly.

"You know what, I don't need the details. In fact, I don't want them." She stepped left, but I followed her. Holding up a hand, Phyre stopped me.

"Phyre, you can't deny this." I don't even know where the plea came from. Cupping her cheeks, the spark between us ignited ten-fold. A bonfire burned between us with only this simple skin-on-skin contact. Thoughts of her under me, forced me to swell. Instantly, I was full length and full of desire. I needed inside this girl. The result would be an inferno.

"I...I have to..." Her fingers circled my wrists and tugged them downward. "I'm not who you think."

"I don't know what to think. I just know that from the moment I saw you, you pierced my tire and my soul. Every moment I spend with you leads me to wanting more and beneath it all I feel I've *known* you for ages, and I want to figure out how. I want to make certain I never lose you again. This connection with you is so real, so present, so intense. It's like...like a...like a fire inside me."

The words surprised me. I'd never spoken in this manner before, but I suddenly felt frantic, as if she might walk away, and I would never know this feeling again. This burning, all-consuming need to be with her: to hold her, enter her, and fill her.

Her brow pinched.

"If you think you lost me, why didn't you ever come find me?"

My hands dropped completely. I didn't have an answer. I didn't know I missed her until she stood before me. Silence feel between us as she rejected my heartfelt words, rejected me.

"You know what? Don't answer that question," she exhaled. In an instant, she stepped around me and was gone, leaving me alone, where I'd been for too long.

PHYRE

The next few days, I avoided Heph. Guilt riddled me at what I'd said to him. I could not blame him for what had happened to me. It was not his fault. Things happened to me, beyond my control. Hestia told me a thousand times those weren't my fault either. It wasn't hard to ignore him. Hestia kept him busy with small repairs around the house, simple things we never got around to. I buried myself in the studio.

Hestia's skill was fire. It's what attracted all of us to her. She knew how to make it and manipulate it to produce beautiful things. Her latest creation included glass beads, although I learned glass designs of any type were a specialty. To the outside world, Hestia's Home was a place for wayward women in need of support and a new path. For all intents-and-purposes, that was true, but it wasn't a place you could find on a map, and it wasn't a place filled with women. The seven of us were the full regime. Six vestal virgins and one leader queen, although not one of us was a virgin, the sacred label stripped forcibly from each of us, sacrificed by the desires of powerful, pathetic men.

Thinking of our history, I worked harder than normal at my station. I had a special-order bracelet I was working on. I stayed late in the studio and fired up early, but not so early that I would wake Heph and be alone with him, since his room was in the upper space of the barn. The extra-large red barn had been converted into six work stations, each equipped with tools for pyrotechnics, including flamethrowers and supplies for making glass beads and baubles. In the center of the open space, a large, open fire heated the room, and Hestia practiced the ancient art of glassblowing, a skill I had yet to master.

Today, Heph stood near her, manipulating precious metals to use for our bracelets. He'd entered the room without my awareness, but when I saw him in shorts, my breath hitched. A metal contraption protruded from his left leg, just below the knee, curving like something to be used as a weapon.

"You didn't know?" Ember asked me, approaching my worktable as I stared. My head shook in response. How had I not noticed it when he was in the shower? Then again, my mind had been elsewhere on his body.

"It was an accident. He was rock climbing as a teen and fell. He should have died." She shrugged as if I should understand. "Some of the girls say he cut his leg loose himself, as he was wedged between rocks. He could have bled to death. Others say he lay immobile for a week, until his father found him. Either way, it's a sad tale. He got that scar on his forehead from the experience as well. The blow to the head alone should have killed him, but as you can see, he's thick-skinned." Heph was a survivor—a lone, rejected survivor—and my body felt pulled to his, wanting to comfort him, recognizing the strength within him so similar to me. A trickle of sweat absorbed on the back of his gray tee. I observed the thickness of his solid leg. The muscles of his biceps flexed as he worked with a long iron rod, angry and red over the hot coals of the center fire. Hestia and he were deep in conversation, but suddenly his head spun, and he caught me staring. His face looked harder behind the protective eyewear. His chin tipped upward like I was some rock star groupie, and he returned his attention to Hestia.

Clearly dismissed, my hands trembled as I turned away. My heart sputtered and clenched in my chest. I couldn't get enough air in my lungs. The room suddenly too warm. The thought of him dying suddenly overwhelmed me.

"Oh God," I muttered as my fist pressed over my heart. "What have I done?"

"What's wrong?" Ember asked, her arm coming over my shoulders.

"My heart," I whimpered. A cold sweat broke out over my forehead. The arm supporting me quivered.

"Phyre?" The sweet sound of Hestia's voice behind me almost undid me. She'd be so upset with me if I slept with her precious man-child. I'd never forgive myself, but at the moment, I couldn't forgive myself for walking away from him, accusing him of things, as if it was his fault that he didn't come to save me from myself.

"Phyre." His rough voice behind me caused me to quiver more.

"I think she's overheated. It's exceptionally warm in here today." Hestia spoke again.

"Air." It was the only word I could choke out. I needed air, and I feared I'd never breathe again because Heph was that air. Only, oxygen fueled fire, and I was afraid. Instantly swept upward, I was cradled against his firm chest as he carried me outside. We hit the crisp, fall temperature, and my lungs opened. Not stopping, he continued to a fire circle between the barn and the house. He sat in an Adirondack chair, pulling me down on his lap. My head fell against his shoulder, and I faintly heard the beat of his heart. My eyes closed to the rhythm. My own heart opened. I'd had a panic attack. I breathed in deeply, inhaling the manly scent of Heph.

"I should get off of you," I said, but my head was so heavy I didn't have the strength to move it.

"Don't go." His arms tightened around me, and my cheek rubbed against his chest. His lips tenderly kissed my forehead. He kept them there, and I wondered what his mouth would feel like on other parts of my body, particularly my lips. It had been a long, long, long time since I'd kissed someone, and I didn't think I'd ever feel the desire to do it again. But with Heph this close to me, the thought consumed me, like fire slowly creeping inside a wall, waiting for the opening to burst into a full flame.

"Feeling better yet?" The cooler air chilled me quickly, and I shivered in his lap. I looked up at him.

"Thank you." The words hardly left my mouth when his lips brushed over mine. At first, he just held them there. The hair around his mouth tickling around mine. But then, he moved, infinitesimally, his lips parted, and mine followed. His mouth searched, and mine shadowed. Lips nipped with gentle sucks and long pulls before his tongue licked the seam and entered me with full invitation. His tongue was thick, like the rest of him, and I sucked it forth, twirling mine around his. Sitting up straighter, I felt the length of his excitement under me, and the spark that started with a kiss flamed to an inferno.

The kiss intensified quickly, building in swirls of tongue and rapid moment of lips. I couldn't get enough of him, or he couldn't get enough of me. Either way, his oxygen became mine, and the fire inside me blazed. My hands wrapped around his neck and I shifted in hopes to straddle him. My body screamed *yes*, while my mind said *slow down*. My long-ignored-core flickered and pulsed like a million candle flames in a ballroom, but my head said *you're going too fast*. My lips didn't listen. My center begged for friction, and the fire struck.

"Ow!" Heph hissed and pulled back, and I instantly removed my hands. His firm fingers caught my retreating wrists and turned to stare at the palms of my hands. Swollen, blackened and steaming, his eyes widened in wonder. The side of his neck, imprinted with one hand, blistered and reddened. I shifted quickly, struggling to get off his lap. He let my legs untangle from over his, but he continued to hold my wrists.

"What did you do?" His tone bit at first, until he looked at my face. Something in my eyes begged him to understand. "What did *I* do? Did I misunderstand? Did you not want me to kiss you?"

"I didn't mean to hurt you." My voice was small, childish and scared.

"You..." He changed direction. "You burned me. But how? Why?" His eyes inspected my hand, and I curled my palm to hide it.

"Are you okay? Does it hurt?" He forced my fingers to unfurl. The skin of my palm was no longer charred, but faded to a deep red. Blisters grew and subsided almost instantaneously. His eyes opened wider, staring at me with a storm of concern and confusion in his dark orbs.

"How..."

"I...I can't explain. I'm so sorry. I didn't mean to, honestly." I tugged back on my wrists, but he wouldn't release me as I stood at his knees. He clenched harder. "I got carried away."

"You got carried away?" He stood, slamming my hands downward, releasing my wrists and raising thick fingers to cover his steaming neck again. My hands ached, smoldering with the heat of what I'd done to him. My heart hurt worse. He spun for the house.

56

"Heph, I'm so sorry," my voice whined, and a tear fell. The waterworks arrived too late to extinguish the fire. He didn't address me, but his solid back facing me spoke volumes.

+ + +

I found Ember in the kitchen and asked for assistance, but I couldn't avoid Hestia. Bandaging my hand, Ember knew it wouldn't take long before it would heal itself. Applying the sacred ointment lessened the chance of scars and soothed the sting as the skin repaired. My concern lay with Heph's neck. Ember's eyes shifted between mine and my hand. Sympathy rested deep in her brown gaze as Hestia oversaw the bandaging process.

"What happened?" Hestia asked, her tone fiercer than I'd heard before, directed at me.

"I didn't mean to hurt him."

"He comforted you. He carried outside for some air. What caused you to react?"

My eyes shifted to Ember. I'd told her briefly the details before Hestia intruded. Heph kissed me; I burned him. Hestia didn't seem to know, although she went to Heph's aid first.

"I...I don't know." I lied. Although in some ways, I didn't know the truth. The attraction to Heph was strong, so strong it overpowered me, and I didn't know how to control it. Caught in the crossfire of wanting to give in, and being afraid this very thing would happen, I panicked, resulting in his scorched neck.

She sighed, bringing a hand to my shoulder and then rubbed down my arm. "I love you." The words startled me from Hestia. It wasn't something we said often, and words I'd rarely heard in my life outside of her home. "And I love him, like the son I never had." She paused, her lips sucking inward before releasing out. Pressed tight, they were white.

"I don't want to see either of you hurt. You've both been through enough pain."

I nodded to agree, although I didn't know enough about Heph to understand.

"I cannot understand what happened, but I need you to separate from him."

"Because of Adara?" I instantly bit, before realizing that wasn't what she meant. She simply didn't want me to hurt him and she wanted me to use my inner strength to walk away from him when I felt out of control. I didn't want to ever hurt anyone again, especially not Heph.

"Adara?" Hestia chuckled, shaking her head. "No, honey, no, because of Zeke." Hestia's hand slipped from my arm, and her eyes lowered.

"Who is Zeke?" I asked.

"My father." Three sets of eyes looked to my left, where Heph stood, leaning against the doorjamb with a large gauze bandage over his neck. His lips tightened, similar to Hestia's, and his eyes looked away.

"He'd kill me if anything happened to you," Hestia's tone tried to tease, but an edge poked through as she stared with concern at her adoptive son.

"I'd hurt him first before he could touch you. Besides this doesn't concern you. My father has plans for me." The words stated bitterly, Heph made a face like he wanted to rinse his mouth after speaking. He looked back at me, questioning hurt and wounded pride filling those chocolate eyes.

"You can't go back yet," Hestia warned. "No matter what decision you make, Zeke can wait."

"But can I? How long do I wait before I get what I want?" His eyes never left mine, hard and penetrating, as if he bore the question into me, wanting an answer I could not give him.

"You aren't ready." Hestia's firm tone surprised me again. Through their eyes, a private conversation ensued between Heph and her that had nothing to do with me. Turning my face away from them, feeling like the sheepish child that I was, I saw Adara on the other side of the kitchen. She mirrored Heph's position, arms crossed, leaning against the jamb for the dining room. She glared in his direction. Maybe I misunderstood. He

58

told me they hadn't had sex. Could I believe him? Had he kissed me to make Adara jealous? The thought dissipated instantly. He didn't seem like the type of man to play those games. I'd known men like that before. I was so confused, I felt like a teenager, despite my years. Twenty-five was surely enough time on this earth to understand men, so I did trust him, which surprised me.

"I'm sorry," I interrupted, addressing Adara. Ember's hand rubbed my arm.

"I'm sorry," I repeated to my knees, as a lone tear dropped to it. Hestia cupped my face and kissed my forehead. I closed my eyes at the comfort.

A presence stood beside me while I sat on the kitchen counter. The warmth of Heph recognizable, a hand caressed up my back, and I squeezed my eyes tight. The tears spilled anyway, and I shook my head. His hand climbed higher, looping under my hair. I heard shuffling of feet but couldn't open my eyes. I didn't trust the waterfall of tears threatening to drown me. His fingers crawled upward, combing into my hair and massaging the base of my neck, as he had done before.

"I'm sorry," I choked out. "I didn't mean to hurt you. I'd never try to hurt you." Falling sideways, he tugged me against him, and the tears I tried to suppress fell in torrents.

HEPH

"Am I the only god without a gift?" I huffed as Hestia and I walked through the woods the following day. A modern descendant of ancient people, my skill seemed miniscule compared to the darkness of my cousin or the brilliance of my brother. I would not inherit kingdoms, as each of them would, if we were able to die. While worshipped in my own right, the populace with my skill grew smaller and smaller in the modern age. Metalwork was a dying art. I didn't understand. "A thousand years old, and I don't have any more skill than working with my hands, but the girl I'm falling for is a goddess with an evil gift."

"Hephaestus," she began. "We don't select our gifts. They select us. Your gift is in your craft. It's still just as important today."

"I'm not going to inherit anything. I'm not Solis or Hades. My craft isn't enough."

"It's plenty. As for falling for Phyre, I don't think that's wise."

"I don't think I have any more choice in that than in manifesting a gift. We don't choose our gifts," I reminded her. "We can't just choose who we love, either. This isn't Zeke and his command to marry someone." I was tired of remembering Lovie. Thinking of her brought me doubt. Marrying a beautiful woman was meant to tame her and secure me. An ugly man like me would only be twice as insecure with such a creature as my wife. I'd always worry I wasn't enough. It was a wasted relationship. She couldn't fulfill me anymore than I could please her. I wanted my own choice, not an arranged marriage. I deserved my own choice. When I thought of Phyre, I worried in the same way. Maybe I was not good enough for her, either.

"Heph, I warned you she was fragile. You don't understand her."

"Then enlighten me," I barked as we crunched down the path to the river at the edge of the property. The woods had turned all shades of yellow, orange and brown. The wind rustled through rapidly falling leaves.

"Hephaestus."

"Enough with the secrecy." I snapped, ready to lose my mind if I didn't have answers for this girl who I wanted to touch, and I thought wanted to touch me, but couldn't. Her fear held her back, and I wanted to help.

"She came to us a year ago, her hands blackened, her nails charred. She'd been attacked."

"Attacked?" I belted. "Was she..." I couldn't bring myself to say the word. I felt sick. Vomit roiled in my stomach. Hestia continued, ignoring my question.

"She holds the power for fire, as all my girls do."

I knew the gift of each girl. Flames could be manifested in any number of ways among them. I don't know how I thought Phyre would be any different. Being at Hestia's Home was selective. Only those with a gift would find their way here. Only those with the gift could stay.

"I'm still baffled as to how she found us. We don't have a revolving door of women. I've only lost one: Adara and Ashin's younger sister, Eshne. Emotionally healed, she prepared to risk the world again. The other girls wanted to stay. I won't force anyone to do anything, including Phyre telling you her story before she's ready."

We broke through the woods to the roar of the river and a long strip of land cleared for archery practice. In the midst of the field stood Phyre, aiming and firing at a circular target several feet away from her. We walked closer, but her focus did not stray. She hit the target every time, occasionally catching the center.

"As for falling for her, I don't want a repeat of Adara." The comment stopped me.

"How did you know?" I faced Hestia with a solemn look on my face. I had betrayed her by sleeping with Adara and keeping it a secret, yet I should have known Hestia knew everything.

"There are no secrets here among the girls. I'm old, but not blind. I saw the affection between the two of you."

"She didn't love me."

Hestia snorted, shook her head, and walked toward Phyre. I could have argued the truth, but I didn't want to betray Adara's trust. Adara had not loved me. Besides, I didn't believe there were no secrets here. Adara's desire to leave stood case-in-point. I guess Hestia didn't know everything. My gaze followed Hestia toward Phyre.

"She is so beautiful," I muttered, catching up to Hestia and watching the locks of Phyre's cherry hair flow in the wind, her concentration firm, her stance tight, highlighting the features of her small stature. "I want her, Hestia, like I've never wanted another soul. I feel it burning inside me. We belong together. Bow and arrow. Candle and flame. However, you want to look at it."

"I don't want this to end tragically for either of you."

"How will it? I can't die." My threshold for this conversation grew rather thin.

"No, but she still can." My heart plummeted to the earth with the thought of a world without Phyre.

"I...I don't understand. She has to be a goddess, to contain such power."

"Any fire burns out eventually, Hephaestus. It's nature. Unless that fire is perpetually nourished, the flame extinguishes."

What if I loved her? I wanted to ask. *What if my love fed the blaze within her? Would she live forever like me?* I ended up not asking as we stepped closer to her target practice.

"You look wonderful, honey," Hestia's motherly encouragement broke Phyre's concentration. She lowered the bow and arrow, aiming them at the packed ground. Her eyes immediately went to the bandage on my neck. My hands slipped into my jeans pockets to prevent the need to cover it.

"Did you need something?" Her quiet tone ripped at my heart. She'd been hiding from me again. Her eyes shifted downward as she toyed with the arrow against the bow.

"We were just taking a walk," Hestia offered. I couldn't take my eyes off Phyre. Her sagging head. Her shrunken shoulders. I wanted to wrap her up and cradle her against me. We didn't have to kiss. She didn't have to touch me. I just wanted to hold her and soak up her sadness.

"Can I try?" I nodded toward the bow and arrow.

"Try? Surely, you know how to do archery." Her agitated tone proved she was unimpressed with my potential mastery.

"I'm not very good." I teased, smiling weakly.

"You make tools and weapons for a living." Her striking blue eyes narrowed at me.

I shrugged. "Just give me a shot."

Handing over the bow first, I positioned the offered arrow along the sight, tugging back on the string and taking aim. Her set was too small for me, and in my fear of breaking it, I didn't pull hard enough. The arrow shot and missed the center, but hit the outer white ring to the left.

"You missed." Stating the obvious, I turned to see her hip hitched and her arms crossed over her chest. Hestia shook her head with a puzzled smile and turned to head home without me.

"It's perception. At least I hit the target. I'll try again."

Setting a second arrow on the sight, I gently tugged the string, pulling tighter this time and taking what appeared as better aim. The arrow shot through the white ring a second time, only this time on the right.

"Close," she snarked.

"I like the odds. Getting closer, but not quite there yet. What's that saying?" I set another arrow, raised the bow and aimed. "If at first you don't succeed, try, try again." The arrow flew, hitting the black ring, but at the top of the circle. "Or is it practice makes perfect?" Another arrow flew, another peg to the black strip, only this time to the bottom of the circle.

She snorted and shook her head, but on further inspection she started to see the perfect design I was forming. A final arrow sailed straight for my last destination: dead center of the red bull's-eye.

"It only took you five tries." Sarcasm dripped from that magenta-plum mouth, and my lips needed a reminder of her fruity mix of flavors. I didn't understand her power. The remorse in her tears after she hurt me proved she hadn't done it intentionally. She feared what happened, and her hesitation to be near me stood as evidence.

"Well, you only have five arrows."

"Someone broke my sixth one." She bit her lip, suppressing a smile.

"Someone shot my tire with it." I couldn't help the curve to my lips in response to the brightening of her pale face. "And my aim is perfect. I hit my mark with each try." We walked toward the arrows protruding from the target. She stalked toward the target and hastily yanked out the first arrow.

"That was north," I said confidently.

"What?"

"My design. The top was north." As she reached for the bottom one, I explained, "South."

I stood behind her as she stretched left. "West," I said. She grabbed the one on the right, and answered herself, "East." She stepped back to stare at the one in the middle. "And the center?"

I reached around her and pulled the arrow toward me, and then handed it to her. One finger rose for her attention, and then placing my hands on her shoulders, I moved her to stand before the target. Closing in on her, I pressed her back, and she stumbled against the target.

"What the…"

"Hold onto the arrows," I commanded softly, noting that she had several clutched in each hand.

"Heph?" She questioned me, lying oddly angled on the target.

"Look at me." The gruff demand came out harsher than I intended. She huffed, trying to hold her ground, but she was going to be my visual explanation. "Lean back against the target and spread out your arms." I slipped my hands in my pockets again to show I would not force her. I needed her to trust me. Blue eyes met mine as she settled against the circular canvas circle. "Spread your arms out."

"Heph," she warned, eyes narrowing again, and fingers gripping harder around the arrows.

"Just play along for a few minutes." My tone pleaded. I only need a minute. Exhaling deeply, she licked her lips. She had no idea what that movement did to me, but she was about to learn. Her arms unfurled slowly, and she lay outstretched.

"I'm not going to hurt you."

"Heph, this is awkward and..."

"I'm not going to hurt you."

Her eyes didn't blink. She stared at me and her throat rolled as she swallowed hard.

"Keep gripping the arrows," I commanded, holding up my hands in surrender. "Trust me. I'd never let anything hurt you," I repeated one final time. Bracing forward, my hands rest on either side of her head.

"You say it took five tries. I'll take as many tries as I can get, but I have perfect aim on my prize." Leaning closer, the throbbing length of me brushed at her core.

"You're my target, Phyre. My compass." I kissed her forehead. Her eyes remained open, watching me, questioning. "My north with your intelligence."

I brushed over her right wrist with my lips, letting my nose trail over the sensitive skin and inhaling the scent of her. "My east with your determination." Her lids closed and then rolled open, lazy and sweet.

"My west with calm patience." I shifted to her left and kissed her other wrist. Then I knelt down before her. Her head rose but her body remained plastered to the target. My eyes never left hers as I lowered to the seam between her thighs. Her breasts rose and fell. Her breath hitched. Holding her focus, I breathed warm air over her core, sending the heat through her jeans.

"My south for sensuality." I kissed her there. When I pulled away, her head had fallen back and her eyes closed.

"There were five shots," she croaked, swallowing hard. She hadn't looked up at me, but faced upward at the sky like a sacrificial lamb. Just watching the peace on her face did things to my insides, like setting the blood to flow, my heart to beat, and my excitement to grow. I stood slowly and lazy lids opened.

"The last shot was the center." I bent to kiss over her heart, covered by layers of flannel and cotton, but beating under there nonetheless.

"You're my aim. My target." I wanted to reach out my hand and drag her to me. I wanted to hold hers, to show her I wasn't afraid of her, but it was too soon. Instead, I stepped back with the soft burning at my wrist and slipped the heavy band covering my skin upward, exposing dark ink over the vein. I shared it with her.

"You're my compass. My home." A tattoo of the ancient mariner's dial covered my wrist. We stood in the northwest and my previous wanderlust nature knew how to discover north in a forest, but this compass tattoo pointed directly at her, the dial trembling at true north for me. Phyre was my destination, my destiny. My skin lit to life, glowing slightly with the direction before me. We remained silent a moment, her eyes staring at the antiquated instrument.

"That compass is alive?" Her voice trembled in wonder.

"This compass recognizes home." My voice faltered with the acknowledgement. On my own skin, I held the answer to all my dreams, my hopes of one day finding the girl for me, as Solis promised one day I would. Before me she stood and the ink recognized her, her magnetism imbedded in my veins. With awkward sliding, she straightened and stood. She didn't reach for me, like I wished, but her mouth warred with a smile. I nodded in the direction of the house. It was time to head back. I retrieved her bow from the ground and faced her. White-knuckled, she clenched the arrows, still held in each fist, now pressed against her chest, and like the arrows drawn to a target, I followed her home.

PHYRE

I was his aim, his compass, his home. The words spun inside me, twisting my insides with pleasure and anxiety. He was those things to me. His nearness gave me comfort, while unnerving me. I'd felt safe all these months at Hestia's Home, but I hadn't felt complete. At times, I still felt scattered, unstable, and restless. Heph soothed that wanderlust in me. He centered me, and I wanted to learn more, experience more, but the thought of hurting him held me back.

He circled around me for days in the studio barn. The heat of the stoked fires filled the place and he wore only a short-sleeved T-shirt. My eyes often drifted to wherever he worked, and I stared at his large body. Thick hands and solid arms contrasted with his softer manners, his tender lips, and gentler touches. Often, my eyes shifted to his covered wrist, imagining the heated skin searching for me.

I was struggling with the drop of some glass, trying to form the right shape for the anticipated, bright beads. My hand shaky, my head filled with thoughts of his nearness, I hadn't noticed when he approached me.

"Can I help you?" His voice startled me, but I didn't flinch as he stood at my back. I stiffened to prevent leaning into him. Shrugging one shoulder was my only response. A tree-trunk arm wrapped on each side of me.

"Here." His voice lowered at my ear as his hands wrapped over mine. "Twist it slowly. Form a rhythm." He rotated my hand in a subtle turn-retreat-turn motion.

"Guide the fire." His breath heated my neck, and his tone deepened. "Now, slide the rod through the flame. Gently at first. Tenderly. Slowly." Each word he exaggerated seductively as his hands guided mine, stroking through the blue fire. "In and out," he breathed.

I swallowed hard at the heavy innuendo, watching as our hands worked in tandem while we spun the mandrel and the glass rod. The fire molded and melted the glass into the perfect drop, reminiscent of rain.

"Eventually, you pick up the pace. You can't rush before that, but then, then you pull out quickly and force it back in." His hand over mine mimicked the motion, prodding repeatedly into the flames in short, sharp thrusts. My eyes rolled shut for a moment, and my head tipped back, brushing his shoulder behind me. "That's my little spark," he whispered, breathing over my neck, and I was lost. The rhythm between my thighs matched the torch of flame blowing before me. My hands tightened on the shaft of the mandrel and the length of the glass. Forcing them together, I imagined Heph and I colliding, the heat of the blue flame a precursor to how I could hurt him, the drip of the glass comparative to the moisture between my legs. Wet and achy, muscles clenched and vibrated with need in time with the heat, producing a thing of beauty at my hands. How beautiful could it be with Heph? Could I use fire to create instead of destroy the man behind me?

His strong hands released mine and slid up my wrists. Circling them with his fingers, he stroked my overheated skin, pushing up my sleeves. The contact sparked more desire. I wanted those fingers on other parts of me. In kind, I wanted the freedom to touch him in response. My eyes closed again briefly. My head fell forward, but my behind pressed back, his excitement evident, a clear indication he wanted me, as he said the other night.

"Little spark," he warned, honeyed and harsh in my ear. His hip thrust forward with enough rhythm to steer me. The brief touch not enough, the friction necessary too near. My backside responded again. His cheek pressed against mine, his large hands still holding my wrist.

"Feel what you do to me?" He sighed on my skin, growing sticky and sweaty. His nose inhaled near my neck. "But the things I could do to you, they would be sweet." Heph could undo me, and I was ready to let him take me right there against the table. Almost. His reassurance didn't surprise me, but Heph would not push until I was ready. Heaven help when I got there, because I wanted to pull him as close to me as I could.

+ + +

Dinner was one of my favorite times of the day, as Heph's eyes often searched for mine. Small smiles exchanged, although we didn't speak directly to one another for days. At my station the other day, I found a quiver filled with six arrows.

May the sixth one guide you home.

He handcrafted them himself of titanium strips. He added real feathers and forged the arrowhead of steel, explaining the process to me when I went to thank him. He hesitated and pointed to the top of the quiver. While I noticed the circular design in silver, with a notch shaped like an arrow and a second shaped like the feathers, I hadn't realized it was a bracelet. Heph removed it and wrapped it around my wrist, squeezing it gently to fit. He'd sized it perfectly. Twisting my wrist, the tip of the arrow pointed at me.

"That's the sixth arrow," he said, leaning toward me. He pulled back quickly, biting his lip, concern in those chocolate eyes.

"It's beautiful." My eyes prickled at the thought of such a gift.

"You're beautiful." Said with such genuine warmth, heat filled me. I'd heard the words before, directed at me in spiteful, degrading ways, but in Heph's gruff voice, each word made me believe it true. I was beautiful.

I stared at the bracelet while trying not to draw attention to it, and Hestia broke into my thoughts.

"It's almost time to celebrate. Maybe the last days of October?" Her eyes sparkled with mischief.

We didn't celebrate each traditional holiday. Every dinner was a feast of gratitude so Thanksgiving seemed nightly. I avoided Christmas but a fall festival celebration sounded exciting. I had witnessed a ritual performed by the girls last year, and was eager to participate this season.

"We could invite the girls?" Hestia addressed Heph, and several sets of eyes looked up, including mine.

"Veva and Persephone?" Heph's voice rose reverently as he mentioned each of their names and I wondered who these two were to him.

"Your little nieces?" Adara's face lit up.

"Yes, but they aren't little girls anymore," Hestia nodded, patting Adara's hand, "but yes, those girls. I suppose I have to invite each of their men, too."

"You'd let Hades come here?" Heph's question perplexed me.

"Hades?" Seraphine's voice sparked, as if she recognized the name.

"Well, I don't think I could stop him." Hestia winked at Heph, and he lowered his head, biting back a smile. A private conversation had transpired about people I didn't know, but the mention of their names pleased Heph. I liked his smile. His teeth were white and bright against the dark scruff around his mouth. My lips tingled when I recalled the feel of that scratchy skin around mine. While I didn't want to hurt him, I did want to kiss him again.

That night I watched him from my bedroom window. He sat outside in the circle of chairs around the fire pit. Adara was present, so I stayed behind. She wasn't angry with me, but she wasn't going out of her way to speak with me. If I couldn't have Heph, he should have someone else who could please him, but the thought clenched at my heart again. Not wanting the panic to set in, I lit a candle and watched the flame to calm me. When I noticed Adara and Hestia said their good-nights, Heph remained and placed another log on the fire. I wrapped a plaid blanket around my shoulders and rushed to exit the rarely used front door.

My intentions unclear, I tried to remain calm as I walked toward the fire pit. Something made Heph look up, and he watched me close the distance. My body trembled, my thoughts arguing whether I could follow through with my plan or not. The fire glowed brightly, the warmth invigorating. Sparks danced, and the wood crackled in the quiet of a dark night.

"It's so beautiful," I said, sitting opposite him. He observed me through the hazy gasses floating around the bright orange blaze.

"Yes, you are," he said softly, not taking his eyes off of me. I swallowed hard as heat filled me. The words encouraged me.

"I wondered if we might try something."

His eyes focused on mine, his chin rested over bent fingers. He nodded once, and I stood. Dark orbs widened with the movement. I rounded the fire to stand before him. His ankle crossed his knee, but he dropped his foot, allowing space for me to stand between his feet.

"Can you trust me, and let me try to control things?"

Shifting in his seat, he sat up straighter and leaned forward, elbows resting on his thighs. His hands twitched to reach for the backs of my knees.

"Okay," his voice croaked.

I pressed on his shoulders and he sat back, assuming my directions. I stepped over each knee and straddled his lap. His hands came to my hips and then fisted, afraid to touch me without my permission.

"You can open your palms," I decided, and the flat of each hand wrapped around my sharp bones. I let the blanket drape over the back of me. Leaning forward, I placed my hands on either side of his shoulders, but gripping the chair instead of his body. My knuckles whitened as I worried I might set the chair on fire, but it was worth the experiment to taste him again. I took a deep breath.

"Let me control," I whispered, and he nodded once more. Chocolate swirls reflected with flecks of gold from the fire behind me. I lowered my head and met his lips. Tenderly, I sucked on the bottom one, letting the tickle of his beard brush my sensitive skin. My tongue peeked out and licked a path, tracing his lips, and his mouth opened. Air expelled, and his hands tightened on my hips. Somehow, I figured Heph had been the one in control of all intimate relations in the past. In this case, he had to trust me.

My tongue retraced the path, slipping forward to meet his. My heart raced, and my center pulsed as I slid over his thighs. A teasing friction rushed through me. If Heph wanted to shift, he didn't, letting me lead. My mouth covered his fully, and he followed me as I nipped at the bottom and sucked at the top. His lips were a perfect bow. I was the arrow ready to go off from just one shot of his mouth.

Scruff hid scars and tickled me. I didn't need to know what hurt him—only that my heart ached that something happened. My mouth tried to give him my sympathy as I kissed him slowly. I took my time to discover the curve of his bottom lip and the dip of the top. My tongue swirled around his large one, learning the movement that would incite an uncontrollable growl from him. Emboldened by the power, my tongue delved deeper. My body leaned forward, my breasts aching to brush over him. My core beat in need of friction. But this night had to be about perfecting a kiss so I wouldn't scorch him. He responded to each call I made with my mouth, drawing out those little rumbles from the back of his throat while my lips caressed his with tender strokes.

I don't know how long we kissed, but the moment the ache between my thighs grew too great, I had to separate. I wasn't ready for more, although my body craved it. With one final kiss, I pulled back, tugging his lower lip with my teeth before releasing him. His eyes opened, and solid chocolate was nearly black with desire. My forehead came forward to rest against his, and I kissed his crooked nose. His lids closed and I breathed him in: campfire and manly with a hint of balsam spruce. I might be his home, but wherever he went was where I wanted to live.

+ + +

"Phyre?" The sweet sound of Flame sounded, as if I were in a dream. My body was surrounded in warm, cozy layers of blankets comforting me, and I snuggled in closer.

"Phyre," her voice whispered harsher, panicked. "You must wake up." Her stressed words reminded me of someone. A voice, little and meek, in need of my protection. Instantly, I sat upright, and extended a hand. Flames burst from my palm as my heart raced. The heat behind me included two large arms wrapped around my waist. He was safety, I reminded myself, but I needed to protect him. In the deep black of dawn, ice blue eyes glared at me.

"Flame?" My voice scratched with sleep. A hand rubbed up my back, and I shivered at his touch. I remained in Heph's lap, my body creaking from the curled position in which I had slept.

"What's wrong?" His gruff tone at my ear comforted me as I stared at my sister through the fire at my hands.

"Flame, what's the matter?" My hand burned, and thick fingers wrapped around my forearm and stroked upward.

"Phyre." The rugged call of my name turned my head, and Heph took a mighty breath. He blew at my hand and the fire extinguished. My eyes met his briefly. His dark orbs filled with concern. I spun back to Flame.

"What's wrong, Flame?"

"You can't get caught out here like this. Hestia would be displeased." My littlest sister was correct. "So would Adara." And thoughts of my oldest pinched at me. Who did I think I was, to take from her a man she still desperately sought? I saw it in her eyes, the way she looked at him with longing. He didn't return the glances, but he had to have felt the weight of them on him.

I quickly untangled myself from Heph's lap, but he gripped my waist.

"Wait!" The hushed tone in his deep voice sent a rush of warmth through the middle of me. I turned back to see eyes roaming my face.

"Tell me I didn't dream it. Tell me it was real."

How I longed to place my hands on his face and touch the scruff around his lips, press fingers to the worry lines around those eyes and trace over his crooked nose. With the steam still rising off my stinging hands, I could not take the risk. My lips had to answer him. Brief and brisk, I pressed forward over his lips, and then unfolded my legs from his lap.

"It wasn't a dream," I whispered, and a slow smile beamed at me like the rising sun. He nodded once and sat back, while I turned to run for the house, with Flame at my side.

"You like him," Flame's high voice whispered harshly next to me. The complex answer was no, it was more than that. The simple answer sprung out of me.

"Yes."

"Hestia will disapprove," she repeated to me. My heart sank as we neared the front door where I escaped.

"I know." My head hung. Hestia did not want us to use Heph any more than she allowed him to experience one of us. But Adara had already crossed the line with Heph in the past, and my heart balanced on the thinness of a stretched string. The arrow aimed, I could not resist Heph as my target.

"Your secret's safe with me." Her hand reached out for mine, wrapping around my burned skin, which healed quickly as the flame had been brief. Feeling the warmth of her hand, a question came to me.

"What have you been up to?"

She shook her head, but I noted her rumpled blonde hair and a goofy smile on her face.

"Flame," I admonished, my voice full of fear and concern. "Where have you been?"

A sheepish smile crossed her lips and the muscles of her face fought to control it.

"The stables." Her answer came too quick, the words almost a sigh. The building was a short trek through the woods. There, four horses resided under the care of the only other man to grace our property on a regular basis. Temple's stable was our only neighbor. He did not join us at the main house, as Hestia was adamant he was an employee, not a family member. His quiet unnerved me as much as the four-legged beasts did. His age was closer to Hestia's, and terrible thoughts flittered through my head.

"Not Temple," I shriek-whispered.

"What? Ewww…" Flame giggled in return. "He's old." He wasn't really *that* old but compared to Flame, old enough to know better. Relief washed over me, but concern still crawled under my skin. What was my little sister up to?

+ + +

As I entered my room, I wrapped the plaid blanket around myself. At some point, I pulled it up to cover Heph and me as we shared personal stories in the night.

"My mother rejected me when I was born," he began. "I was slow. Well, slower than I am now, and she didn't want to take care of me. I later learned she did it to spite my father. He'd had a daughter with his first wife, when my mother thought she would be his next wife." Heph sighed, and I stared at the campfire, listening to the beat of his heart while he spoke. "My father took me in. He took us all in. He has so many children I've lost count. He has trouble, shall we say, keeping it in his pants."

I chuckled at the thought, and his fingers stroked through my hair.

"You think that's funny but it's true. His gift to the world is procreation and the sky."

"The sky?"

"My father rules it."

"Isn't that from some Greek myth...?" My voice trailed off. Who was I to question him, with my flaming hands and ability to produce fire?

"It is. My brother Solis will inherit it, should anything ever happen to Zeke. I, on the other hand, am only what you see."

My hand stroked down the front of his form-fitting T-shirt, feeling confident I could touch the cotton but not his skin.

"I like what I see," I offered quietly.

He hummed against my hair and kissed my forehead. We were quiet for a moment, and the pause encouraged me to speak candidly next.

"My parents died." I swallowed hard at the memory. "It was Christmas. Candles burned throughout the house to give it a festive feel. One night, one remained lit, and I carried it to the tree to see it better. The twinkling, miniature lights remained on. My parents had gone to bed. I set the Christmas tree on fire, and the house went up in flames. My family didn't get out in time, because rather than call for them, I watched

Heph

the tree burn, mesmerized by the blaze." I shrunk into Heph, waiting for him to reprimand me for not seeking help, for not realizing that fire was deadly. He kissed my forehead again, holding his lips there.

"The flame was so beautiful, and I felt a strange peace watching it burn. It comforted me, although I had nothing to fear in my life. The walls engulfed in flames, curtains alit, ceiling blazing, and still I stared. When they found me, the fireman said it was a miracle I survived. I don't know how I did."

"You're a survivor, huntress." He interrupted me, but I continued, lost in memory as I watched the low flame over the campfire dance. "I went into foster care at first, but when the father wanted to touch me, and I burned his chest, I was sent to another home. I passed from place to place, lighting small fires whenever my anger or fear arose." Memories flipped through the pages of my mind, turning slowly as I lit each corner of the paper, watching them vanish in smoldering flames. "Eventually, I went to a state home. As soon as I could, I ran. I travelled by back roads and wandered into homeless shelters. I made my way the best I could, to get here. Then one night...one night..."

"Shhh, you don't have to tell me more. Not yet. Not ever, if you don't wish to." His lips returned to my forehead, lingering there, and I twisted to breathe in more of Heph. The scent grounded me. He smelled like home. My center, I thought, without sharing the words with him. I nodded to let him know, I wasn't ready to relive the memories. I only wanted this memory and I closed my eyes.

Hours later, I paced my room, afraid Hestia would be angry at Heph. That she'd blame him somehow, when it was me who went to him. I never worried before that she'd make me leave, but I panicked that she'd kick me out of the home because of what I did with him. I kissed him; he let me. A soft knock at my door ignited my fears. Opening it, Hestia asked to come in and closed the door behind her.

I sat on the bed, still wrapped in the plaid blanket, holding the last of Heph's fragrance to me before Hestia made me leave. My head fell forward awaiting my sentencing.

"It appears my Hephaestus is quite taken with you."

I nodded without looking up.

"I'd like to know how you feel about him."

"I don't want to hurt him."

"I don't want you to hurt him either," she said, helping herself to sit next to me. "But I also don't want him to hurt you."

I looked up at her words.

"Heph…is special. Kind of like you, but more like me."

"He mentioned something like that last night."

"You have to understand, he's lived a long time, a long life, and most of it alone."

At twenty-five, I felt ancient when I should have been carefree. I hadn't felt alone in the last year, but there were times I was lonely. Although he looked around thirty, I didn't care how old Heph might be.

"He's had interest in a multitude of women with promises broken. He's rather confused, I fear."

"What happened?"

Hestia nodded and brushed at my hair. "That's not a story that should come from me." She smiled to soften the blow of not sharing.

"What had he promised Adara?" I asked quietly, still encouraging answers.

"He promised to return and marry her. He'd take her to Zeke's estate as his bride. She doesn't think I knew, but there isn't much I don't know. He didn't return, until now."

"Did something happen at this father's estate?"

"Zeke kept him home too long and Heph let the relationship fail, though I don't completely fault Heph. Any relationship involves more than one person." The accusation sounded awful. Heph seemed so disinterested in Adara upon his return. How could he do that to my sister? But then a new thought struck: could people go back to what they had, once they give it up? The question haunted me. Hestia believed in second chances. She preached it often. Did Heph's feelings for Adara still linger? I didn't want to believe it. The concept made me sick, and bile clawed at my stomach. Heph claimed a sense of familiarity with me.

He'd lost me, somewhere in his history. I had to believe his interest in me was genuine.

"It seems Heph didn't know what he wanted until he saw you." The words made me smile, though it conflicted with my thoughts.

"Why didn't he come searching for me?" I asked innocently. The concept confused me. So many nights I felt alone as I searched for a place where I could feel safe. Was Heph looking for me while I looked for him?

"I don't think he knew where to look for what was missing from him."

"But here he is." I sighed, toying with the edges of the blanket wrapped around me, reminding me of our night together.

"Here he is. This will always be his home." *Home*. Heph said I was his home. His center.

"I think he returned here each year hoping to find balance in his life, to center himself. And this is the year it might actually happen." I sat up straighter at her words, and she brushed back my hair. Hestia was so maternal.

"He might not have searched the world for you, but at one point, he did search the world, and it was cruel to him. Maybe you were what he was looking for, but he got lost along the way. He gave up on himself. I need you to not give up on him." She tapped my knee for emphasis. "He'll need to learn about you, and you'll need to learn about him. It's more than the fire in your hands that will need control." She winked at me, and I turned bright pink to coordinate with my hair.

"I don't think I'm there yet."

"But you will be. Heph is still a Cronus. He has needs. He's sweet and he's innocent, but he's more man, and he hungers. Starve him, and he'll stray." My brow pinched at the metaphor. Was she implying that Heph would lose interest if I didn't sleep with him? Or perhaps there was more to her meaning, something deeper, related to her? Either way, the implication was clear. If I didn't give into my desires for Heph, he wasn't going to wait for me.

"I'm not endorsing promiscuity. I'm just giving you my permission for exploration. Heph could help you discover what you need. He helped Adara, but he also broke her heart." Would Heph break mine? I questioned everything, and my heart began to crumble with the thought.

HEPH

I was the happiest man in the history of the planet as I worked the metal over the fire. Today, I made new shoes for the horses at Temple's stable. He needed a blacksmith, and as long as I was present, the work was good for me. The fire stoked, the heat oppressive, my thoughts fired back to my little spark and her exploratory kisses. My morning shower helped relieve what she did to me, but it wasn't enough. Her kiss had only nurtured a tiny flame when I wanted the campfire: sweet and smoky.

I stood centered toward the ovens, working the metal, watching it turn a brilliant hot orange and wondered again at the history of my huntress. Burning down her house as a child, she had to be forgiven for the misunderstandings of her gift. I sensed she felt cursed from the destruction. What other evils had she encountered? Older men wanting to touch a child turned my stomach to stone. Teenage boys horny and hot burned my insides. And then, whatever the crowning moment of disgust that brought her to Hestia's Home made me wish I could spear someone with the hot poker of my blade. I'd kill anyone that tried to harm her again.

I hadn't spent any time with my girl during the day. Her subtle smiles and shy glances at dinner twisted me inside, and I missed her. When I returned to my room after dinner, Phyre sat on the edge of my bed, the blanket from the night before wrapped around her in a way that pinned it to her side like a dress. My lips curled at the bare arm exposed on one side, her creamy pale skin looking soft and smelling sweet, but I questioned her intentions. She chewed her lip, but it was not the delicate bite that endeared me. Her eyes avoided mine.

"What's going on here, Little Spark?"

Her shaky laughter didn't sound right.

"Hestia sent me."

My brow creased. "For what?"

Delicate fingers with short nails picked at the plaid fabric over her.

"She said you wouldn't remain interested in me if I don't sleep with you." Her voice trembled and the words cut.

"What?" The question rolled out like trees dropping after a lumberjack's cut, slowly falling and then a crash. Did Hestia think so low of me as to offer this girl to me? Did she think so low of Phyre to suggest she give herself to me? I stared, unblinking, my fists clenching and unclenching at my sides. Something was off.

"No," I barked. "No, that's not true. No. Forget it; I'm not sleeping with you." I brushed past her for the bathroom, needing space, needing a moment to collect my thoughts. I turned on the water at the sink and splashed my face, ridding the thoughts of desire that stiffened me, reminding myself of the argument that solidified my answer. I didn't only want her physically; I wanted her everything.

I re-entered my bedroom to find her perched with one hand on the barn-red blankets. Pristine white sheets curled down from the numerous pillows. Instantly I envisioned spreading her there, admiring her hair in contrast to that innocence.

"Let's go in the other room." The command was harsh, although my intention was not. I needed to separate her from the bed before I changed my mind and agreed with Hestia. She stood slowly and entered the small living room. Taking a seat on the edge of the couch, my heart dropped. I panicked that the next few minutes would define us, and it would end the same way as Adara and I. No reciprocation of unrelenting love. I could give devotion and security, but I wanted love in exchange.

"I didn't mean to upset you," she said, still not looking up at me. I knelt before her, placing my hands on her covered knees.

"Tell me what happened?"

"Hestia came to see me. She gave me permission to pursue you." Her voice faltered. "Experiment, she said. She implied I would not be able to keep you interested unless I gave in to you."

I wasn't a fast thinker, so it took me a moment to collect my thoughts. Did Hestia think by giving her permission that Phyre and I would not happen? Did she foresee that I would turn Phyre down or did she predict Phyre would never proposition me? Was this some kind of motherly reverse psychology?

"Let's start with the experimentation. Is that all you want? Do you want to see what you can do with someone? With me?" Could I be her toy? My immediate answer was yes. The afterthought was no, and my heart fell to my knees aching on the thin, rug-covered floor.

"No. I mean, I want to try things with *you*. I want to see how far I can go. But I only want to do them with you." Her eyes remained downcast, and she bit her lip in the way I liked. The thick pad of my finger tipped up her chin. Her blue eyes shone like the deepest part of a lake, and I wanted to plunge in.

"Have you experimented with others?" I had to know. Who had she been with in the past?

"I...I'm not a virgin." She shivered and swallowed hard at the thought. Her eyes closed briefly. I didn't wish to bring haunting memories into this conversation. This was about us, not the past.

"That's not what I'm asking. I want to know if there are other men in your life."

She laughed bitterly and replied, "How?"

I understood her hesitant reply but after Lovie, I needed to know if there was any other. I nodded my understanding and my lips twisted, holding in a retort referencing Lovie. Again, this was not the past.

"Let's start with the next thing. My interest in you. I can't even measure the feelings I have for you. No tool exists to take the width of my affection or the length of my interest. I want to know you. All of you. When you are ready to share it with me."

A slow smile grew on her permanently cherry-magenta lips.

"But..." Her smile drooped as I spoke. "I need to know, what is your interest in me? Is it only experimentation?" I couldn't be used again. I had no doubt Hestia knew of the affair with Adara. She allowed it to happen, knowing it might fail, hoping it would fail. But for who? Me or Adara?

"I..." Her hesitation brought back instant memories of Adara rejecting me. I sat back on my hunches and hung my head.

"I feel safe with you. I trust you." My head rose slowly to meet her wide blue eyes. "And the flame in me fizzles when I think of not being with you."

Sitting upright, my hands cupped her cheeks. I'd startled her, and I cursed myself for my eagerness. I didn't want her to snap and react. I paused, drinking in her eyes before lowering my lips to sip on her. Those fruit-flavored lips were the sweetest I'd ever tasted, and gentle sucking was not enough. My tongue slipped over her lips, savoring the taste like a child licking up the last of a delicious flavor, hoping to make it last as it lingered. Her tongue flicked out to meet mine, and the invitation ignited a blaze. Plunging forward, my tongue stroked over hers, sparking flint to rock and bursting into flame. Our mouths danced like the light around logs in the night fires. We lapped and we crackled, and the shells of our hearts cracked. I kissed her like I'd never kissed someone before— eager, anxious, and thrilled to experience her.

In our kissing, she had leaned back, and my upper body rested over her. My chest crushed her breasts, ripe and firm under the plaid blanket. My mouth fell to her jaw and trailed down her neck.

"Heph," she moaned, and I continued to blaze downward.

"Heph, I…I…" Panic filled her voice, and I pulled back inches from the swell of her breasts. My hands rose in innocence, and I sat back to meet her eyes. Her hands clenched and unclenched at her sides. I never even realized she wasn't touching me. Our mouths melding and molding was enough.

"I'm sorry," she whispered.

"Please," I begged. "Please don't be." Her knees pressed on my sides, and I noticed the plaid blanket dressing rose, exposing long legs of china white. My eyes shifted to the space exposed to me.

"What are you wearing under there?" My head tilted, lips crooking in question. With eyes still connected, I lifted the plaid blanket to see a peek of bright Christmas red. She had on my underwear.

"Phyre," I swallowed her name. "What else do you have on?"

"Nothing else…" She exhaled, and I sucked in the air. My eyes rolled back in my head.

"You're killing me, Little Spark." I flipped positions with her, swinging up to the couch and dragging her into my lap. Cradling her over my thighs, my hand reached for her ankle and stroked upward.

"The fire almost came, didn't it?" My concern that I frightened her returned. Was the kiss too aggressive? Too suggestive? Could she sense how much I ached for her?

"When I feel out of control, I can't always think like Hestia taught me. I forget to focus, but I tried this time. I didn't want to burn you—I wanted to touch you."

"Let's try this," I offered and held out my thick arm. Long sleeves were rolled to my elbows, exposing thick forearms marked by working with fire. "You take control again. Rub over my skin." As I hadn't experienced her touch in this manner before, the first tender brush of her palm made me flinch. The coarse hairs on my arm stood on end. She pulled back as if I shocked her, and I chuckled.

"I'm sorry. That was me." I kissed the side of her head, hoping to encourage her to try again. The tips of her fingers tickled the thick hair on my arm. Like playing a piano, her fingers worked back and forth over imaginary keys, hitting each note as she stroked over me. My breath calmed, but my pulse raced. I could not control the length pressing into her hip. The tenderness of her touch turned me on like the dial of her flamethrower. The first twist and I burst forth, ready to create or destroy. In her case, I only wanted to design something never forged before.

Her fingers spread, and her palm flattened. Her eyes closed as she rubbed from wrist to elbow. She lifted her hand, and my eyes focused on her face as it came to mine.

"I don't want to hurt you," she whispered with a trembling voice.

"I don't believe you will. I trust you." The words closed her lids and her lips parted as she cupped my cheek and let her nails scrape tenderly over my hairy face. Her cheek came forward, mouth smiling, as she rubbed her face over mine, enjoying the scratch of my beard. A subtle moan escaped. I wanted her mouth on me. I wanted so many things, but I would let her lead.

Her hips rocked, rolling against me, and I stilled under her.

"Heph, I…" Her breath hitched and her face released mine. "Hold my hands back," she whispered, and she held them together in front of her at the wrist. I covered them both with one of mine and dragged them over her head. Arching her back, she pressed into me with the round of her ass.

"Heph," she breathed, and my free hand went to her knee. Dragging upward, I curled around her inner thigh and travelled north to her core. Brushing over the soft cotton, already moist with her arousal, I pressed firmly, and she sighed. Her eyes were closed, but sensing mine, she opened those bottle blues and stared at me, begging me to touch her. Her brow twitched, as if questioning my hesitation. Letting her know I'd do anything she asked, I pushed aside the red briefs and plunged into her like my crafty tongs dipped into fire. Her back arched upward, her hands straining on the handmade manacles, holding her palms flat to one another, she let me take charge and master her. My finger dove deep, reveling in the heat of her, and lingering in the warmth. The pad of my thumb found a separate nub of pleasure and her hips rocked over me.

Subtle huffs escaped her lips, as she mumbled my name, begging me to get her there. A new flame was lit inside her and cresting sparks only teased her.

"Let me have your fire, Little Spark. Give me the blaze."

Her back curved and her head fell back as she bit her lip holding in a scream. Her legs stiffened and thighs clamped, holding me in place against her. Her eyes rolled back and I wanted to know what she envisioned as she exploded over me. Floating like smoke, drifting up to the sky, she fluttered back down like loose embers and relaxed over me. Her head rolled, and she kissed my forearm, pressed near her head, as she stretched over me.

"Heph, I…I've never experienced anything like that before. Never."

My heart soared with pride that I could give her that first. I wanted to be her first at everything, as I knew she'd be the first for me. First and last.

PHYRE

Resting in Heph's lap, my lids grew lazy and closed momentarily. Like a satisfied kitten, napping in the sun, I stretched and purred. Aftershocks lingered as the embers died down. Heph smiled at me, but I worried I hadn't satisfied him and I sat up abruptly. Balancing on one thigh, I looked over my bare shoulder at him. The plaid blanket draped over me in a sultry dress, replica of a Grecian goddess, or more like a Scottish princess. Ember helped me, belting it at the waist, and speaking words of encouragement.

"You can do this. Trust him." Confiding in her, I told her what Hestia said. Ember stared back at me in disbelief, and then told me she knew what to do. Here I sat, staring into the warm eyes of a man who just gave me something I'd never experienced before. A sensation I wanted to experience again, but now it was his turn. I slipped off his lap and knelt before him, pushing his knees apart, feeling confident to touch the denim covering.

"Phyre, you don't have to do this." He sat up straighter, placing his hands on my shoulders.

"I want to. Please." My eyes begged him to let me. Satiated and empowered, I didn't want to lose my nerve. He slowly sat back and watched as I unbuttoned his jeans and unzipped it to free him. Boxer briefs in forest green greeted me. I smiled and he helped me lower the material to his hips. Springing forth, I inspected him. I'd never paid attention to a man before. Previous experience proved only one function, one purpose, from the men who approached me. This would be different. This would be me controlling him.

I didn't trust myself to wrap my hands around the thickness of his length. This was going to be a first, as well. Placing my hands on his knees, I pressed up and lowered my lips to him. My tongue swiped over the salty tip, and he flinched. I pulled back and looked up for assurance to see his eyes closed, his expression peaceful, his lips curled.

"Heph." He opened his eyes instantly.

"I need to ask you to bind me again."

"What?" He choked, and my eyes brushed to the thick leather strap around his left wrist.

"Strap my hands so I can't hurt you."

"Phyre, no, I trust you." His eyes begged, pained at the thought.

"Heph, please. I don't trust me." I didn't believe I would hurt him intentionally, but I didn't trust the excitement I anticipated in bringing this large man to his knees, figuratively. The power of that thought set my palms to prickle. "Please." I whispered.

Heph unsnapped the thick strap and I placed my hands behind my back. Lowering my head, he reached over me and wrapped my wrists. I misjudged the length of the leather and the fit was snug, but I couldn't move my hands, and the cuffing relieved me. He sat back, and I noticed the large compass tattoo he'd hidden under the covering. The north end pointed at me, reminding me of what he said. I was his true north. His skin blazed and the glow encouraged me. My eyes turned to his, but his tenderness redirected me. My mouth returned to cover him, drawing him deep, learning the way to bring him pleasure and claim him. If I was his little spark, he was my soothing flame, and I wanted to take comfort in the blaze of his heat.

+ + +

The next few days passed with silent stares and subtle caresses, but I did not climb the stairs to his room again. I missed his touch and wanted to taste him again, but I didn't want to raise suspicion with Hestia. Permission or not, I didn't want her to think I was Adara, and that I was using Heph. In preparation for the celebration Hestia wished to throw, we gathered leaves, ironing them in wax paper and stringing them from the kitchen ceiling. Hestia made a wreath of yellow, orange and brown foliage and decorated the iron chandelier in the dining room. Garlands in fall colors draped from mantels and down the center of the table. The adornment gave off a holiday feel and festivity filled the air. I wasn't certain there was a theme, other than a celebration of harvest, bounty and fall. Winter would be on us soon, and I feared Heph would leave. He wasn't here this time last year when I arrived. I'd just missed him, or he had just missed me. Either way, I told him I was found by him now, and I privately prayed to remain in that position with him: Found and home.

When Persephone Fields and Veva Matron arrived, the energy of the house rose twentyfold from just two additional girls. Solis Cronus was their escort and quite opposite his brother, Heph. Slimmer, but still broad, his booming voice and tan stature filled the room. His sandy blond hair and honey colored eyes scanned the room and every girl sighed, wishing he would pick her, but his eyes always landed on one girl: Heph's sister. With acorn-colored hair and unusual sapphire eyes ringed in turquoise, her curvy body and sassy mouth instantly endeared Veva to me. It took a moment to learn that while sister and brother to Heph, Solis and Veva were not blood-related to one another. Persephone was the quieter of the two women, her smile sweet but hesitant. Her blonde hair and blue eyes embodied innocence, but the tenderness of her expression hinted at a secret knowledge. We had a surprise for her, but we were sworn to secrecy. It had not arrived yet, but Hestia did not show a trace of panic, as always.

"It's a pleasure to meet you." I didn't extend my hand, and Veva looked down at my clenched fists. I didn't touch people willingly, and my hesitation stumped her. Every other girl eagerly hugged her, pulling her close, remembering her as a child. Before me stood a woman, and one important to Heph, but I couldn't touch her.

"You're new here?" The statement was a question, and Veva searched my face for signs of something. I didn't understand her questioning glare, and my fingers twitched with the need to protect myself. The warmth at my back as I remained standing in the breakfast room told me Heph was close.

"Phyre arrived last year in the winter," he explained, his hand stroking down my hair, sending a signal to his sister, and her eyes opened wide.

"I thought you were going to patch things up with Lovie." The words tumbled out of her mouth and my back stiffened. Veva closed her eyes and Persephone hissed her name under her breath.

"Who's Lovie?" I asked through clenched teeth and a forced smile. The fingertips at the base of my back made me flinch, and instantly Heph removed his touch. We stood in the small space of the breakfast room, now overcrowded with three additional people, and the walls suddenly caved in on me. The heat of the hearth fire too great, sweat built at the edge of my hairline.

"She's no one," Veva lied, shaking her head. Solis spoke up in his booming deep voice. "She was— *was*—Heph's fiancé, the cheating *bi*— ."

"Solis!" Hestia snapped. Persephone covered her forehead, shaking her head vigorously. The tension in the room closed in on me, crushing me.

"You were engaged?" The strangled sound of Adara at the doorway cracked through the thickness, like shifting plates below the earth. The room rumbled in heartache.

"I..." Heph coughed behind me. Adara glared at him over my shoulder. I stared at her, the hurt cutting deep into her dark eyes.

"Heph, how could you?" Seraphine admonished, standing, anticipating Adara's retreat. Instantly, Adara spun for the kitchen with Seraphine in tow. Veva looked at Heph over my head, mouthing, *I'm sorry*, and my heart froze. That saying of hell freezing over? It happened within me, the heat of my flames crystallizing into frozen waves, and I shivered.

"Phyre." The tender voice of Heph behind me did nothing to warm me. I stepped forward, addressing Veva.

"I look forward to your stay. Excuse me." I stepped past her and exited through the side door. The moment I hit the fresh air, I ran like I hadn't run since that night: the night I needed all my energy to get here, as fear chased me, and a man died because he lied to me.

+ + +

I sat on the edge of the roaring river bank, casting out stones from the gravel under my fingers. I didn't care that my jeans slowly drew up the moisture from the bank and the wetness seeped deeper than my skin. Cold filled me. Heph had been engaged. While I vaguely remembered overhearing this, it hadn't processed. Why hadn't he told me? I thought it was only Adara, and yet there had been someone else. How many lovers did he have? How many marriage proposals had he offered? How many women had he loved before? This was more than a man who sowed his seed, aimlessly restless. This was a man with intentions to settle, not once but twice, with different women, both in the same year.

My heart ached so fiercely, the stabbing scissors effect opened to snip and cut and carve out my heart. I bent at the waist, feeling sick at the thought of his touch. The way he caressed me. The words he spoke. I believed him, like I had believed others, and he hadn't been truthful. Pretty words and tender strokes, and I had given into to hope. I turned to my side, bracing both hands in the cool, gravelly soil on the edge of the water. My fingers dug deep, suppressing the instinct to burn, holding down the spark ready to ignite and set the forest on fire. My heat raged. My heart ripped. But I did not cry. No, no tears fell to extinguish flames. Frozen behind my eyes, they remained.

Taking deep breaths to hold back the bile rising, a thundering sound filled my ears. The river raced, and the noise of water rushing over rocks heightened. The volume rose like a thermometer, hovering over me like a fever. A vibration rumbled the earth beneath my hands, and I watched as the little stones under my fingers knocked subtly together. My palms vibrated. My arms quaked. I looked up to see the river rising, forming into a shape. A motorbike sped toward me, the whine of an engine and the roar of the river mixing into one. The nightrider, dressed in black, came into full form and raced in my direction. I couldn't move. I stared at the strange figure as the image of rider and bike grew. The noise took over all senses, and I held my breath as he jumped the river bank and landed feet from me. Spinning in the gravel, rocks arched and sputtered, cascading over me. The back tire spun three-sixty before coming to a complete stop. The engine cut as pebbles rained down on me. Removing a helmet, a dark head of hair, flipped back, and a bluish face with bluer lips faced me.

"Are you okay?" he breathed. His black hoodie, open at the chest, exposed a dark T-shirt underneath, accessorizing dark jeans and heavy boots.

"I...I'm fine." My stutter was a new thing, but I didn't know how to respond to the stranger before me, piercing me with sapphire eyes, shades darker than his skin. A white scar cut his face from forehead to chin at his hairline and a slice over his lips matched. His eyes narrowed in concern.

"Are you one of Hestia's girls?" Surprised that he knew her, or potentially recognized me, I didn't answer as I slowly rose, ready to take aim at him with my hands. My arrows remained in my room. The beautiful new set matched a new bow Heph had forged for me. My heart couldn't think of him, in my fear. My eyes did not leave the stranger.

"Who are you?" My voice sounded stronger than I felt, my palms flat as the need for protection took over my broken heart. My blood boiled, fueling the flame as it rolled through me for its destination. A spark at my left hand let me know I was almost there. His eyes didn't miss the sharp light.

"Fire." His eyebrow rose. "Definitely one of Hestia's girls." My shoulders dropped as I stared. My head tilted just the slightest in question. "Allow me to introduce myself. I'm nearly family. My name is Hades."

+ + +

We walked in silence after introductions were made. My eyes continued to shift to the blue creature, human in every way but color, who stalked beside me. We cleared the trees to see people gathered around the fire pit. More chairs were added to accommodate the growing number of guests, but quiet murmurs did not present a rowdy celebration. As we drew closer, Seraphine screamed: "Hades!" Springing from her seat, she ran for the man we were anticipating, but I did not expect. No one had mentioned his color, or the fact that he would arrive by way of the river. Seraphine surprised me further by lunging at the man beside me. He chuckled as he caught her, and she muttered something into his neck. Staring in wonder, the greeting was not what I expected, either. I had imagined another girl approaching him in such a manner.

As if on cue, the side door opened and slammed shut. Blonde hair effervescent in the night slowly moved toward the couple embracing. Her motions calculated, her grace refined, Persephone kept her eyes forward as she moved evenly to Hades and Seraphine. Hades released Seraphine instantly, my blue-haired sister stepping back as Persephone approached.

"I'm sorry, I'm late," Hades greeted his girl, who stared unblinking at him in the dark.

"You're here. You can be here? At Hestia's? At my aunt's home?" The questions surprised me as I eased away from them, but not far enough to miss their conversation. They definitely had an audience, as all eyes were on them.

"I can be here." He reached out to brush back a loose hair in the evening breeze and held his hand behind her ear. She nodded slowly, her head lowering, and Hades bent at the knees to look up at her.

"You aren't excited to see me." The question, stated as a comment, came so quietly only those closest could hear him. Seraphine stepped further away. I turned away from them.

"I am," Persephone said quietly. "Yes, I am." Arms encased her hips, and he lifted her to his height. Her arms wrapped around his neck, and they stood in an embrace that broke my heart. Love radiated from her, encircling his dark presence, and my eyes swung to Heph's without thought. He sat in the same chair where we slept nights ago. His posture the same: an ankle crossed over his knee, a hand propping up his chin. He hadn't acknowledged me.

"Phyre, come join us," Veva called out pleasantly. Heph remained closed off.

"I think our new friend has had quite the shock in meeting me," Hades spoke, and his voice sounded like water over river rocks.

"You have gravel in your hair. Are you alright?" Ember asked and my hand rose to find small bits of pebbles stuck in my hair.

"What happened?" Heph sat forward, finally looking at me.

"She was my welcoming committee; I found her by the river." Hades' tone remained cheerful, attempting to cut through slices of tension. He stood with his arms wrapped around Persephone, holding her to his side. Shivering with the cold that seeped through my jeans, I smiled falsely.

"If you'll excuse me, I seem to have gotten wet by the river and need to warm up from the chill." Heph moved as if I might sit with him, but I walked on the outside of the circle, suddenly feeling like I'd never fit in, and headed toward the house for my room, to burn a small candle and release my heartache.

PHYRE

I had missed dinner and returned to the kitchen as the late-night thief that I was. Most people gathered in the living room now, which was easy enough to avoid as I exited the main staircase and turned left for the dining room. The breakfast room with the giant hearth held voices, too.

"Why can you be here and not other places?" Persephone's voice whispered. "Why do I not know these things?"

"Because Hestia is like family, and the river connects here. It simply never crossed my mind to mention it."

"But a river connects to my home, too." Her voice turned argumentative, and I knew I shouldn't be listening. I walked to the entrance of the dining room, and found Solis and Veva kissing in the dark. Turning about, I crossed the kitchen for the sink, feeling hostage to the spectrum of relationships—lust and arguing.

"You aren't at your home. You're in California now," Hades tone soothed. A heavy sigh fell after the comment.

"That was quite a greeting." Persephone's tone turned edgy, and I wanted to close my ears. I knew nothing of Seraphine's friendship with Hades, but Seraphine had been here for years.

"She's an old friend."

"Old friend," Persephone snapped. "That was more than friendship."

"I kind of like it when you're jealous. It's sexy." Hades chuckled, and my heart snapped at the laughter. Somehow, I knew Persephone did not appreciate the compliment.

"I'm not trying to be funny or sexy. I'm serious. Who is she?"

"Persephone," he warned. "Don't do this."

"I knew there would have been others. I mean, look at you, but still, I haven't had it put in my face."

"There aren't any others," he sighed, and I smiled, but then I thought of Heph. How many others had he had? At least two and that was only in the last year. He'd hinted that he was much older than he appeared which only meant more time to experiment and appreciate others.

"I…" Persephone's voice hung and I knew I really didn't want to hear what came next. "I kissed someone. Well, he kissed me."

The silence weighing from the right outweighed the embarrassment of walking in on Veva and Solis kissing to the left. I took the risk they were still making out in the dining room and crossed to the entrance. Thankfully it was empty. If I slipped quietly, I could wrap around the dining room into the hall and hit the stairs without anyone noticing me.

"Okay, boys. Where is Hades? Time to get out."

"What?" Solis chuckled as I hit the first stair and climbed slowly, listening to voices filled with love.

"No men in the house. You know the rule."

"Then Veva can go with me."

"No girls in the barn, same rule applies."

"Hestia," Solis admonished, a tease to his tone, and I imagined him batting his eyes in flirtation. He seemed like a man who knew his way around women. That must be the Cronus' brothers' inheritance.

"Unless you're married, no." I could picture Hestia shaking her head, not falling for the charm of Solis Cronus.

"We're engaged. That's close enough."

Squeals of excitement followed the announcement, and I was thankful I'd reached the top of the stairs, finding solace in the solitude of my room, heart shattering at the thought that I would never marry.

HEPH

I did not think things could get any more messed up: Veva blurting out about Lovie, Phyre running off, Adara's accusing glare. And now, Hades in a total lather about something Persephone did.

"She said she kissed him."

"Were those her words?" Solis asked as the three of us sat in my small living room. Hestia's secret stash of alcohol flowed between us. I wasn't much of a drinker, but when I drank, it had a purpose. Tonight, it dulled my aching emotions.

"She said, '*he* kissed me.'"

"Who?" I asked. Hades swiped a hand through this dark hair. I wasn't as close to my cousin as Solis was. They were long-lost best friends. Being more of an outsider in my own family, I didn't visit cousins and relatives. I could hardly keep track of all our relations.

"I didn't ask. I stormed out as soon as she told me."

"Dude, did she like it?" Solis' face dropped after he asked. Shaking his head, he said, "Never mind, this is messed up."

Hades and Persephone had a strange relationship, in my opinion. They wanted each other. It showed when they were together, and yet something kept them apart. Hades was a god, for goodness' sake, he could make anything happen. But then I thought of myself, and realized, well, almost anything. I couldn't make the girl I loved, love me. I hadn't made any of them love me. The past no longer mattered, though. I only wanted the one in the present to be my future.

"And you," Solis turned on me. "You're as fickle as Romeo."

I stared at my brother. He knew I didn't understand the reference. I wasn't practiced in academics or literature. I worked with my hands. I had a trade.

"Meaning?"

"*Oh Rosalind*," Hades said.

"Who's Rosalind?"

"One day, it's *I love this hot girl at Hestia's* and then suddenly you're engaged to Lovie. And then, I hear you banging Callie in a shower stall," Solis admonished.

"How did you hear that?" I snorted, embarrassed and confused how he knew I took her quickly there last summer.

"It doesn't matter. What matters is you can't make up your mind. Two beautiful women stood there with their hearts crushed tonight. *Two*. Dude, you must have some serious Cronus to work that magic."

"I don't have magic." I hated when Solis spoke to me and didn't make sense.

"He means, you're like your father, with all your women." Hades' took sympathy and explained, but he didn't sound pleased to clarify. I'd never been compared to my father or the prowess he had to produce the multitude of children on the estate in California. Olympic Oil encouraged sexuality.

"I am nothing like Zeke."

"It doesn't look like it. Two women. Two hearts. What did you do?" Hades asked. I hung my head. I touched a girl and told her I loved her, to learn she didn't love me. I touched a second girl and never said the words that scared me. Now, she closed herself off to me. I didn't understand women.

"I screwed up, as Solis would say. Adara didn't love me. Neither did Lovie."

"I'm sorry, man. What about the other girl? Phyre, she looked devastated." Hades' curious tone surprised me. Had he seen something I hadn't?

"I don't think she'll speak to me at the moment." He nodded in understanding.

"Thank gods, I have Veva now." Solis smiled brightly and tipped his drink. I'd never seen my brother so happy and my sister nearly beamed with joy.

"Engaged? How did I miss that?" I asked.

"It happened right after Lovie…" His voice faltered. *Right after Lovie was caught with her rear in the air and another man taking her.*

"I'm sorry, dude." He meant the apology, but the reminder stung. Cheating hurt. Lying did, too. Phyre should have known I had been engaged. How did I fail to tell her? The answer was clear. The same way I tried to avoid speaking of Adara. I was such a disaster with women.

"You need a grand gesture. You're a god, for heaven's sake, give her sunshine and rainbows."

I stared at my brother. "Where have I heard that before?"

"You said that to me." He paused, raising an eyebrow, refreshing my memory. "To get Veva back."

Ah, I nodded. I couldn't recall saying such a thing.

"I want to ask Persephone to marry me," Hades blurted. Solis and I stared. How could that be possible, with where he lived?

"How will you do that?" Solis asked, lowering his glass and shaking his head.

"I don't know, but my parents worked it out."

"Dude, your parents are miserable," Solis commented, offering no consolation.

"I know," Hades sighed and wiped a hand through his dark hair. "But so am I, without her."

The room grew silent as we each held our own thoughts.

"Didn't Hestia want this to be festive? I don't feel festive. I want my girl," Solis said, slumping back and downing the rest of his drink. A hesitant knock came on my door and I stood to open it, too hopeful it would be a girl with cherry-rosebud hair. Instead, I pressed the door wider to present Persephone. Hades stood instantly, taking the two quick steps to reach her and took her in his arms. All would be forgiven as soon as they talked. Her feet dangled as he lifted her straight upward and walked her into the hall.

"This is such bullshit. I'm going to get Vee." Solis set down his glass. Opening the door, Hades and Persephone were already gone. Solis tapped the wood and looked back at me.

"It's going to be all right, dude. They'll both come around." With that, he closed the door. I only wanted one of them to come around, and I feared that one would not come looking for me.

+ + +

Foolishly, I searched for Adara first when everything happened, feeling a sense of obligation to explain myself. Adara deserved the truth. I didn't want her to feel how I felt, despite the fact that she rejected me. The truth included how I felt beholden to my father, who took me back in after I tried to run away. In search of someone, *something*, I would never receive, I bore the scars of that journey in both my missing leg and my cut-up face. Zeke took me back after my mother rejected me. Twice. I owed him everything, but Adara didn't need all those details. She only needed the ones I offered.

"You didn't love me, Adara." I paused watching her dark eyes widen. "My lack of return came additionally from a promise offered by my father. If I married the girl, he would give me a portion of his estate. I'm not greedy by nature, Adara, but I wanted his recognition."

She nodded her head in understanding. She was one of the most selfless people I knew, taking charge of her sisters and bringing them here. She appreciated praise of her good intentions. It's why it made it so hard for her to just ask Hestia to leave.

"I was a fool. Zeke felt he owed something to her mother. An ugly man would do her good, he told me." Adara flinched at the comment and her eyes shifted away, confirming something I had already known. It wasn't my face that attracted Adara.

"I think it had more to do with taming her. Too many men wanted her. She was beautiful and lively." Adara's head began to lower, and I knew I offered too much. She was equally beautiful, if not more so, but Phyre outshined them both in my eyes. I couldn't let thoughts of Phyre cloud my explanation, though. I walked on sensitive ground as it was.

"I promised him I'd marry the girl. He thought an ugly man would not be jealous of attention she received from others." How wrong my father was. From the moment of our engagement, I sensed Lovie's too-sweet tone and tender flirtations disguised her true intentions with other men. Distracting me with the hope that a beautiful woman would love me, I fell for the temptation. Sensing her deceit, I faltered when Callie approached me last summer. She'd been a steadfast girl of interest. She let me take her anywhere, and her willingness confused me. Having my way with her in the shower stall confirmed that marrying Lovie was a mistake. We both lived a lie, only Lovie got caught before I could break the arrangement.

"Over time I knew she didn't think of me as anything other than a means to an end." Adara flinched at the mention of her own intentions.

"Heph," she warned, but my hand rose to stop her as we sat across from one another in Hestia's formal living room. The gathering room was her small, cozy breakfast space. This room was a formality. "Heph," she continued, ignoring me. "You aren't ugly. You're kind, and you're good. You're gentle and sweet. You don't understand..." Her voice drifted off, and I shook my head.

"I do. Time had passed for you and me. When you couldn't return my love, I didn't see the point. It hurt. Lovie's rejection didn't surprise me, but it only stung. I wouldn't have returned here, knowing how you felt, but so much happened at once: meeting my mother and finding out about my sister, and then Lovie. I just needed to come home. Being here grounds me. Hestia grounds me..."

"Phyre grounds you." Adara's eyes sharpened.

"Adara," I growled in warning. We weren't discussing Phyre.

"Don't. I see how you look at her. It's how you looked at me. You want her, like you wanted me. You think you love her, like you thought you loved me. I only know one thing for certain in this story, Hephaestus. I was wrong. I loved you, and I didn't know it until too late. I'd never had love like that before. I longed for you when you left. Seeing you again, it rekindled everything inside me. I missed you. I want to be with you."

The words shocked me, but it was too late. My heart had changed.

+ + +

After the night of silence from Phyre, I sought her out the next day, but she hadn't come from her room. Hestia allowed her to stay upstairs, although she typically refused to let the girls wallow. She agreed Phyre might have caught a cold sitting on the wet riverbank for too long. I found it impossible that a girl who could produce fire would be chilled, but I let it slide. Hestia wanted the women to live a life as normal as possible; perfecting their gift was part of that normal. After that, she treated them as humans.

"A day in bed never hurt anyone," Hestia teased as she poured me coffee, her cheery tone so opposite her words. Hestia did not believe what she spewed. Life wasn't all work, but she abhorred laziness. She didn't appreciate cowardice either, but I couldn't fault Phyre. I was the one who hadn't been brave enough to mention my recent past.

PHYRE

To my surprise, Hestia let me stay in bed. I used my monthly curse as an excuse. Lying on my side, I stared at the window. A gray sky filled the fall day. It was the perfect day to linger under the covers. My mind meandered over the night's events: learning the truth of Heph's engagement, knowing he went to Adara first, meeting Hades, catching Solis and Veva kissing.

My thoughts drifted to my late-night visitor. Veva had come to the door.

"Can I talk to you?"

As I nodded my assent, sitting up in my bed, Veva entered and began.

"I want to apologize."

I blinked in confusion but she blazed forward.

"I've only known Heph a short time, even if he is my brother. I instantly fell in adoration of him. I love him." *She smiled sweetly, like a proud sister, and helped herself to the edge of my bed. The candle at my bedside danced in the slight breeze from the open window.*

"I'm so sorry my mouth got ahead of me. It happens sometimes. I react before I think."

I smiled slowly. I knew the feeling.

"I've never seen the gleam in Heph's eyes like he had when he looked at you. And I crushed the heat in yours, when I burst out information you clearly did not know."

I began to shake my head, ready to speak when she raised both hands, waving them at me.

"No, listen. He didn't love her. It was an arrangement of some type. Heph did it only to please his father. That's what he does. He tries to please others."

She sat up straighter at the thought.

102

"I mean, he doesn't go around trying to please women, just does what he thinks is best to satisfy others." Both hands covered her mouth. *"I'll shut up now,"* she muttered behind her palms. I couldn't help the giggle that escaped me. One hand came forward to my crisscrossed knee. *"Please forgive me. And don't hold the situation against him."*

I turned away, looking at the simple candle flame. I'd misunderstood the situation, and I misunderstood Heph's intentions. I cursed myself for falling for him, because that's what was happening. I was the blue flame from the thrower, torched and burning for more of him.

"I don't really know Heph either, and I can't fault him for loving another girl." My fingers picked at the quilt over my bed. *"I just misunderstood his intentions with me."*

"I can tell you, Heph isn't calculated like that. He doesn't form intentions. He acts and walks away. The fact that he stood behind you, stroking your hair? That was not Heph. That was not random. That was my brother falling in love."

My head sprang up.

"How can you know?"

"Oh, honey. I don't think we ever know. We can't see it coming, and then, boom, *you're flying over a valley, holding on for dear life, hoping to make it to the other side."*

My brows pressed so tight they kissed.

"But once you get to the other side…the things you learn. The things you experience. It's…it's heavenly." She exhaled deeply, and a blush rose on her face. I smiled and looked away. I don't think I'd ever carry that expression. I liked Heph, liked him a lot, but love was a whole new level.

A second knock came at my door and bright blonde hair popped around the wood.

"I can't take it anymore." Persephone entered and shut the door silently behind her. *"I don't mean to interrupt, but I need to go see him. I don't know why I sprang all that on him."* She addressed Veva, and I

tried to pretend I didn't know what I knew. In an instant, she told me the shortened version.

"Hades and I are...complicated. Separated. I tried to go on a normal date. Be a real girl. I'd been talking to someone in class, and we'd been to a few study sessions together. He was pleasant and attractive. I think I thought if I gave it a try, something might spark."

I sat up at the comment.

If at first you don't succeed, try, try again.

Heph had done that with me. His patience proved he'd let us try. But when I thought of all his marriage proposing, my heart ached. Maybe that's what he meant. The more he proposed, the closer he'd get to getting it right. Did it even work that way? I had no idea. I'd never had a relationship. I had failed attempts at intimacy, and one night of misplaced trust.

"What happened?" I asked.

"He kissed me, and I let him for about five seconds. It wasn't Hades, and I knew no man would ever compare." Her head lowered. "That makes me a bad person, doesn't it?" Her voice lowered as well.

Veva's hand covered her friend's as they both sat on the edge of my bed. My room was becoming a confessional slumber party.

"Honey, he told you to live. He wanted you to have experiences. You were doing what he wants."

"What about what I want?" Her free hand slapped my bedcoverings. "Ugh," she groaned. "I don't know why I let him keep doing this. Each time I think I'm finally accepting that he will not be part of my life, he returns. My heart can't take the rollercoaster. I want off the Ferris Wheel." Her head flopped dramatically onto my bed.

"What happened with the other boy?" I asked sheepishly. Was it so easy to disregard someone else? She waved dismissively.

"I never liked him. It was just an experiment."

My heart dropped. I didn't want Heph to think he was only an experiment to me. Was I only an experiment to him? I liked him. He meant more than some trial-and-error romp, not that that's what Persephone had.

"I'm so tired of this, tired of denying myself." Persephone groaned again. "He told me he wanted me to live, but I'm tired of living without him."

That thought stopped my memory. I was tired, too. Tired of hiding and not knowing who I was, who I could be, and what I wanted. I wanted to live freely, and for me that meant giving into what I felt for Heph. It was going to hurt when the fires with him blew out, and he left me behind at Hestia's, but I would not be Adara. I would not wallow in the pain of losing a man. I would enjoy every second Heph gave to me, if he would give me more. I would not let my life burn away to ash, but rise up, like a flaming Phoenix reborn. *Tomorrow*, I decided, as another cramp claimed me.

+ + +

I rolled under thick covers to see the dark black of night and felt a malleable wall behind me. Startled, my head spun to find Heph sleeping, over the blankets, next to me. I twisted completely to face him and stared at his large face. The bright spotlight from the barn reflected partially into my room, and his features outlined in shadows. His breathing was shallow, and his crooked nose didn't appear so bent. I risked a fingertip down the curve of it, and his nose scrunched with an itch. I smiled to myself and fluttered shaky fingers over the scratchy scruff on his cheek, cupping upward to his ear and sliding down to his jaw. His nose twitched again. My thumb brushed tenderly at his lower lip, and his hand came up to swat away the nuisance disturbing his sleep. I drew back before he touched me, and his eyes opened abruptly. Staring back at me, blinded by the light behind me, his eyes appeared glassy and uncertain of his surroundings. After a turn of his head to the ceiling, he fell back to his cheek on my pillow, biting his lip.

"Hi." The groggy sound of his voice did things to my insides, and I melted against the sheets.

"What are you doing here?" I whispered. "You aren't allowed to be up here."

"I haven't seen you all day. You're avoiding me." Caught at the truth, my lids lowered to avoid the intensity of his gaze. Heph was right. I'd been hiding all day.

"We need to talk," he said, but then he paused, waiting for me to speak. The first thing on my mind burst quietly out of my mouth.

"Do you love her?"

"Lovie?" He chuckled, and something on his face answered for him. "No. She is beautiful, but not for me."

I nodded in understanding, although I didn't understand. How was a beautiful woman not for a man like Heph? He was incredible. Tender and kind. And terribly good looking, to me.

"What about Adara?"

His silence worried me and I feared for the worst. He had loved her.

"She's more complicated. I thought I did, but she didn't love me. When I realized it, I already had plans to leave, so I left. I did not return as I promised. There is nothing left between her and me." He'd been looking at the ceiling again as he spoke but his head rolled back to face me. Our eyes met and we stared at one another. In that moment, we shared something I couldn't describe fully. He was begging me to accept his answers, and willing me to understand. A shaky hand reached for his cheek again and my thumb returned to his lips. He kissed the pad.

"Hestia says you're sick."

"It's a woman thing." I smiled sheepishly and removed my fingers from his face. He grabbed my wrist and dragged it back to his scruffy cheek.

"Oh...*oh*...are you okay? Can I do anything?"

"How?" I giggled, knowing the logistics of my condition could not be helped.

"I don't know. Don't you suffer nausea, headache, aching of the lips and stiffness for more than four hours?"

I stared, unblinking, before I burst into laughter and turned my face to suppress the sound in the pillow. Finally recovered, his smile filled with white teeth beamed back at me.

"No, Heph, no."

"Oh. That's just me then." His hand slipped to his waist, and he adjusted his pants. My eyes travelled south.

"Want me to rub your back or something?" Shifting my eyes back to his rugged face, my body relaxed at the sweet gesture.

"I want you to kiss me."

My request was met tenderly at first, hesitant as only Heph could deliver, but quickly it heated. The fires stoked inside me. My breasts ached for his touch; my stomach fluttered with need. Knowing I couldn't follow through on anything other than kissing intensified the desire. Our mouths molded and meshed, warming one another as Heph slipped a knee between my covered legs. I kicked at the sheet to release me, and one leg looped over his hip. A thick hand cupped under my knee, hitching my leg higher as our tongues danced and our lips waltzed. Not certain how much time passed, I was out of breath when he finally released me. Hesitant to touch his face while my concentration was in the kiss, my hands remained placed over his rolled shirt sleeves, but itched to climb and feel the heat of him.

"I should probably go before I stay all night."

The exaggerated pout of my lip warranted another round of crackling kisses and sparking embers that could not be taken to the next level. Drawing back from me, he said: "You should go downstairs. You missed dinner. I'll sneak out after you leave."

With a final peck, I rolled out from under his leg, missing the weight of it over me and stood. His eyes roamed my attire. My comfort clothes were a long sleeve T-shirt and his red boxer briefs.

"You're killing me," he chuckled as he rolled to his back and rubbed exaggeratedly over the thick length at his zipper. Stepping toward the bed, determined to get at him and relieve the pressure for him, his hand rose to stop me. I'd climb that man like an oak tree and build a house to live there, if need be.

"No," he chuckled softly. I smiled at his playful tone and retrieved a robe to cover me. Once covered, he perched up on an elbow and we took another moment to drink each other in. Looking at him was like sipping hot chocolate on a cool day. He warmed my insides. Finally turning to leave, he called out my name softly. His large frame filled my bed as he sat upward and stretched his long legs.

"You are so beautiful." With those words, I didn't care who he loved before, because in that moment, I felt like he loved me.

+ + +

Downstairs was a bevy of activity despite the late hour. Seraphine spoke to Adara in the breakfast room while I quietly gathered some leftovers for my midnight dinner.

"He loved you," Seraphine said.

"I was too late." Adara's sad tone froze my motion of scooping out salad on a plate. "When he told me, I didn't tell him that I felt the same. I panicked. If he knew the truth of why I wanted to leave, he wouldn't have felt the same way about me."

"You didn't know that. You should have trusted him. You trusted him with everything else." Seraphine's husky voice sent home the image of Heph with Adara, and I released the lettuce between the tongs in my grasp. I didn't need to hear this. Heph had assured me it was over, and I had to believe him.

"What about you?" Adara chuckled without much humor. "That was quite the greeting."

I imagined Seraphine shrugging a shoulder and tipping her head to swipe back the dark hair with blue streaks. Her eyes matched the color, and the wideness of them would tease back at Adara.

"It was nothing. It's been a long time since I've seen him. Hades was there for me at a low point."

The silence for a beat assured me they understood one another.

"We've all been there." Adara's voice fell softer, and I wondered if there were more details to Adara's escape than I knew. Her youngest sister was almost raped by the drunken slob who was Ashin's husband. Adara killed him when she couldn't get him off her sister. Eshne recovered enough over time from the experience, and I'd learned she didn't want to stay at Hestia's. She didn't possess the gift, and being here was a constant reminder of what had happened, when all she wanted was to live a normal life and forget the whole situation. Ashin, on the other hand, felt beholden to her older sister for saving her from a difficult marriage. Unsupervised at a young age, she'd made a huge mistake in accepting his proposal. Adara claimed she had her own issues at the time, but rectified the situation when it all came to a boiling head.

"You still need to go," Seraphine said to Adara.

"I know. But I don't know how. I don't know where to even begin to look."

"Heph would still help you."

"He would," Adara sighed. "But I can't ask him. His interests lay other places."

"Phyre?" I straightened at the sound of my name and left my dinner plate on the edge of the counter.

"I see the way he looks at her, like he used to look at me. I gave that up because I was afraid to tell him the truth."

"He'd understand. Tell him now."

"I can't."

What truth? I spun at the pressure of eyes on me. Spinning back, I saw Ember leaning against the dining room door frame. Our eyes locked for a second as I was caught eavesdropping on sisters.

"He won't last with Phyre any longer than he was with you," Seraphine spoke confidently. "Look at this other engagement fiasco. How many other women wait for him?"

All my bravado and confidence fell to my stomach and the salad before me repelled my senses.

"He isn't like that," Adara defended.

"How do you know?"

The silence that followed answered Seraphine's question. We didn't know much about Heph's life outside of our home. How many others awaited his return with empty promises and filled hearts?

HEPH

Leaving Phyre's bed left a hole in my chest, and I woke grumpy from another night of lonely rest.

"I saw Callie before I left. She asked about you." Solis' stood beside me, his words burned deep. Callie was a sweet girl, but not for me. How did my life become this tangle of women, yet not one of them wanting the real me? Not the escapee. Not the false fiancé. Not the lusty lover in a shower. Then my thoughts slipped to Phyre.

"I want you to kiss me." The sweetness of her request did things to me. My heart thudded. My dick stood at attention. She wanted me, and it felt different, inside me. Heat lingered and embers of lust burned, but it was more than fire that warmed me. Her fingers on my face let me know she took a risk and trusted me. She believed in herself not to hurt me, and that gave me comfort. She felt safe with me. Home.

I worked while Solis watched, wiping at his brow in the heat of the barn.

"I'm not interested in Callie and you know that."

His eyes shot forward, and I spun to find Phyre behind me. My smile grew tenfold before falling to my feet. What had I said to deserve the look she gave me?

"Who's *Callie*?" The fierceness in her tone lit the fire in me. I was tired of explaining myself. Tired of the misunderstandings.

"A girl from home. No one." I spun my back to her, but she stabbed me with her next words.

"Is that what you'll say to her about me? A girl from Hestia's. It was nothing." I dropped the iron, ready for a fight, but her slender back and waving hips told me to stay back.

Fuck this. I removed my apron and followed after her.

"Hey. Hey!" I shouted as she picked up her pace, rushing out the barn and briskly walking for a path cut in the woods. I knew where this trail led, and I hadn't been there yet this visit. "Don't you dare say you're nothing to me! When I look at you, I see everything I want."

She tossed her hair over a shoulder as she stomped ahead; keeping her back to me when I'd just spilled my heart angered me.

"I'm tired of explaining myself," I barked. "What about some truth from you? How many lovers have you had?"

She spun to face me, fire in her eyes.

"None. To have a lover you'd have to have someone love you first." Spinning back to the trail, she marched on, and I followed her lead.

"What? You said you weren't a virgin."

Her hand rose to dismiss me, and Hestia's tale returned to me.

What happened to her?

She stopped so abruptly I almost smacked into her, but almost as quickly she spun and stomped forward. Taking large steps, I matched her pace but fell behind her, giving myself a second to cool down before we reached the temple. A circular structure of marble and stone, the twelve columns and open dome roof set the place apart from the rustic barn and country home of Hestia. Built a long time ago, this space was Hestia's private spot for reflection and worship, but over time she allowed her girls to find solace and peace here, if needed. Phyre was almost to the marble steps when she spun on me again.

"You want to know what happened to me?" Her breaths rose so quickly, I could see the beat of her heart within her chest. "I was...I was..." Her eyes closed, and I didn't need to hear the word. "He was there, and I didn't want him to be. So I burned him. Alive." Her breath hitched before lowering to a sob. I stepped closer but her raised hand stopped me. No tears fell and she caught her breath.

"I don't know why I believed him. He told me I was safe with him. He took me across the state of Idaho. I'd traveled all the way here from the East Coast. I was so close, and then him. I believed in him. But the back seat..." She exhaled, blowing out air through hollow cheeks. "He pulled me into the back seat along the highway." Her head shook.

"Phyre, stop," I warned, but she continued.

"I heard him scream and call me names. I don't know how I escaped from under him. By some grace of the gods, I got over the front seat, locked the door, sealing him inside and sparked the gas tank. I didn't look back, Heph. I let him burn in hell like he deserved for what he did to me."

My heart ached, but more importantly, I wanted to rip down the structure behind her. I wanted to throw giant stones and crush the trees surrounding us. I wanted to tear the grass from the earth. I quivered and quaked with hatred for a man touching her in such a manner.

"There were only a few others before him. Ones who said they loved my hair, thought me beautiful. Ones who said they'd help me. None of them understood me." She raised both hands and shook them before me. "How could they understand? I'm not normal, Heph." Her voice trembled, but still no tears fell. "I bet *Callie* is normal."

Stepping into her space, she stepped back and hit the edge of a column.

"I don't want Callie. And I don't know why I'm coming across sounding like a player, because I'm not. There's only one person I want." I reached for her face, brushing my fingers into her hair. My other hand followed and pinned her cheeks so she would look up at me. "I only want one girl, Phyre. You." My lips brushed over her mouth, but hers remained still.

"I'm going to be your secret, right? Another Adara, as you aren't allowed to be with me. And then you'll go away and never think of me again, Heph."

"I…" I wanted her to come with me when I left.

"I can't go with you, Heph. I don't know how to be out there," she waved in the direction behind me, "and you cannot stay here." She was correct. I couldn't. This was Hestia's Home for women. I was only a visitor. I shook my head, but her hands covered my wrists and removed the gentle grip I had on her face.

"I'm already a dirty little secret, Heph. I don't need to be yours as well." She brushed past me, and although I reached for her, I let her slip from my fingers. My head hung as she walked away.

+ + +

That night the fire burned in the pit and again we sat around it. Hades and Persephone quietly sat holding hands, her head on his shoulder. Veva nearly sat on Solis' lap. The other girls watched, some with longing, others with regret. I thought of Phyre, who sat opposite me, near her youngest sister, Flame. Her voice spoke of regret. She wasn't normal, but that's what I loved about her. She was broken, but I could mend her. I wanted to take her horrors and burn them alive. I wanted to lock the door and keep the demons away for her. I wanted to protect her from ever having to face such sin again. But her avoiding eyes told me I would not win her over.

Hestia had her rules, but there was no denying how I felt about Phyre. Phyre's eyes travelled to mine through the smoky flames, and then quickly flicked away. She chewed at her lips, and my mouth watered to nip her there. I just wanted to hold her. I wanted to assure her that everything would be alright. We could work something out. I looked at my cousin Hades for inspiration. I didn't want to feel hopeless like him.

Suddenly, headlights from a vehicle swiped over the yard. The sharp rumble of gravel nearing the home sent the girls into panic, each reaching for the other's hands. I stood with fear for their safety. Slamming doors and heavy crunch of feet startled us all. Instantly, Hestia stood beside me.

"By gods, is nowhere sacred from him?" Solis grumbled near my back as a large man, similar in stature to myself, with good looks like Solis, approached our modest gathering. Another man followed beside him, equally as imposing.

"Hestia, I hear you are harboring a fugitive." The booming tenor of his tone, reminding me of Solis, revealed our father standing before us. To my left, Flame fled from the circle, her powerful legs, pushing fast for such a tiny frame.

"Hades, go after her," Zeke demanded.

"I'll follow you," Solis offered, and the two began a brisk walk toward the woods where Flame disappeared.

"Zeke, how dare you?" Hestia admonished, her best attempt to scold apparent on her face. "You know we are all fugitives here." Her arms fisted on her hips, her thin dress rising upward in her stance.

"You know I love you like a brother, but what is the meaning of this?" She swiped a hand dismissively before her. Her attention caught as she took a double take at the second man. He approached her, kissing her tenderly once on each cheek.

"Beautiful as ever, Hestia." Her eyes followed his withdrawal.

"How long has it been, Pollo? How wonderful to see you, again, too." Something stopped her, and she turned on Zeke once again. "What's going on here?"

Pollo had blond ringlets of hair, in contrast to the snow white of the man next to him. Smaller in height, his body was slimmer. His smile was bright, like he'd just told a joke, and the laughter lingered on his lips. At the sight of something behind us, that mouth lowered and puckered in consternation. Solis tugged a young man at his side, while Flame marched next to Hades, and Temple, the stable guard, followed behind. A gathering crowd filled the yard.

Flame's face was streaked in soot, her hair wild, with a piece of hay stuck to the side of her head. On further inspection, an odd-looking creature stood under Solis' protection. My eyes narrowed to take in the sight. Subtle horns stood higher than his dark brown hair. His chin was covered with a goatee. His chest rose, bare despite the chill, and hairy legs stood atop hooved feet. He was half-man, half-goat, and I blinked as if in a dream.

"Who's this?" Hestia asked, stepping closer to examine this strange appearance.

"A thief," Pollo snarled.

"Step into the light, my child." Hestia held out a hand to guide the creature, who stood the size of a man, but looked the age of me. Crossing closer to the fire, the full essence of his strangeness heightened, as if he had morphed and got stuck half in each form. This couldn't be.

"Who are you, child?" Hestia soothed.

"My name is Pan."

"And what have you to do with Flame?" The sharpening of Hestia's tone concerned me. The accusation was clear. Flame had been sneaking off to see this young creature and with that came consequences.

"It wasn't for me." His eyes shifted to Flame and back as his voice trembled with a bray.

"I tried to help," Flame defended, her head suddenly high, defiant, despite the hay sticking from her hair.

"You wanted to help *him*," Pan snapped, peering at her. Flame lowered her head.

"Still, if he was going to hurt you, I would have stopped him."

"Oh yeah, how?" The words cut Flame, and her eyes flared. The blue danced with righteous anger, to prove who she was and what she could do.

"Flame," Phyre barked, attempting to redirect her sister's attention. Flame's head whipped to her sister and they stared, a silent conversation ensuing. Flame nodded once, collecting herself.

"Just trust that I would not let Puma find you." Flame offered, weakly.

"And who is Puma?" Zeke's voice boomed in frustration.

"He's the thief, not me." Pan defended, struggling under the hold of Solis.

"Return what you stole, and Pollo will forgive you." Zeke demanded.

"I don't have anything, I swear." Pan's wild, black eyes returned to Flame, pleading for her support.

"I can vouch for that," Temple offered in his masculine voice. A quiet man by nature, I felt safer knowing Hestia had someone like him near to protect her if need be.

"If you don't have them, who does?" Zeke asked.

"I do," came another voice, and behind Pan stood a stunning man with a leonine face and whiskey-colored eyes. "I'm Puma."

Dismissed from the trial about to ensue, Flame and her entourage of two were escorted to the house with Zeke, Pollo, and Hestia. The rest of us remained in wonder at what Flame had done and how these two young men were involved.

+ + +

I was afraid to leave Phyre that night. The girls huddled close, and eyes drifted to the house often. Her eyes reached for mine and then looked away each time I caught them. I wanted to ease the tension, but did not know how to help. In small groups, people stood separate from the fire for a few minutes. Hades and Persephone headed for the woods. Solis and Veva turned for the barn and the room next to mine in the loft. Adara, Ashin and Seraphine went for the house. Only Ember and Phyre remained.

"I guess we should go in as well," Ember hinted after a few minutes of awkward silence. Ember. How appropriate her name for the coloring of her hair and the dying flame of the fire. She seemed to be the closest to Phyre; alliances formed even among sisters. Her eyes searched her friend's, and Phyre pointed to direct them to the house. My fists clenched at my sides, fighting the desire to capture her and drag her to my room.

"Phyre," I choke-coughed. "Could I speak to you?"

Ember walked away slowly, but I guided Phyre to follow. I didn't want her walking alone outside the house, for some strange reason. Learning of the nearness of two strange men did not settle well with me. As we stopped just outside the front entrance, Phyre turned to me. Reaching for her hand, I noticed her trembling.

"What is it?"

"Nothing," she shivered, but her eyes lied. I lifted her hand and opened her curled fingers. Placing her palm to my lips, I kissed her there. Her breath hitched, and I withdrew, but did not release her. My thick fingers dragged over her soft palm pad, tracing over deep lines, sensing the heat beneath the skin. I continued to caress the inside of her hand,

and then flipped it as if examining the veins that fed her life. The pad of my thumb stroked over her thin skin.

"I don't want you to go to bed angry with me." I could not draw my eyes from her hand. "I just want to go to bed with you."

Our eyes shot up at the same time.

"To sleep. I want to hold you in my arms as I take you in my dreams." I stepped closer to her. "Give me your fears."

Her head shook and lowered to rest on my chest. My arms wrapped around her and drew her near. She trembled against me; I figured the presence of my father and the situation with Flame frightened her.

"I don't want to leave you tonight," I said, and her hands came to my flannel shirt and fisted in the fabric, tugging me closer to her cheeks. She hadn't spoken to me, and the desire to carry her away to my room returned.

"You shouldn't sneak into the house. Not tonight. And the loft is too crowded. I'll see you tomorrow, Heph," she said, pulling back from me.

"Promise?" My voice nearly squeaked, like a teenager reaching puberty. Fear filled me that I'd lose her in the night. She stepped back and wrapped her arms around herself.

"Tomorrow."

PHYRE

The arrival of Zeke frightened me to my core for two different reasons. On the verge of breaking, Ember followed me to my room.

"Are you okay? You're shaking." My hands trembled, and my fingers tingled. I needed the flame to calm me. Ember's presence held off the opening of my private stash under the cushions at my window, since it was a blatant disregard of the house rules.

"Zeke is Heph's father." I stated the obvious. Similar in stature, Heph stood larger but Zeke's aura outweighed the height difference. His booming voice and angry brow as he spoke of Flame and fugitives scared me.

"He's been here before. I guess I had forgotten you haven't met him." Ember began. "The friendship goes back a long time between Hestia and Zeke. She's older than him, and much wiser, but she lets him think he has the upper hand." She winked. "Something about three sisters and three brothers. Each boy loved a girl. In Zeke's case, he loved two of them. Hestia was not one of them. The number of his children rivals the stars, Hestia jokes." I nodded, knowing Ember rambled to soothe my trembling and force my concentration from the man on the first level who was demanding an explanation of our sister, Flame, and her nightly wanderings. She also distracted me from another man, who wanted me to come to him tonight. I needed Heph. I wanted him to hold me and tell me things were fine, but I fought the urge, afraid that giving into his comfort made me weak. A shaky hand swiped over my forehead, and Ember didn't miss the trembling.

"What is it?"

"When the lights filled the yard and the heavy stomping came at us, I thought I'd been found." I looked over at my sister. We never had visitors this close to the house without warning, and Hestia often spoke of an invisible force that kept us safe. Her teasing tone made me take the words as jest. Heph was the first vehicle I'd ever seen stray so near. It was part of the reason I attempted to stop him.

"After all this time, I feared someone had finally found me and knew what I'd done to Randy." I hadn't spoken his name in a year. The hatred I felt in trusting someone so easily and then being taken advantage of erupted inside me at the mention of his name. "I would be damned for the sin I committed, only to meet him in hell."

"You aren't going to hell for protecting yourself." Ember crossed the room and covered my shoulders with tender fingers. A gentle shake attempted to re-enforce her words. "No one is going to find you here. And no one is going to take you away from here." Our eyes met. It was never going to be safe to leave, and Heph would go eventually. "Unless you want to go." Her voice faltered. We talked among ourselves at times about the world *out there*, but for the most part, the world at Hestia's was peaceful and problem-free. It hadn't crossed our minds too often that more existed beyond the woods. We had each seen *the more* and it wasn't pretty.

"He can't stay." I whispered so softly I wasn't certain Ember heard. Nodding her head proved she did.

"You really like him, don't you?" Her brow pinched.

"It's more than that. I think I love him." A tear slipped from my eye and I briskly wiped it away. "That's silly, isn't it? I don't really know for certain how he feels about me. I don't really know him. And it's only been a few weeks."

Ember's hands slipped to my wrists, circling them and holding onto me, encouraging me to speak freely.

"But whenever I'm near him, I feel at peace. He…he centers me. I've felt restless at times, but when I'm near him, it disappears. I want to crawl in his lap and live there. Make him my home." I laughed hesitantly at how ridiculous my words sounded, and yet how true, as another tear dripped down my cheek. Ember wiped it with the pad of her hand.

"My dream for all of us is that feeling. Whether from our home or from a man. I still believe in love, although it doesn't exist for me. Not in a conventional way. I suppose I'm more like Hestia. I'm truly happy here. I don't have a desire to be touched by a man. I'm perfectly content alone." Ember paused a beat, and my brow pinched in question. She couldn't mean that. We weren't actually alone at Hestia's, but there were moments of loneliness. Had she not felt them? "But I know Adara feels differently, and I can see you do, too."

"I guess none of it matters. I don't feel safe to leave alone, and it's not that I'm unhappy to stay. I just...I just...Heph..." I didn't know what to say further. I couldn't describe how it felt. His touch on my skin. His mouth on my lips. The way he looked at me. "Heph will have to leave either way. He can't stay here." The thought brought me to my second fear from Zeke. As his father, knowing he arranged a marriage for his son, Zeke's appearance reiterated that Heph lived another life. He didn't belong here and I sensed Heph would leave our home sooner than intended. Panic filled me, erupting into fear that I'd never experience Heph in the way of my dreams, if he left too soon. How futile to waste time fighting with him if I couldn't keep him here—and I couldn't. Hestia's Home was for women.

"Maybe you and Adara should leave together. Take a break, a vacation. Go out and see what you think you are missing." I stared off from Ember. I couldn't be with Adara. Her silence the past weeks spoke of her disapproval at whatever was happening between Heph and me. Her quiet also whispered her disappointment. She'd had the chance to leave with him. He could have taken her away, but she failed at her escape. By not loving him immediately, he left. *Would the same happen to me?* If I didn't give into my desires, would the flame burn out too soon?

+ + +

Hestia planned a special feast for dinner the following night. The festive ritual would occur afterward and I felt privileged to partake in the dance of worship to the fire goddess. We girls were giddy with excitement, but Flame remained in her room. We didn't learn much more of her meanderings other than she harbored Pan in the stables and Puma out in

120

the woods. Playing both boys, she tried to help form a truce between two obvious rivals. I would guess they each adored her and someone would eventually get burned in the triangle of friendship. Zeke and Pollo left sometime during the late hours for rooms at Temple's stable, a place I avoided as a former city girl who was afraid of horses.

"Dammit." Reaching for a pot, it clattered to the brick floor and a thin layer of water splashed outward. I bent at the waist to pick it up and swore again. "Shit."

One hand held wrapped in the other, the sting of a fresh burn boiled on my palm and the edge of my thumb. Ember stepped to my aid.

"What are you doing?" She giggled with her non-scolding tone.

"I was trying to help. I boiled water."

"And you burned yourself?" Ember tugged my hand to the sink as she questioned me, but she should have known better. I was a nightmare in the kitchen. Picking up the pot, Heph stood near enough for me to get a whiff of his balsam pine scent. I didn't know where he came from. He placed the metal cookery on the counter near the sink, and looked into the pot, where minimal water remained.

"Did you burn boiling water?" He chuckled, and I turned to give him a scathing look. "You can make fire, but you can't cook?"

I bit the inside of my cheek. The warmth of his eyes washed over me, bringing me instant comfort after a restless night. "Well, you can make weapons, form artistic sculptures, but your aim sucks."

He burst into laughter. His laughter grew louder like hammers pounding wood, and I found I liked the rhythm of it as it beat out of his chest.

"Phyre, you know my aim does not suck. I explained it to you." His eyes playfully stared at me, daring me to take his meaning. "I have a strategy of hitting around the target," he said, drawing a circle in the air around my head, "before taking aim at the center." His finger pointed at my heart—the center of his target. It ached to be speared by him. The arrow already punctured me deep with a wound I was certain to never recover from when he left. I was sorry for my outburst the day before, shouting my history at him and then walking away in frustration.

If we were to build anything between us, we would have to remain a secret, even if I didn't want to be another notch in his belt. He'd already had an affair with Adara. As much as they thought it was concealed, Hestia knew of its failure. I didn't want to be a failure either, but I'd fail myself if I didn't give into the desire I had for this man, who surprisingly cupped my face, in the middle of the kitchen and kissed my forehead.

"God, I love you," he chuckled at my ear, and my heart leapt. I stared up at him, the words on the tip of my lips when another clatter broke the spell. We both turned to find Adara near the large six-burner stove. "The expression on your face, I mean," he corrected louder, and I turned back to him. His eyes shadowed a bit. "I love the expression on your face."

His hands remained on my cheeks and my shoulders lowered, not even realizing I had tensed at his words. He pinned me in place with the intensity of his eyes. I couldn't move, despite the awareness we were the center of attention in the kitchen. I had a sense of Ember near me by the sink, and Adara remained by the stove. Hestia had walked into the room from the large dining room, and Ashin worked on the counter behind Heph. But none of that activity mattered while he looked at me like that, holding my face tenderly between his large hands. His head lowered, and my lids closed. His breath warmed my face, and just when I thought his mouth would touch mine in the middle of the chaos, Seraphine called his name.

"Heph, can you help me elongate the table? It's rather stiff at one end." Her words rattled in giggles as she teased, and Heph turned a deep shade of red. He kissed my nose, despite the audience. So much for secrets, I decided, as he stepped back to help assist with the table for our additional guests.

+ + +

Dinner preceded our celebration. Flame returned to the fold, her transgression not mentioned. Whatever happened would have to wait for later explanation. Zeke and Pollo joined us with chatter from Zeke's estate, Olympic Oils. I watched Heph, who ate with an ear to his father, ignoring the gossip and rumors while waiting for news that involved him. There was no mention of the girl to whom he had been engaged, and I sighed with thankful relief as our meal progressed. The feast shifted our energy, filling us not only with good food but the laughter and cheer of good company. The energy of love between Solis and Veva, and Persephone and Hades, covered our table and we toasted to love in any form: home and hearth, family and friends.

Gathering in the yard after dinner, we formed a circle of sisters, and unheard music danced in my head. The forest became our instruments, strumming out the opening chords with the faint rustle of leaves waving in the wind.

So the song goes
Of a girl who is gone,
Somewhere, she lost her way.

My feet found the rhythm I'd practiced for weeks. Instantly entranced, I moved. A simple drum beat in my head as I held my torch and stepped toward Ember, my partner. Not looking at one another, but lost in our own worship of our gift, we circled arms and spun in opposite directions.

Follow the flame,
It knows the way
To safety free from harm;

Releasing one another, the tempo increased, violins strung through the whisper of trees rustling, calling to me, and I turned to face the dark limbs. Arms spread wide at my sides, I twisted left and then right when the blare of bagpipes crunched from the cold leaves at my bare feet. Nature played the rhythmic sounds that entranced me.

A home for the fire
A hearth for the heart
A place for the weary to stay.

With a sway and a skip, my fire sisters and I shimmied and slithered in a circle, intricately weaving amongst each other in silent praise.

Dressed only in white, with mountain laurel crowns on our head, we danced like princesses, offering up soul and body to our protectress.

Be who you are
Free from the harm
Let the fire sway.

My arm swung graciously outward at my side, reaching for one sister and then pulling back in search of another. Consumed by the sisterhood and the swirl of the flames in my torch, I twirled and tiptoed over the damp grass as the music of nature played on.

So the song goes
Of a girl needing home,
The brave will find her way.

The drum of the wind rumbled on as the pipes from the leaves at my feet hit a crescendo too high, and over the earth, my feet did fly, carrying me away in my head. Time stood still while we moved, as I became one with the flame in my hand.

To be who she is
To live how she pleases
To see her fire as strength.

We drew closer to our destination, pacing the dance without thought as we travelled the trail to the temple hidden in the woods. The foliage skittered in response, whistling with a whirl as the final string strummed in the trees, and the last beat of a drum brought the sounds of nature to a sharp end.

Set the flame free
Dance round the rings
Let the fire sway.

We stood, breathless and anxious, with our gift in hand as the final words hummed from silent lips.

So the song goes
A girl found her home,
The light, within, her way.

We circled the set of columns structured as twelve large pillars representing twelve months under a domed sky. The river roared a background waltz as we fell into step and surrounded the marble structure. Each sister stood outside her set of pillars, separate from one another, but then in unison we turned and entered the gaps for the center. A stone basin filled with kindling lit instantly as we bent in worship to the wood, sacrificing itself so we may spread our flames. The fire whooshed upward, igniting instantly and filling the small space as six faces watched our inner gift take flight. The space lit to orange and yellow, dancing in shadow over our cheeks as eyes twinkled in wonder at the power before us. When Hestia entered, we turned one by one to leave, letting our mother have a moment alone with the flame.

In exhaustion and exhilaration, we walked home silently, allowing the experience to wash over us. A smaller replicate of the fire burned in the fire pit in the yard, surrounded by chairs awaiting our return. Heph sat among the seats as did Hades and Persephone, Solis and Veva, and Zeke. They watched the dance as quiet observers, knowing they witnessed something sacred, but separate from them. Wine was passed by Zeke as we sat. Hestia would not return for a while.

As the ancient ritual settled around us, a new tradition occurred. Seraphine would sing to us. Her guitar rested near a stump and she reached for it when the timing seemed appropriate.

"Solis," she prompted. "Care to join me?"

"Oh, I can't sing." His laughter boomed breaking the last of the lingering thoughts for celebratory fire and the first of the crackling spirit of flames.

"Oh, he can," Veva giggled. "Trust me, he can sing."

Solis shook his sandy blond hair and nodded at Seraphine to pick something. If he knew it, he'd try his best, he said. To my surprise, he instantly knew the tune, a song of longing, a call for home, and a need for connection with another. Instantly my eyes found Heph's over the smoky aura of the flames. The meeting of our eyes formed an intense moment, similar to his watching me in the woods the first time we met. *Do I know you?* he asked, and my heart leapt with *yes*, before I realized the answer. Something within him spoke to something in me that first day, and I had wasted days in between. I couldn't wait any longer.

Heph

When the song ended, Seraphine broke into more soul piercing songs, folksy and rich with her smoky, flirty tone. The atmosphere shifted but I remained on edge. My heart thudded under the white shift. I didn't want Heph to get away from me. If all I had was one night with him, I wanted to take it and keep securely wrapped within it. I would not drag forth the past, nor would I smother the future. As the night drifted on, the more restless I became. Eventually, I excused myself to watch a private flame, in need of reflective quiet and solitude to calm the volcano threatening to erupt within me. I lit the candle in my room, and sat at the window, letting cool air seep inward to suck out the smoke. Shortly after taking my window seat, I noticed Heph's broad back standing at the entrance to the studio barn. He stopped for a moment and turned in my direction. Hands at his sides, the slightest of nods gave me the courage I needed to seize the night.

PHYRE

My heart raced as I ran from the house for the barn. Not bothering to check for witnesses, I slipped through the large sliding door. The wooden structure awash in darkness did not deter me. I knew the way. I followed the rough wall to the stairs and took them two at a time to the loft. The first door on the left stood closed with a thin ray of light seeping under the door. I knocked but didn't wait for an answer. I cracked open the door as I did the night I watched him pleasure himself. That image of him consumed me and my heart nearly leapt from my chest as I curled around the door, closing it quickly.

"Hang on." The gruff voice of Heph carried through to the living room. The light from his bedroom illuminated the small space. Instantly, his presence filled the doorframe as he buttoned up his jeans. Standing shirtless, his head rose slowly and drank in every inch of me still clothed in the white slip of a dress, pressed against the door to his space.

"Phyre." His voice breathed my name, and I sprinted for him, afraid I'd lose my nerve if I didn't just leap from the flames licking inside me. He met me halfway in the dark room, and my arms circled his neck while my legs trapped his hips. His mouth crushed mine, and my hands snaked over his head, holding him to my face. Lips rushed with licks and sparking sips of sensitive skin on cheeks and necks and jaws. He carried me to his bed, and we fell in a tumble to cool sheets under a too-bright light.

"Let me get the light," he muttered between sucking my chin and nibbling at my neck.

"No," I exhaled, afraid to let him out of my arms. His large body half-covered mine. A heavy leg perched between my thighs, and my hips forced friction as desperation ached at my center. With a tender push, I pressed Heph to roll on his back, and my legs straddled him. Instantly, my core met the length of him, thick and thrusting upward against me. A guttural sigh escaped my lips. I was lost. My hips rocked, rubbing the damp, thirsty center of me, parched from a year without drink, over the seam of his jeans.

Sitting upward, my hair tumbled forward. A thick hand rose and wrapped long strands around his fingers.

"You are so beautiful." The compliment was filled with awe and something more, something I longed for, but didn't dare to ask aloud. *Do you love me, Heph?* The words rang desperate in my head. The devil side of me decided she didn't care for an answer. I rippled over him, allowing my hips to take control, flickering at the wick beneath my thighs. My thoughts lost in a smoky fog of desire, I pulsed over his thickness, anticipating the spark.

"Heph," I ground his name through clenched teeth as I concentrated on the uncontrollable passion slowly erupting inside me, volcanic and ready for release. Tumbling and tickling up my skin. Curling and folding at my knees. Climbing and crawling over my thighs. The edge of the lava, ready to leap.

Little Spark, I heard shouted, but muffled through the roar of magma, licking and lapping at my inner walls. I ignored the cry, letting my body roll onward: rubbing, searching, seeking a path I'd suppressed.

Phyre, cried somewhere in the distance, garbled, as if said through thick wood. Wood that burned and bent under the power of seductive flames, kissing and cursing in its destruction. I could not respond to my name. My body fell forward, gripping at anything to tether me as the eruption neared the mouth of my core.

Suddenly, the world spun and I dropped several feet, landing with an *umph* on something hard. Instantly, something heavy covered me entirely, and I rolled to my side on the coolness of the wood floor. Tender pats and heavy beats rumbled over my body as the sound of my name filled my ears, like being underwater and breaking the surface.

"Phyre?" The strained voice of Heph questioned me. Breathing heavily, my eyes focused on the ceiling as I heard the shuffling of feet near my head.

Too heavy, I whispered in thought. *Too hot.*

A blanket rested over my body, smothering me, as the smell of burnt fabric filled the air. Rolling to my side again, I tried to lift my upper body, pressing down with my hands to sit up. Instant pain rippled over my palms and shot up my forearms. My elbows gave way, and I tumbled downward, smacking my face on the floor.

"Phyre!" My name roared to life as thick hands covered my shoulders and pressed me back. I stared upward as Heph knelt over me. My eyes blinked in confusion. A heavy palm brushed over my forehead, cool to the touch. My face felt warm, and my skin dripped with sweat.

"What happened?" My throat croaked the infamous question, choking on the words as if I'd inhaled smoke.

"Fire." His gruff voice whispered in concern. He tugged on my shoulders, lifting me upward to a seated position, and the blanket over my shift slipped to my waist. My trembling hands lifted to my eyes to find them blackened and smoldering.

"What did I do?" Tears instantly filled my eyes and clawed at my throat. I turned to Heph, finding a storm within those sweet chocolate eyes. "What did I do?" My voice shrieked in harsh quiet.

"You set the bed on fire."

I couldn't even cover my face with my hands in embarrassment. I simply hung my head. Instantly, hoisted into the air, Heph carried me into the bathroom and stepped into a lukewarm shower.

"Should I get Ember?" His voice trembled as he held me pressed against him under the weak stream.

"Don't leave me," I whispered and his lips brushed my forehead. He set me on my feet and lifted one hand at the wrist to hold it under the stream. It burned at first, and I flinched.

"I don't want to hurt you."

Suddenly, something occurred to me. "Did *I* hurt you?" My eyes scanned his partially clad body. The solid structure of his chest, the hard ripple to his abs, and the strength of his biceps glistened with sweat. Rivers of water slithered over his glorious skin.

"Did I burn you?" Tears continued to fall as did my voice. *How could I do this again?* I'd practically attacked him when he was no threat to me.

"I'm fine." A thick hand brushed over my hair, partially hit by the spray. Looking down, I saw my sodden dress, smudged with ash in places, charred in one spot, forming a burn hole large enough for a fist. Heph's jeans grew darker as they soaked up water on one side of him.

"I'm so sorry."

"I'm fine." Lips came to my forehead again, pressing tenderly against my clammy skin. "I think we just need to cool you down."

"I ruined everything."

He responded only by shaking his head as we stood under the stream. After a few minutes, I shivered.

"Hang on a second." He stepped from the glass enclosure and exited the bathroom. Returning, he lifted a flannel shirt for my attention before hanging it on a hook at the back of the door.

"When you're ready," he spoke sheepishly, looking at the tile floor while I remained fully clothed in the shower. "I'll wait in the living room."

My heart ripped from my chest the instant the door closed, shutting him off from me.

What have I done? I wanted to scream, but the truth of the details lingered, as if in a dream. The excitement, the desire, possessed me, and the fire remained uncontained. Without concentration or thought, the flames broke free as my body craved something it hadn't had before. Heph's touch gave me a taste. Now, my body wanted a feast. In my desire to consume him, my gift nearly did. A living, breathing thing, fire has its own hunger, and I'd been on a diet too long.

I could have set him on fire. I could have killed him. A sob crept from my throat and smoldering hands covered my lips. My head rest against the glass panel as tears streamed faster than the shower spray at my back. My gift was a curse, and it ruined everything.

HEPH

I sat with my head in my hands as my elbows rested on my knees. I heard her silent movements as the shower shut off and the door creaked open. She stalled near the bed, and I knew what she'd see. Scorched sheets, a burned pillow, and a blanket used to smother the flames. Her hands clenched so hard into the material I thought I wouldn't get her free. The sound of crackling still rang in my ears where her hands had been placed on either side of my head. The image of her over me, taking her pleasure, melted under heat into a girl who no longer recognized me, a woman who didn't need me as more than a vessel to bring her to completion. I'd lost Phyre in the process, and she set one instead.

Her white knees rested level with my face and I slowly looked up at her dressed in one of my flannel shirts. Hanging too long, the arms rolled and rolled and rolled to expose hands still raw and red from what happened.

"What happened?" I mumbled, staring upward like a troubled child. *What had I done?*

"It isn't you, Heph. It's me." The words struck me. How often I'd heard them used in excuse. Lovie said them after getting caught with another man attached to her. Adara said it while I nested inside her. Callie hinted at it, until I was claimed by another. Nameless, faceless many over the years, over the too many years, said the same words to me.

I sat back with a huff and I sensed her hesitation. She wanted to straddle over me and yet she held herself back. Sitting forward again, my thick hands circled behind her knees and she fell into my lap.

"I'm so sorry," she whispered. "I'm so sorry," she said. Her head came to rest on my shoulder. "I ruined everything." The sadness in her tone rang as deep as the confusion in my heart. *Didn't she want me?* She came to my room. She leapt to my arms. She pressed me to the bed.

"I would never hurt you." The words tumbled out as if they needed to be said. *Did she try to hurt me because she thought I was taking advantage of her?* Her head shook wiping away my thoughts.

"I didn't mean to scare you."

"You didn't," I lied, the crack of fire still ringing in my ears. "But can you tell me what happened? What did I do?"

Hands rose and then fell, knowing she couldn't touch my scratchy beard with sensitive skin.

"It wasn't you. I lost control." Her face pinked and her eyes lowered. "I lost control," she said softer. "I wanted it so much. I wanted you so much, that my mind took over. No, my body did."

I didn't know whether to smile at the thought or whither in defeat.

"Did you come?" The crassness of my question surprised even me.

"I don't think so. It was more a matter of getting there. It's been so long since I've been with someone." She closed her eyes with the thought before continuing. "I just let go…too much." Her head hung. I couldn't help touching her, and I brushed back her wild hair to see her face, kissing her cheek without conscience.

"Was there something I could have done? I lost you there." Thoughts riddled my mind. Not what had I done, but was it me? Was she repulsed by my figure? My face? The many scars on my body from accidents with fire and the fall from grace off the mountain. The one that caused injury to my leg. She hadn't even seen my leg without the prosthetic yet. How much more would that repulse her?

"I…I don't know. I don't think so." Her brows pinched. "I was in control the other times, but tonight I got carried away. Maybe it was the dance and the ritual." Her shoulder shrugged, and my too-large shirt slipped, revealing a pale white shoulder. My lips reached for her now-cool skin. Lazy eyes looked seductively at me, longingly, but I didn't wish to tempt fate a second time tonight. Sensing my decision, her legs squirmed over mine.

"I should go," she muttered, but I tightened my hold on her back and clamped a hand over her bare thigh.

"Just stay with me." I tipped us sideways, knowing we couldn't last the night on my cramped couch, but not willing to release her yet. "Let me just hold you."

She nodded in response, pressing a kiss to my chest. Her sore hands rested on my skin, and I longed to take her pain. Her forehead settled over my heart and I wrapped my arm tighter around her as our legs tangled together to keep us on the cushions. With my lips on her hair, I breathed in her scent; smoke lingered with the fruity fragrance of her, and I sighed, feeling any potential to fill her dissolve into flames.

+ + +

I heard voices later in the night and extradited myself from Phyre. My heart ached once I uncurled from her. Sound rose up the stairs, echoing off the vaulted ceiling below, yet Phyre remained heavy in sleep, and I imagined the loss of fire tired her. I slipped on a shirt and crossed back through the living room. For some reason, I took a second look at Phyre, tucked in the couch, wrapped in my flannel shirt. Her hand smoothed the leather as if searching for something, reaching for someone, and my heart flipped with hope that someone would be me. The voices outside my door severed the pull to Phyre and I exited quietly.

"You're stealing my sons." A subtle laugh with a hint of seriousness travelled up the boards to my loft. I stepped quietly down the stairs to find Zeke with Veva in the large studio. Veva and Persephone were not allowed out here any more than Hestia's girls, but like Phyre, and Adara before her, the rules were obviously not followed.

"I'm not stealing anyone," Veva bit back, a little sharper than I'd heard her use before with Zeke.

"Solis is marrying you and moving off the estate." He placed one finger over the large digit of his other hand, ticking off the offenses. "And now Heph is falling in love with a girl he can't have."

I stood taller, pressed into the shadows of the partially hidden stairwell.

"How does that make me stealing him?" Veva chuckled without humor. "He's a grown man, and he can love who he wishes."

"No, he can't. He can fuck who he wishes, but love remains on my estate. Lovie awaits his return. Their relationship has been a longstanding agreement. Heph thinks he can have other things as he watched you and Solis come together, but he can't. By default, it's your fault."

I bristled at the thought.

"Heph can have whatever he wants of life. Lovie doesn't deserve him."

"Neither does this girl. And no, he can't." His hand waved dismissively toward the barn door, indicating outside. My fists clenched at my sides. *How dare he speak of Phyre like that? How dare he speak of me?*

"What makes you God?" The thought stopped her. "You can't make him, can you?" Her voice faltered. New to the discovery of me as her brother and the history of our family, Veva was still learning our ways. Zeke's power was infinite, if he wished to enforce it.

"I can make anyone do what I please. I can be very persuasive." His hand raised and he brushed back a hair, curling it behind her ear and lingering on her neck. "And you're going to help me return him to the estate." To some, it may have seemed fatherly. To me, it appeared seductive. Veva's shiver hinted at the same thought. My body sprang to action. I jumped the remainder of the steps, landing with a hard clank of my metal foot on the cement floor of the barn. Zeke's eyes looked over at me. Surprise filled his older face. He spun Veva to stand before him, holding her as a human shield.

"What are you doing here?" I barked. Zeke's hands rested on Veva's shoulders.

"I'm only talking with my future daughter-in-law." His booming tone warned me to step back. My eyes shifted to Veva's, which opened widely.

"It didn't sound like a discussion. More like demands."

"We were just discussing you, and how Veva wants you to return to the estate."

Vee's eyes opened wider, and she tried to shake her head, but Zeke's hand on her shoulders tightened.

"She misses her big brother."

Veva took the hint and dipped her head to agree. While newly introduced to one another, Veva had been consumed with Solis from the moment she set foot on our estate. Zeke's words were false. I'd heard his reasons for bringing me home, but I didn't understand why, why he couldn't let the relationship with Lovie go.

"Plus, Lovie wants to speak with you. She'd like to apologize."

"There's nothing she could say to me to change my mind. I'm not going back."

Zeke pursed his lips. "Hephaestus, you've always been a good man, but you aren't the smartest. When a beautiful woman wants to talk to you, you listen to her."

"Zeke!" Veva shrieked, struggling under his hold.

"A beautiful woman who wants to reconcile with you cannot be kept waiting while you dip your wick in a candle that can only burn you." I hated the metaphor. If only he knew I hadn't entered Phyre, and didn't foresee it ever happening. I shook my head. It wouldn't matter to me. There was something about her that drew me to her. An ignorant, ugly moth attracted to the brilliant, burning flame could not be prevented.

"That other girl might be beautiful," Zeke continued, and I hated the implication that he'd noticed her beauty. "But she can't be what you need. She can't understand who you are. You need your own kind."

Veva shook her head again, wincing at Zeke's hold. "I'm not like you, and Solis loves me. Don't listen to this." My brows pinched. Phyre was more goddess than I was god. Maybe Zeke had it wrong. Maybe I wasn't enough for her. Sensing my insecurity, Zeke went there next.

"You could never give her what she needs, either. She's a free spirit. She needs to burn. She can only hurt you."

"No," I huffed but I thought of the flames near my head. I wasn't afraid to be burned. I bore the scars of loose fire and hot sparks all over my chest and arms, but Phyre was different. She was alive. She needed freedom. *Where would we go next?* I couldn't stay at Hestia's. She couldn't come outside Hestia's with her power.

"She would never hurt you, Heph," Veva answered, defending Phyre without fully knowing her. Then she winced.

"Let her go," I snapped, realizing Zeke still pressed Veva to him. He released her quickly and she stumbled forward, reaching out for me. I tucked her into my side as she sputtered and coughed.

"I'll kill you for hurting her." I spun to face my father, whose bright blue eyes blazed back. "Are you threatening me, son? After all I've done for you."

Guilt struck me like a lightning bolt. My father knew where to punch. Rejected from my mother, my father took me to his home. Not in a fatherly manner, but in the way of collecting children like one would collect rocks. He filled his estate with his offspring. Being one of many, I was grateful the home remained even after I ran away. *Once.* The world was cruel to me, and after a stiff scolding, Zeke took me back. It was the second time my mother turned me away.

"Your mother didn't want you, Heph. I'm the one that took you in." Hera's rejection set deep, but Hestia soothed the sting. Hestia's love hid the pain, until Zeke choose to remind me of his, exerting his greater authority over me.

"How dare you?" Veva snipped, standing straighter and loosening from my hold. "Don't speak of her to him." Veva and I shared the same woman who birthed us, but we did not share her as a mother. As our mother, she filled that role only for Veva. "She did this to him because of you."

Zeke's temper flared instantly and a finger pointed at Veva reinforcing his words.

"Don't speak of things you don't know." The tremble to his voice proved Veva stood correct and the rumors I'd been told were true. My mother gave me up because she couldn't face me. She couldn't face the reminder of *his* unending infidelity. He ripped out her heart and in attempts to protect her own, she sent me away. Only mine broke, too. We were a bitter triangle.

"Don't point at her with that tone," I hissed, pushing Veva behind me, protecting her as the brother I wanted to be. I knew that voice from Zeke. He was gearing up for things Veva should never see. Zeke stepped closer to me.

"Don't take that voice with me." His threat would still me in the past, but with Veva to be protected and Phyre in my room, I drew strength I didn't know I possessed. I stood taller, taller than my father.

"I'll speak how I wish."

The strike surprised me. A sharp lash of his hand, full of electric energy, and my body jolted with shock. The sting instantaneous and then done. My heart stilled, but a gasp of oxygen revived me. I blinked. The slow closing and opening of my lids was the only movement my body could make before feeling returned to my extremities. My father had only hit me once before. A boy who ran away in search of love from a mother, he slapped me to remind me love lived where he was. His home. Not hers. The vibration on my face at my current age should have made me laugh. Instead, it hardened me.

"I don't need this shit. And I don't need you."

"Heph!" Veva's heartbroken voice cried behind me, but I went cold after the momentary heat of my father's hand on me. I charged for the barn door and plowed straight ahead toward the darkened trail to the stable. My car remained parked there after replacing the tire. Temple's home being on the edge of Hestia's property, it was safer to leave the vehicle there than closer to her house. I stomped through the black night and the cool mountain air, barefoot, my heart laid bare as well. Hatred toward my father ripped at my chest. The pain of my mother and the reminder of her abandonment tugged at the loose cords of arteries. The final pinch came at the thought that Phyre could not control her gift, and I would never be what she needed. I didn't feel the cold. Heat filled me with insecurity and I needed escape before I'd combust.

PHYRE

I woke in a chilly room, minus Heph and my dress. Taking a moment to recall the night, my hand covered my forehead. Just as quickly, I removed my palm and stared at the raw welts intermingled with tiny puffs of skin. By day's end, they would vanish. Until then, they would be a strong reminder of what I'd almost done. I cursed myself. I didn't deserve to want things. I didn't deserve to want Heph.

At the thought, I sat up slowly, feeling a strange loss, as if a piece of me went missing. I used the bathroom and cringed at the sight of the scorched linens and singed pillow. After using the facility, I returned to the room to remove the sheets and fold the blanket. Something didn't feel right again, as I stood on the opposite side of the bed. The naked mattress marked as well by my capabilities, my eyes drifted over it to notice the wood floor. Scanning left to right, something was absent. It took a moment to recall tripping on a case, sprawled open and erupting with clothing. Red boxers flashed through my mind. The "something missing" became clear. Heph's case was gone.

Quickly, I balled the sheets and carried them downstairs to the studio where the large fire pit softly smoldered. I placed the ruined sheets over the embers and watched as they burst into flame. Hugging the red blanket to my chest, I inhaled Heph's manly scent: balsam pine. My heart ached, his loss slowly settling in but not yet registering with me. I turned for the door, not concerned at the obviousness of where I'd been or with whom. I entered the front door and took to the stairs instantly. I climbed slowly, sensing I walked to the end of something. Life as I knew it. Life as I wished it to be.

Entering my room, Adara stood facing my window. The casement cracked, but no flame lit the candles on the ledge. In my haste to get to Heph, I'd forgotten the open window and my stash of candles. Exposed, I waited for Adara to admonish me: for fire in the house and the flame I stole from her.

"He's gone." The words spiraled through the room, taking their time to reach me and take root. She didn't move her eyes from the window, caught in some memory as she stared at the red barn feet from my room. Slowly, she turned to me. "I'm so sorry."

Her words broke me and I swallowed hard. A tear trailed down my cheek.

"How do you know?"

"He left this morning. He sent Solis to get his things."

Why didn't he wake me? I wondered. *How could he let me sleep?*

I wanted to argue he'd return, but the gentle, dark haze of Adara's eyes watching me, fought my claim. This is what Heph does. He leaves. He isn't allowed to stay anyway, I reasoned in my head, but staring back at Adara, the truth was clear. He left without taking me with him. He didn't want me.

I nodded as if Adara and I spoke. We hadn't really talked since Heph arrived. Six weeks without much of a word from the girl who mothered me almost as much as Hestia. Guilt washed over me at stealing her man. She shook her head as the tears fell faster.

"I'm sorry," I mouthed, but her sorrowful stare and her sudden embrace told me my sadness outweighed an apology.

"Me, too," she whispered against my hair, stroking over it like a mother would. "Two broken hearts don't make any of this right." A sob escaped as my arms wrapped around her waist.

"What did I do?" I cried, knowing he left because of me.

"Nothing. You did nothing wrong," she attempted to assure me, but she was wrong. I'd scared him, tough and large as he was. The threat of burning him alive in the heat of passion was certainly not attractive. He ran to escape telling me. He didn't wish to face me, but the more I thought of this explanation, the more irritation festered. *How could he walk away without telling me?* I'd understand, but I wanted to hear it from his lips. I wanted him to face me like a man. Instead, I deemed him a coward.

+ + +

November led to December and the cold settled in by January. Restless and ornery, I circled the yard, perfecting my archery only to curse the target and its whispers of centering. I finished my schedule of baubles and jewels to swear at the torch flame for its reminder of first touches. My arrow wrap bracelet still choked my wrist. Torture that I inflicted on myself, as I still wore the silver band he made me and stared at the arrow, wondering when it would point me home. I loved Hestia's Home, but the loss of Heph made me wonder if here was where I was intended to stay.

In some ways, I understood Adara, and her desire to leave. This couldn't be all that we were destined to be. While Hestia was happy, she was clear that she lived her life before she settled here. She'd had two marriage proposals: Pollo being one of them, we learned. Idon, Zeke's brother, being the other one. She hinted at sexual contentment, and Temple crossed my mind. Catching the eye of Ember as Hestia revealed these things one night at dinner, her glance suggested my thoughts were not alone. Hestia had ways to fulfill herself, and it didn't always involve being in isolation. In fact, the suggestions reminded us all that love existed, if we wished, or we waited, whatever the case may be. I sensed Adara had waited long enough. Now, she was ready to look for it, as her youngest sister Eshne had.

An invitation to visit her sister arrived: a break from the bitter, damp winds of the Pacific Northwest replaced with the sunny disposition of beaches in California. For years, Adara declined the offers, so I was told. But this year, the invitation included the announcement of her engagement. Ashin desperately wanted to attend and Hestia decided a small vacation might be in order to give us all a break. Never one to not think of work, Hestia included it as part of the deal.

"There are three glass beaches along the coast. Old city dumps turned trash to treasure. Beach glass abounds on those shores." Hestia winked. "You can't take the supply but the hunt is half the fun. It might inspire some designs."

She turned to me and eyed my hair.

"Ruby red is the rarest of gems to find." Her eyebrows wiggled. "I challenge you to search for the perfect match." She patted my hand as she eyed my hair. "Sometimes we need to seek out what we've lost." I didn't understand her meaning.

She didn't speak of Heph's departure, not surprised or disappointed by his absence three months ago. Hades had left the night Heph disappeared, and Persephone followed with Veva and Solis the next day. At least *they* said good-bye. Zeke spoke with Hestia in private before taking his leave. He did not address us girls, which was fine by me. His presence disturbed me, especially when his eyes drifted to mine in sorrow before sharply looking away. I didn't understand the expression on his face, nor did I care to interpret it. He hugged Hestia and left by way of Temple's stables.

Three months later, my experience with Heph seemed like a lifetime ago. The flames that burned inside me subsided each day without him. Long suppressed, they burst to life in a new way with the experience of a gentle lover, not the casual and callous ones of my past. Separated from my love, the flame receded, recklessly dormant under my skin.

Huddled in heavy coats, thick mittens and caps, we set out on our journey, shedding our layers as we drew closer to the border of each state. I hadn't ever been to California, and I was curious how the landscape would change. I pictured palm trees lining highways and perfect blue skies, but we hit Highway 1 under gray skies and thick, ancient trees. Traveling south, the scenery mesmerized me, and I stared out the window in wonder at the stark contrast between rock and sea. The bright blue ocean roared below as rocks reached great heights on the opposite side as we rode the winding highway road. My thoughts drifted like the waves with all that happened to me and how far I had come. Heph or no Heph at present, he'd opened a door for me. My heart unlocked, leaving me ready to welcome what might come next. Knowing I had the potential to control my gift, I just needed the right person to take the adventure with me.

"It's so beautiful," Ember chattered. It was her turn to drive our industrial van with three full rows for the five of us. Hestia chose to stay behind with Flame, who didn't trust herself to leave. I caught the lie in her eyes. She had two men to attend, and the thought of leaving them to their own devices frightened her.

Ashlin wiggled nervously, anxious to see her younger sister. Adara remained pensive in the front passenger seat. We talked after Heph's departure, and she explained to me that she loved him, but not the right way. That's why he left her. He figured it out, and her love wasn't enough. She wanted him to take her away from Hestia's. She wanted him to take care of her, as she was tired of being the responsible one. A hint remained of something more to her tale, but enough was said to realize, she recognized her error in her feelings for Heph and his willingness to help her no matter what.

Seraphine sat reserved next to me, a flood of memories racing by like the landscape, as she told us about being a musician on the road, when her gift struck. A girl in a band on their way to the top, when the place they played mysteriously burned to the ground. *Electrical wiring*, they faulted. *I got angry at the manager of the club*, she clarified as we rode south.

I had been the anomaly. I'd had the gift since I was young. I just didn't know what to do with it, other than harm someone. After the accident with my parents, each mark, each scar, and each burn came at the expense of those who tried to touch me or love me, Heph being the most painful example. When Randy raped me, his death was the pinnacle of my hatred. When Heph tried to love me, the eruption of my fire was nothing in comparison. Each harmed in their own right, though; I repelled men, and for good reason, I decided.

We pulled up in front of a quaint bed and breakfast, located hundreds of feet from the sea but its presence still apparent as a back drop. We each exhaled in relief, ready to stretch our legs and inhale the salty, ocean air of California. Not as warm as I expected for January, but not as cold as our home up north. The gray sky had shifted to bright blue upon our arrival, and the promise of an adventure lay ahead. Commands were shouted out.

"I'll check us in."

"I'll get our bags."

"I'll search the map for the first beach."

As I followed Ashin to collect our numerous bags, she stopped and called her sister's name. Adara stopped several paces from the van, her arms crossed and her back to us. Her attention was focused on the restless waves of the Pacific, thundering and rolling on rocks below, a sharp cacophony of sounds. She took another step forward when Ashin called her name again. Adara halted, but her motion came reluctantly, as if she was pulled by an invisible force to the sea. Her head twisted in recognition of her sister's voice, but her body remained facing the ocean ahead. Her arms uncrossed and fists lowered to her side. One final concerned cry of Adara's name and whatever held her spellbound to the waves broke. She turned back for the van and assisted with the luggage.

Checked in and assigned rooms, I ended up roommates with Ember and Seraphine. It didn't matter, as the bedroom attached to another, where Adara and Ashin would sleep. Their sister Eshne planned to meet us here. As we awaited her arrival, we sat on our balcony.

"It's so peaceful here," Ashin sighed, staring out at the waves. Adara's eyes glazed over as she looked in the same direction as her sister.

"I can't believe I haven't tried to get here earlier," I said, thinking of my great journey across the United States to reach Hestia's Home. The ocean hadn't even been a thought. I just wanted to get as far away from one coast and reach the other.

"California is heaven, that's for certain. But the sun is sinful." Ember snorted after the comment, and I didn't understand some pun she'd made. A soft knock at the door told us Eshne had arrived. Cheers and hugs followed all around as my sisters-by-fire greeted a girl I'd never met. She embraced me as if I were part of her family. Family with my sisters was familiar to me, but this was something more. I'd never had a stranger, who knew of my gift, hug me so hard. It gave me hope that she greeted me like I was part of something bigger, greater than just Hestia's Home.

"It's a pleasure to meet the newest sister," she said, releasing me. Her warm smile shone brighter than Adara's firm curve or Ashin's shy curl. This girl was brightness, but definitely related to them, with her raven black hair and ever-present tan skin. A strip of lavender streaked down one side, and Adara's fingers hesitantly curled over her sister's purple tresses.

"What's this?" Her voice shook in question, with a touch of fear. Eshne smiled sheepishly.

"Let's sit."

A lunch had been brought to our room, and we filled the balcony with our chatty seven. Through the course of the meal, Eshne spoke of her impending wedding. Adamant that her sisters attend, Eshne explained the marriage vows would be exchanged soon.

"I'm pregnant." The squeal following her announcement sent up another roar of congratulations and more hugs. However, Adara remained frozen in her chair. Her eyes pierced her sister with fear.

"What of the gift?"

Eshne sat slowly, following the hard eyes of her sister.

"It's under control."

"You received the fire?" Ashin stared at her sister, caught between excitement and astonishment. "When? How? Where?"

Adara brought the interrogation down a level. "What about the baby?"

"I'm not concerned." Eshne sat taller, facing her oldest sister by blood with stiff shoulders. "Malek is thrilled, and I'm under the best care."

"Malek is *human*."

"He is." Eshne's lowering eyes hinted at her own doubts. Suddenly feeling like an intruder in very private matters, I looked at Ember for support. Seraphine interjected with her own thoughts.

"I think we'll let you three talk, and head out to the first of the glass beaches. Adara and Ashin, there's nothing you'll miss that we won't see tomorrow when we go to the second one."

Adara dipped her head in gratitude, but Ashin's eyes followed us, as if willing us to take her away. I couldn't spare her feelings, as I assumed her younger sister Eshne would need the support. Adara seemed ready to pounce into motherhood mode with the grand inquisition for the youngest sister.

After saying our congratulations, although a bit more somber at the moment, we left the three sisters and hit the highway again for the beach. The land belonged to an old glass company, the space near the water turned into a trash heap during a time when garbage could be dumped into the sea. We took in the glittering array of rocks and glass once we climbed the short heap to the beach. Suddenly filled with laughter, we ran for the edge of the water like three carefree children. The sound of our giddiness filled the air while squawking seagulls dipped and dived for treats along the shore.

Releasing one another, we separated and walked with a new mission. Eyes glued to the ground, we hunted for unusual shapes and brilliant colors. I had my instructions: ruby red, cherry glass, something to match my hair. The concept was like finding a needle in a haystack—daunting, but exciting, like the prospect of buried treasure. After a short time, I decided to sit, staring off at the rumbling ocean, watching the soothing waves crest and fall, crashing harshly against the rocks and crawl like a clawing hand at the rocky shore. My thoughts drifted at the peaceful scene, so I hadn't heard the tell-tale crunching of feet approaching me. A shadow filled the space next to me and a hand lowered.

"Is this what you're looking for?"

A large, thick palm held an edgy shard of glass, glinting with cherry-rosebud color. It was perfect in color, though unstructured in form. Raising a hand to shield my eyes, my gaze climbed and climbed and climbed. The hint of his voice familiar, I found my hope confirmed.

"Heph?"

Large knees cracked as he squatted beside me, still holding out the highly-sought gem.

"Phyre," he exhaled, his broad forehead wrinkled in concern. His white teeth nibbling at his lip above heavy scruff.

"What are you doing here?" My voice rose with too much excitement and I coughed to cover the croak following my eager tone.

"I'm searching for treasure." Melting chocolate eyes hesitated as he stared at me. I bit my lip, holding back a smile. My head turned to face the rolling ocean.

"Why here?" My voice lowered, and my eyes watched my hand randomly scoop up a handful of rocks and glass.

"Because you're here. The treasure I finally found, but lost." My heart crashed to the shore, like the waves before me. Heph sat next to me, and his hand came to rest on my lower back.

"I'm sorry," he started, but I dismissed the words with a raised hand.

"Don't." The words came out harsher than I intended, but I didn't want to hear his explanation. Three months he'd been gone, and my heart finally decided to let him go, like the leaves falling from trees in autumn. Yet sitting next to me, buds of hope forced through dormant wood, threatening to open too soon.

His hand slipped from my back.

"The words aren't enough," he stated softly. He stared out at the ocean and my eyes shifted sideways to see him deep in concentration.

"Zeke," he offered. "He does this thing with me, and it always works." My head rose slowly to take in the stern expression on his face. "He makes me feel guilty. I shouldn't give in. I'm a grown man, older than dirt, but he gets me every time."

I blinked at him, surprised at the admission.

"You aren't old," I burst out, sounding ridiculously incensed, as that wasn't the issue at hand.

"I'm older than you might think. Old enough to see fire's first flame, but it doesn't matter. What matters is I've been alone too long and listened to him too often. And I miss you."

I knew Heph was like Hestia, part of an ancient people; their lives were longer than most. The things he must have seen over time, the hate and the heart of humans. I couldn't imagine it all. I stared at him, and he finally turned to face me.

"Tell me I'm not too late."

Was he too late? My heart leapt to say no. My body ached to agree, but my head overruled.

"I…I don't know," I offered weakly. Where did we go next? That's what concerned me. As if reading my thoughts, he responded.

"I wondered if we could spend time together. If you'd let me see you, while you are here?" The sweetness of his tone did things to me. I nodded consent without even thinking.

"Thank you," he exhaled, reaching for my hand and opening my palm. Cupping it with his, he placed the red glass in mine and curled my fingers over it. "Keep this for me."

"We aren't allowed to take glass from here," I said, sounding like a rule-abiding teenager.

"It already belongs to me." He stood with ease despite his large body and offered me a hand to help me stand. I slipped the glass into my pocket and took his hand. Stumbling as I stood, I fell against his chest. Hands resting on his T-shirt-covered chest, I shivered at the connection.

"Aren't you cold?" The whipping wind re-enforced it was not beach weather.

"I'm always warm when I'm around you."

My breath hitched, recalling our last night together, but there was no malice in his comment. In fact, the curling of his lips and the dip of his head confirmed it as a compliment. I couldn't help but smile in return.

+ + +

I shouldn't have been surprised to learn Heph not only knew where we stayed, but he had a room there as well. He asked me to meet him for dinner on the patio at seven. I had to tell my sisters, and none of them seemed surprised except Adara. For her, the heartache could not be disguised. He returned to me, and I had no idea what that even meant, but the fact that he came here was more than he'd done for her. My heart wanted to feel for her, but it was too full of anxiety and anticipation. Ember helped dress me in a white dress that accentuated my hair. The material was sheer over the arms and chest, hinting at my breasts. It hung to my knees with heavy embroidered designs.

"Where did this come from?"

"Heph sent it." Her voice was soft, dreamy almost. "It's so romantic."

"It is, actually," I sighed. I smiled, biting my lip. My hand drifted over the material, feeling sensual. I admired the details again, realizing the design included flames and leaves intertwined.

"You look beautiful." Ember spoke to me through the reflection in the mirror.

"I feel pretty," I whispered. "But I'm nervous."

Her eyes met mine in the mirror. "Why?"

"I've never been on a date before." My head lowered in embarrassment. I couldn't recall a moment of ever being treated to dinner or a movie. Holding hands on a walk. Kissing under stars. Any experience I had involved setting myself free from a bad situation or giving into desire only to run away the next day.

"It's going to be a special night." She winked in the mirror, and I smiled wider. The thought of Heph, handsome and sexy in jeans, waiting for me to meet him, warmed my insides. I'd never felt this way. The flames didn't lick inside me for escape, but filled me with comfort and warmth. It felt like I was going home.

I replied to Ember, "A first."

HEPH

I paced the patio, recounting in my head the details. Candles. Lots of candles. Dinner. Wine. Talk. We had to talk, but when she crossed the stone pavers, all thoughts left my brain. I stared, tongue-tied, as a vision of sugar plums, glistening and ripe for pleasure, approached me. I swallowed hard. I'd never done this before. Trying to make an apology was hard work.

"You look beautiful," I breathed. Her curving lips responded.

"So do you." I blinked in shock. "You're very good-looking." My eyes widened in surprise. No one said that to me. She stepped too close to me, and my thoughts fogged. "In fact, I think you look sexy." My mouth dried, and a giggle crossed her lips as she watched my throat roll.

"Are you teasing me?"

"I'm not teasing." Her hand, planted on my chest, swiped downward and pulled away. Her tone lowered with her eyes. "I'm sorry, that was probably a bit much. I'm nervous." She giggled again.

"Me, too." My hand rubbed over my head. I didn't know where to go next. Her head swung to the table.

"It looks beautiful." Breaking from my spell, I pulled out the chair for her and motioned for her to sit. I took my seat and poured some wine for each of us. Raising the glass to my lips, she said, "We should toast something."

I blinked again. I was messing this up.

"What should we toast?"

Her head looked upward at the star-filled sky.

"A beautiful night."

"A beautiful girl," I replied and brought the glass to my lips. She smiled slowly, and I downed the glass, thirsty, frightened, and nervous. She set her glass on the table, untouched.

"We should talk," she said, and I set my empty glass on the table near hers. Silence filled the space.

"I…" We both spoke at the same time. We laughed together.

"You go…" We started again collectively, and laughter filled with tension continued.

"Ladies first," I said, dipping my head. She nodded back and began.

"I've never felt like you make me feel." Those weren't the words I expected her to say. "I don't have expectations of anyone in life, Heph. But I expected more from you. I still don't understand why you left without telling me."

I sighed. "I told you on the beach. My father."

She stared at me, and I knew it wasn't enough.

"He can make me feel guilty for his generosity. Even though he's the parent, and he should have wanted me, he reminds me of his 'kindness' too often. As if I'm not grateful."

She watched me, waiting for more.

"My mother didn't want me. I reminded her of Zeke, whom she loved, and he betrayed her. He isn't a faithful man, and he has so many children, even I've lost count of my siblings. Solis is my best friend of the lot. Zeke just likes to reinforce my allegiance to him by manipulating me."

"Why did you return, then?"

"I didn't want to lose you."

She sighed, and her shoulders fell. "I thought I frightened you."

I laughed bitterly. "A fire doesn't scare me, Little Spark. I've seen much bigger flames."

"Is that what happened to you?" Her eyes drifted to my leg. We hadn't ever discussed it.

"I was mountain climbing, making my way across the country. I felt desperate for space and answers. I wanted to know why...why my mother didn't want me. After finding her, and being rejected a second time, I took risks to prove to myself I was stronger than they all gave me credit for. I'd been beat-up, stabbed, chased, and abused." I circled my face with my finger. "And then, I fell." Visions flashed through my eyes of tumbling down the rock, and then the world going dark. I woke under a blazing sun. I'd been out for days. "My leg was trapped, broken and swollen. The only way to move was to break the leg again. I slipped out, prepared to die, when Zeke found me, taking me in a second time."

Her hand reached for mine, and I curled her tiny fingers into my palm. How I longed to hold all of her against me. Holding her hand was a huge step. The flames within could burn, but for now, the heat of her hand calmed me.

"When he brought me home, he smacked me around. Hitting me to reinforce his love, he said. He wanted it hammered into my thick skull that home was where he lived and nowhere else. He alone loved me, and I would only find love on his estate. The rest of the world would not understand me. Understand us." Modern descendants of gods would be hard to explain to the new world.

Her hand squeezed tighter in mine.

"But I still don't understand; you walked away from him, if you came here. You're stronger than you think." Her smile brightened to reassure me, and I wanted a taste of those magenta-rosebud lips.

"Well, Solis told me to get my ass back to Hestia's."

Her brow pinched, and her hand slipped from my grasp, but I chased her fingers and tightened my hold.

"So Solis made you return?"

"Actually Veva. She scared me more than him." I chuckled at the scolding Veva gave me. Filled with love and good intentions, she ripped me up one side and down the other, telling me how much she admired me and adored me, but running away proved I was thick-headed. Then she laughed, knowing she'd done the same thing.

We're more alike than I thought, big brother. Her words filled me with joy.

"So Veva sent you here."

Not understanding her meaning, I smiled larger.

"Actually, Hestia told me where to find you."

"Hestia?"

"I'd gone back to her home. It's really more my home, happy and comforting, than my father's estate."

She shook her head. "I see," but something told me she didn't.

"What about Lovie?"

The question surprised me. I was here for her; didn't she see that?

"What about her?" I snapped. Phyre's eyes shot up to mine, and her hand tugged to release my grasp. Questioning ocean-colored eyes peered into mine.

"I'm not going back to her. We had our time. It's over."

Her hand relaxed in mine.

"Phyre, I want to begin again with you. A new story."

"I want that, too."

I slipped from my seat and fell to a knee. Cupping her face, I leaned up to kiss her. My lips twitched with excitement: a child eager for the sugary, sweet taste of a treat. The connection was tender, hesitant, and new. She returned the kiss like she'd never kissed me before, and I felt the separation.

Tell me I'm not too late, I had asked. *Was I?* I wondered. I deepened the kiss, asking her without words to accept me. Her hand cupped my cheek as only our lips touched. Pulling back from me, she stared with smoky blue eyes, questioning where we stood.

"It's only you." It seemed futile to keep talking when she needed my action instead. Sitting back in my seat, dinner arrived, and we ate intermittently between speaking of our pasts, avoiding things too heavy like her travels to the Pacific Northwest and my adventures through the United States.

She laughed her fire-crackling laughter, and my heart warmed as she smiled at me. I'd never been on a date before, and if I was human, I imagine this night was what romantics wrote about in books. The starry night, the chilly air, the fire nearby. Good dinner, great wine, and better company. But the night came too quickly to an end, when she said she thought she should go, and I didn't want her to leave.

My hand reached for her, respecting her wishes, and I walked her back to her room. We stood outside the door, hands caressing over fingers and wrists, tracing palms and intertwining digits.

"I guess I'll see you tomorrow." Her eyes on her hands, rubbing over mine. I wanted her to sense the irony. She wasn't burning me. We touched without fire, but the blaze was in my veins. I wanted her.

I leaned forward and kissed her lips softly before drawing back.

"Good night," I said, and with strength I didn't know I possessed, I stepped back as she entered her room and closed the door.

PHYRE

I stood outside Heph's door, my hand rising to knock and then lowering. My forehead came forward to rest on the wood as my heart raced. It was after midnight, hours after he sweetly walked me to my room.

Could I do this?

Should I do this?

Ember questioned me the second I returned.

"I didn't expect to see you." Her eyes hesitantly roamed over me, before her mouth spread into a wide smile.

"What happened?" Her laughter didn't pull me away from the door, my back still pressed to it, holding the knob.

"It was...heavenly," I sighed. The night had been perfect. It was everything and more than I expected from a date. Slowly my head rose, and I stared at Ember. "And he walked me back here."

Tender eyes watched me. "Did you not want to go with him to his room?"

"He didn't ask me."

She nodded slowly, and then her head popped up. "Did you want him to?"

Before I could think, I breathed: "Yes." We stared at one another, my back still on the door.

"You know, I love you, right? And I want what is best for you." She paused. "Heph is good for you, Phyre. Trust him."

Could I do this? I questioned again as my forehead pressed against the door.

Should I do this? I answered my own question by taking a deep breath and raising my fist. The thought of losing him in my life made me want to take charge of my own. I wouldn't waste another moment separated from what I wanted. I rapped quickly on the wood. The door opened almost instantly to a bare, broad-chested Heph in jeans.

"Phyre," he breathed, and my name on his lips assured me I need only strike the match, and the flame would ignite. He stepped back, allowing me entrance to his room. The space was larger than ours, more like a master suite, complete with a fireplace where a small fire warmed the chilly night. The door to his balcony remained open.

"What's this? Why are there so many candles?" I questioned, taking in the hundreds of wax pillars, unlit and gothic, but statuary, around the room, standing guard over the bed.

"It was wishful thinking." He shrugged one shoulder and crossed the room to stand in front of the fireplace. I followed slowly, taking in the display.

"Wishful thinking for what?" My voice lowered, the sound sultry and uncertain.

He shook his head at first, taking a small crystal glass from the mantel and sipping the amber-colored liquid.

"Tell me. Please."

His eyes came to mine.

"I made a wish. For you. Tonight."

I stared at him. Should I curse at him for assuming I would sleep with him so soon? I couldn't. I'd wanted that, too. In fact, from all that happened with Adara, I selfishly decided I needed to take what I wanted before I lost the chance. That's why I stood here.

"What are you doing here?" His tone was sharp, cutting a little as he stared into the fire.

"I…" I swallowed, knowing this was the moment. Set free the risk. "I was afraid, if I didn't take tonight, I'd never get another chance. And I'm afraid I'll never feel again how I feel about you. And I wanted…" I didn't get the chance to finish before his lips covered mine, drinking in my words, reassuring me tonight would not be a mistake. After our lips melted together, dripping with desire and sparking the flame of passion, he drew back, breathless.

"We need to take it slower." My words weren't a warning. They spoke the truth. I didn't want to lose control. I needed to prove I could do this, and I wanted it to be Heph. I wanted Heph because I loved him. Without words, I wanted to show him I loved him.

"Why are there so many candles?" I looked around again at the white display.

"I thought if we lit the candles, the flames would calm you, and it would hold at bay the one within you." His eyes questioned mine, hoping he hadn't hurt my feelings. Biting at his lip, I smiled and tipped up to kiss over the tender skin.

"That was very thoughtful of you. And romantic."

His brows shot up.

"I'll light them." Stepping away from him, I pressed the pad of my thumb with the tip of my index finger and the wick sparked. I looked at him over my shoulder, my lips curling with anticipation as I lit another pillar. Heph followed opposite me, lighting the candles on the other side of the room. It took several moments for all the flames to dance, and the room filled with romance. A midnight opera. A gothic hall. The room whispered of sensuality. I met Heph at the end of the bed, but he pulled an armless chair to stand before the fire.

I watched as he slowly unbuttoned his jeans, revealing Christmas red boxer briefs beneath. A nervous giggle escaped me.

"I replaced the pair I was missing." His clarification came through in a gruff voice, raspy and warm, a raised eyebrow teasing me. He watched me as I stared at his bare skin, and I drank in the hard display: thick thighs and broad chest, with heavy arms that bore a new design on the inside of his wrist.

"Why do you have a plum and a pear on your arm?"

"They remind me of you. You're a fall flavor, and I want to taste you." Dropping to his knees before me, he lifted my dress, slipped down my underwear, and kissed the mound at the apex of my thighs.

"I've never…" I wanted to tell him I'd never done this before, but his mouth on my center sucked out my breath. My hands covered his head as his tongue entered me. My legs trembled, but I ignored the shaking. The spread of his tongue, warm and wet, sparked the pressure inside. Like slow rolling magma in the earth, the heat rose and the

156

temperature soared as Heph tasted my core. The heaviness built, and my insides rumbled as the eruption drew to the peak. Bursting forth, I tipped back my head and cried out Heph's name, the sound of it steamy and seductive as my orgasm ripped through me and slipped over the edge, pouring down the mountain like a slow-rolling tide. Unsteady after the release, Heph stood to support me.

"You have on too much clothing."

He spun me to undo the two dozen tiny buttons on the back of my dress. His thick fingers fumbled at first, and then worked faster as more skin was exposed. I held my breath, knowing he was about to see the full exposure of me, a hidden truth of who I was. His breath didn't hitch as others had, but trembling fingers traced over deep scars and puckered skin, not afraid to touch.

"When the fire roared in my home as a child, I didn't even feel the pain. Pressed into the wall, I never noticed the flames at my back. I didn't know how to heal myself then, so the scars remained."

Lips hit my back, sucking and kissing over heavily damaged skin. I'd seen it in the mirror. The skin raw and etched like a poor design of scratches and scrapes. As his mouth covered the patchy puckers, my dress slipped from one shoulder and then the other, cascading down my pale arms before sliding off my wrists. Falling to the floor, I stood naked as he spun me to face him.

"You take my breath away." His words washed away the devastating memories and his mouth on me cleared any negative thoughts. Scrubbing off the dirt of the past, Heph continued to kiss my jaw, my neck and my chest. His mouth travelled downward, and he took one full breast into his mouth. I nearly jumped out of my skin at the pleasure, as his tongue swirled over a peaked nipple and he sucked the heavy globe. A fiery current triggered my lower belly to flicker again.

"Heph." I swallowed his name as he moved to my other breast, paying homage to tender skin and another tight bud. He stood and returned to my lips, kissing me like he needed my oxygen to breath. Our mouths molded together, melting into one another again and again, like the glass beads heated by flame. Pulling back from me, breathless once again, he stepped back and removed his loose jeans, taking his red boxer briefs with them. His hands came to his hips, daring me to take him in, teasing me with what I'd miss if I didn't. My eyes travelled to the intricate design of his leg, a mastery of metal artwork.

"You're sure about this?" he questioned, a hint of fear I'd reject him.

"Are you sure about this?" A brief flash of our past crossed my mind.

"Trust yourself not to hurt me."

There wasn't a question in my mind. My eyes leapt to his metal leg again and back to his scarred face.

"There is nothing I'd prevent more than hurting you. I've never been more certain of anything in my life. I want to be with you, Heph." My words were heavy, hoping to assure him I wholly accepted him. "Everything about you I find miraculous and beautiful."

He stepped back, nearing the chair by the fire.

"We're going to let you control this, and use the chair for stability."

I nodded slowly, noting he'd thought out how to make this work for us. He sat, and I walked toward him.

"You are the sexiest creature I've ever seen." His eyes watched my movement, caressing over my hips, and crawling down my thighs. He bit his lip, the one that tasted me, the one that kissed me like I was on fire, and I loved him.

I stood before him, and he tugged at my waist.

"Straddle me." Opening my thighs, I spread over his.

"My feet don't touch the floor," I giggled nervously.

"You're going to float anyway."

He dragged me to meet the length of him and we both groaned at the connection of skin on skin. My hand came between us and curled around his velvety skin, rippled and tight, accentuating his excitement. His head tipped back as I stroked him several times. A low groan rolled from his throat.

"Press up on your toes." His hands, gripping my waist, lifted me effortlessly, and balanced my center on the tip of him. His eyes didn't leave mine as he lowered me, slowly filling me.

"So deep," he sighed, his eyes rolling shut.

"So full," I whispered.

His hands at my hips moved me, developing a rhythm like a slow dance or a blowing flame. I hissed with excitement as I swiveled over him. Thick hands slipped to my backside and pressed against me.

"Bull's eye," he whispered, as the length of him completed me, dragging slowly inside of me.

"Home," I answered, as my channel clenched over him.

An arrow to a bow, he shot straight at my heart, and our connection hit the target. Branded forever, Heph's name tattooed on the vessel keeping me alive. Every flame in the future would whisper his name, because no moment would top the warm sensation of him buried inside me. Heph was my home.

Slowly, the heat grew again, surprising me how quickly I could reignite. Smoldering embers are not a dead fire, and Heph was a match, sparking a second blaze. My hips no longer needed his guidance as I rocked over him, rolling rhythmically like the beat of our goddess ritual. The music of our union filled my ears and a new ritual took place. Heph matched the drumming and called out to me as I burst forth a second time, encouraging him to follow. Warmth seeped inside me as he stilled, forcing my thighs to crush his. I took a peek at where he joined me, knowing no union would ever be the same.

My head fell forward, resting on his as we caught our breaths. Sweat rolled down his temple, and a trickle curled down my back. The flickering flames of the candles danced around us, celebrating our union, witnesses to the glory. Heph's mouth reached for mine, and we kissed with lingering lips, our hearts settling and our breath catching. He slipped me off of him and placed me on the bed. Returning to help me clean, he curled me into him afterward, hands on his chest and head over his heart. He stroked my hair until his arm fell heavy and slipped from my back.

Heph

Sensing his sleep, I whispered over his calm heart, lips affixed to his skin.

"I love you, Hephaestus."

HEPH

"I love you." The words lingered in the smoky air of flames blown out and fragrant candles, flickering over my heart and warming my insides. *I love you*, I responded in my thoughts, certain she heard me. But when I woke to the pounding at my door, and not a trace of her presence but melted candles and dripping wax, I believed I imagined the night.

"Heph!" The banging on my door rattled the frame. "Heph, I need Phyre!" Hopping to the door as I slipped into my jeans, I found a pacing Ember standing in the hallway. Her eyes travelled past me.

"Heph, I need Phyre. And you. You come too."

"I…" I didn't know where she was. "What's going on?"

"I'm so sorry." Breathing heavy, her hand covered her chest. "I hate to interrupt, but it's Adara. Please, come quick."

Stepping back into the room, I reached for a shirt and slipped into shoes.

"What happened?" I asked, panicking myself at the loss of Phyre and the concern for Adara.   "Adara. She…she walked into the sea." Ember's breath caught, and her hand covered her mouth, holding back a sob.

"What?" I bellowed, tugging the door closed and following after her.

"She didn't come to dinner. When I went to check on her, the balcony door was open, with no sign of her. I had a strange feeling something wasn't right. Just a gut feeling." Her fist covered her lower belly. "Seraphine headed toward the beach. When she found her, she called out for Ashin."

"What happened?" I asked again, racing toward the beach where the iridescent glow of something large and green bent over a body on the rocky shore. Ashin knelt near the huddled body, sobbing and rocking as the green creature curled forward to cover Adara. Seraphine beat on his back, slapping frantically at the scaly skin.

"Get off of her! Get off of her!" Seraphine shrieked.

"Hey," I shouted, reaching the rocky shore and sprinting the final steps to Adara. Suddenly, I stopped. "Triton?"

Not breaking his motion, pumping on Adara's water-sodden chest, my cousin bent to cover Adara's mouth, breathing into her. The irony of my cousin working to save the life of a woman on the shore startled me. Typically, he took the breath of those consumed by water, releasing them to the sea.

"What happened?" I asked a third time as Ember caught up to our gathering. *And where is Phyre?*

"I found her in the water." Triton sat up, continuing to work on her chest. "Come on, baby, breathe." His endearing demand surprised me.

"Do you know her?"

"No." He pressed again, and water spurt from her mouth, choking her in a flood of salty spew. Triton turned her sideways, allowing the water to pour from her lips. Placing her on her back, he lowered to cover her lips. It was more than giving her oxygen. My cousin kissed her, and Adara's mouth responded. The kiss was brief, and Triton released her slowly. Their eyes held one another as he pulled back, and finally looked up at me.

My raised eyebrow questioned him.

"She was in the water," he repeated, and then his eyes shifted down to her. His green-skinned hand covered her forehead and brushed back her dark hair. Adara's eyes remained on her savior, but Ashin fell on her sister.

"What were you thinking? What were you doing?" Her sobs fell harder, and Adara's head turned slowly. A limp hand came to the back of her sister.

"Who are you?" Ember asked, eying the strange coloring of my cousin.

"I'm Triton. Heph's cousin. Man, what are you doing here?" His jovial face broke into a wide grin despite the tragedy before us.

"I'm...this is Adara. One of Hestia's girls."

"Hestia lets her girls leave the home?" His questioning black eyes fell back to Adara. Their eyes held one another and I felt uncomfortably like an intruder on something private.

"Maybe we should get Adara up to the hotel." Ember's voice behind me startled me from my observation of my cousin and my ex-lover.

I bent to lift her at the same time Triton scooped her up in his arms. He stood without effort, holding her close to his chest.

"You can't go up there like this, can you?" I nodded to the bed and breakfast, knowing my green- skinned cousin could not walk among the humans with his odd coloring. He needed time to morph, and we didn't have time to wait.

"Are you a fish?" Seraphine asked, regaining her composure after beating on his back while he tried to save her sister.

"If I were, I'd be fish pâté by now, from the beating you gave me." His smile spread across his face, and Seraphine stared at him and his teasing tone.

"He's not a fish. He's my cousin. His father is Zeke's brother." The girls stood around exchanging glances while Adara rested in his arms. Taking note of their compromising position, he stepped toward me and handed me Adara.

"Take care of her." His voice faltered as he looked at her. "Stay out of the deep end, baby," he said to her. He spun and quickly ran for the ocean, gracefully diving into the waves. An iridescent glow filtered at the surface before disappearing into the dark water.

"What is he?"

"He's a god," Adara stated.

"Uhmmm…mmm…mmm…" Seraphine replied. "That he is."

Ember began to laugh, and the sadness of the moment broke, while Adara soaked my shirt in my arms.

"Let's get this fish to your rooms." I tried to tease, but the question of her presence in the ocean lingered among all of us. As we barged into their room, I noticed Phyre sitting on her bed through the open door. Instantly she stood and stepped toward us.

"What happened?"

Laying Adara on the bed, I brushed back her hair, feeling the weight of Phyre's eyes on me.

"I'm sorry," Adara croaked, looking up to me, her throat rough from the salt water intake, and her hand cupped my cheek.

"There's nothing to be sorry for," I said, brushing back her hair. Looking back, I caught Phyre watching me. Her eyes drifted to Adara and back to me. The sorrowful expression on her face tore at my heart. She misunderstood, but guilt ate at me. Did Adara try to kill herself because of me? Seraphine's voice interrupted Phyre's troubled gaze.

"We need to get her changed," the spunky, blue-streaked girl said.

Phyre looked away from me, and on that note, I took my leave, worried once more that I had lost Phyre forever.

HEPH

The next day, I dressed quickly and went to the girls' rooms. Swollen, red eyes met mine.

"Ashin, what happened?"

She shook her head and opened the door. Adara sat up in bed, the covers pulled over her waist. Instantly, I noticed the second room sat empty.

"Where did they go?" I addressed Adara.

"They left. Seraphine wanted to get to Hestia. Ashin decided to stay with me." Her sad dark eyes looked at me. "Our sister is getting married." The words hit me hard. "And she's having a baby."

Images of tiny girls with cherry-rosebud hair filtered through my mind. I didn't even know if it was safe for Phyre to carry children, and I'd never thought of having my own until that moment, but none of it mattered, as Phyre was gone, and I still didn't understand what happened.

"Why didn't you go back with them? You could have returned later for the wedding."

Adara's eyes shifted to the open curtains, draped around the large glass door.

"I wanted to stay. It's time, Heph. I can't keep hiding at Hestia's."

I looked at Ashin, who sat on the second bed and lowered her head.

"What are you hiding from?" The question came from somewhere deep in me.

"Life, Heph," she smiled weakly at me. A new thought struck me.

"What were you thinking last night?"

She shrugged a shoulder and the guilt of her disappointment seized me. *Had I done this to Adara?* I asked myself. Did my return and subsequent rejection drive her to such extremes? Surely, jealousy could not be the reason she walked into the ocean and hoped to drown.

"I…" she paused, clamping her lips tight. After the midnight swim, her true color returned today. Adara shook her head, and a tear dripped from Ashin once again.

"What secrets do you keep?" I sat next to Adara, my hand coming to her covered knee. Her head shook as her eyes closed briefly. "You can tell me anything, Adara. After what we shared, I still consider you a friend. Practically family. Let me help you." My eyes watched her face as a silent tear trickled down her cheek. Beautiful skin, soft and supple once under my rough hands, she could have been everything to me. I would not have denied her anything, but Phyre confirmed that I deserved more. I deserved more than giving of myself to someone who only half-heartedly wanted me. When Adara refused to answer, I moved onto another question stabbing at me.

"Did Phyre go with them?"

Adara's head swung back to me.

"She did. I'm so sorry."

Why? My head screamed but my mouth didn't ask. In some ways, I knew the reason. Phyre had her own guilt. She felt the same as me. Adara had tried to kill herself because of the lost love, the happiness of her family around her, and the future she didn't see.

"I'm here for you," I offered and a slow smile crossed Adara's lips. Lips that once worshiped my body but did not whisper *I love you* in the night. Her hand reached for mine and slipped into my palm.

"I know, Heph. I know."

+ + +

Three months passed.

I escorted both Adara and Ashin to their sister's wedding, taking pleasure in the pride they found in honoring her day. They walked her down the aisle, giving her away to her human husband, Malek, who seemed like a decent man. Still slender, a tiny bump at Eshne's belly hinted at the growing pregnancy. No one in attendance seemed to care she was pregnant before the wedding, too wrapped up in the happiness shared between the loving couple.

Adara looked lovely in a dress of leaf green, while Ashin wore something sunshine yellow. The contrast to their typical darker shades, clothing of jeans and flannels, brightened Adara's mood. Day by day she smiled more and lost the far-off stare. Ashin wanted to return to Hestia's Home, as she told me in private, but I didn't think it safe for Adara's fragile feelings yet.

"I want to go home," Ashin whined one evening. I'd moved the girls into a small cottage on a short street that dead-ended with the beach. They shared a room while I took the second bedroom.

"I know, but not yet."

"How long, Heph?" Ashin sighed heavily. "California is beautiful, but I don't want to stay here. I miss Flame." Attached to the younger girl as a substitute for her own sister, Ashin had a special bond with Flame. Being estranged from their younger sister for a few years, she didn't feel as protective of Eshne as Adara had. In fact, the attraction of her wayward husband to her younger sister still stung, feelings suppressed but present. No one wants to feel as if she is second to someone else. I thought of Adara. She would have replaced Lovie for me, and I replaced her with Phyre.

Guilt cut through me at the thought of Phyre. At first, I cursed her for leaving without an explanation. Then I swore at myself for not following her, trying to figure out what happened, but I'd already chased after her once. I came here because of her. I remained here because of Adara. Only Phyre burned in my thoughts, my destiny flickering like a lit candle where I made a wish for love. I did not hide my feelings for Phyre, although I didn't speak of her absence. I hadn't followed Phyre, in that moment feeling a greater sense of duty to Adara and a commitment to Hestia to take care of her daughters.

"It's almost spring. Everything will be in bloom," Ashin added, her thoughts far away, up the coastline, in another state. Taking in the sunshine and the rolling sea waves, I had to agree my thoughts matched hers.

"Did you ever call her?" Ashin asked breaking into my thoughts.

"Call her?"

"You know, on the phone." I stared at Ashin, so similar to her sister, and yet a softer look graced her face.

"No." I snorted, like it was a ridiculous thought.

"It's the twenty-first century."

I stared at her. I didn't have need of a phone. There was no one I wanted to call. When I lived on the estate of Olympic Oil, everything I needed was there. When I travelled, I didn't have a care or concern. I didn't own a cell phone.

"I...I wouldn't know what to say." Time had passed, and again I'd let another relationship fail; only this one lingered, deep in my heart. In trying to do right by Adara, I let Phyre slip away. I often thought of our night together: the feel of her around me, the touch of her hands on me. My hand came to my forehead, scrubbing as if holding in a headache, wiping away the thoughts of her tenderness.

"Don't you miss her?"

"With every breath I take," I whispered. At a shifting-sound behind me, I looked up to see Adara standing in the patio doorway. Her arms crossed, she smiled softly. It didn't reach her eyes, but her eyes didn't look as sad. Being in California was a good fit for her. The warmer temperatures and sunny days brightened her face.

"I think you should go," she said, shifting her gaze to the ocean behind me. "She's waiting for you."

"She left me." I paused. "And you don't know that."

"Yes, Heph. Yes, I do." Her smile remained the same, frozen in place as she turned away from me. Ashin looked at me, her curved lips silent, but her eyes spoke the truth. Adara knew about waiting, and I did, too.

+ + +

"What the fuck are you thinking?" Solis stormed the cottage door, passing me for the small living room one night. Veva followed, but stopped to kiss my cheek.

"Well, great to see you, too," I muttered. "What are you doing here? How did you find me?" I asked louder.

"We heard you were still here. Zeke knows everything. More importantly, where is Phyre?"

"Home." The word snapped from my lips.

"Home? Hestia's Home? Then isn't that where you should be?"

"I'm helping Adara." Relief washed over me that the girls were on a walk outside.

Veva stared at me. "I think you're hiding."

"From what?" I snapped.

"Love." The word hung in the air between us like a rain cloud.

"I thought you loved Phyre," Veva's voice softened.

"I do." The words tumbled out. I hadn't told anyone, not even Phyre. I should have told her my feelings that night. Maybe she wouldn't have left. Maybe she wouldn't have misunderstood. I should have told her, only I thought I'd have the next day with her and every day after that.

"I'm confused. You love Phyre, who isn't here, but you're here, helping Adara." Vee's eyes narrowed. I stared at my fast-talking sister, her hands on her hips. Her sapphire eyes rimmed with turquoise gleamed at me. Solis came to stand by his girl.

"There…there was an incident with Adara, and after Phyre left, I decided to stay."

"Phyre left?"

"Yes."

Veva's arms crossed and her foot tapped.

"Oh, boy, not the foot tap," Solis teased. My sister glared at him, but he winked in response.

"But you love Phyre?" Veva repeated.

"Yes," I sighed, not certain where she was going with this inquisition.

"So why are you here again?"

"Ad…" *Adara*, I was about to answer, but Veva raised her hand.

"No, no, don't answer that. Adara is a big girl. She can take care of herself. You're hiding, and I won't let you. You get in that fast car of yours, and you get your ass to Hestia's."

I stared at my sister, her arms waving dismissively toward the front door, as she glared at me.

"I love you, Heph." *But you aren't the smartest guy*, I expected her to say next, reminiscent of my father. "And you deserve a woman who loves you. She's waiting for you. You know about waiting, right Heph?"

"Solis always said the right girl was waiting for me." The moment the words crossed my lips, my heart pinched. I did know about waiting. Waiting to find the right girl to love me. *Oh god*s, did someday come and go? Did some night as well? A hand came to my forehead to rub the crinkled skin and puckered scar.

"I messed up, didn't I?"

"Yes," Veva sighed.

"Not yet." Solis interjected. "You need a grand gesture," his tone mocked me. "I remember someone giving me that advice. Sunsets and rainbows, I think he said, because I'm a god." Solis' reminder of me telling him to take advantage of who he was and go after Veva was being used against me.

"I don't know what to do."

"We're here to help you," Solis said, placing a hand on my shoulder. "But first tell me what happened with Adara."

PHYRE

Heph's body ran warm, and I needed some air. Pulling up my hair, I entered the balcony and stared out at the rolling, black ink off in the distance. The water had a powerful sound, so different from the quiet of the woods around Hestia's Home. The only moving water I'd ever heard was the river, softly rippling, versus the harsh rolling of the waves in the ocean. Cool air blew around my neck, chilling my skin covered in Heph's shirt. I hugged my arms around me, holding in his scent, recalling his body moving with mine. A smile crossed my lips with the memory, and my body longed for a repeat. Turning to glance over my shoulder, I saw Heph still resting, his chest rising and falling peacefully as he lay stretched out on his back.

I twisted back to the yard and saw a figure in white crossing the lawn. Squinting to take in the sight, I noticed dark hair blowing at her back and the fluttering of thin material around long legs.

Adara?

I pressed my hands on the bannister and stared off at the lithe body, gracefully floating over the grass, as if in a trance. She walked slowly, methodically, and I recalled our practices for the fire goddess ritual. Adara was an elegant dancer, but something about her movements concerned me. I glanced back at Heph, still sleeping, and although my insides warmed at the thought of curling up next to him again, I sensed a call to my sister.

Turning back, Adara crossed a greater distance and her hair blew wildly behind her. I ran from the room, exiting the back door of the inn, and raced over the sharp grass. My feet cut at the dry pricks under tender pads, but I moved forward, pulled toward Adara.

"Adara!" I yelled, reaching her moments before she crossed the edge of the property, and took the steps down to the beach. On a natural cliff, we were several feet up from the shoreline.

"*Adara,*" *I called again, grabbing for her arm as she ignored me. Spinning her to face me, her tear streaked cheeks surprised me.*

"*Adara, honey, what's wrong?*" *Softening my tone, I attempted to calm her, although I trembled with fear. Her eyes looked wild, skittish, and roving.*

"*I can't take it anymore.*" *The tone of her voice was eerie and sad.* "*Everyone's getting what they want, except me.*"

Her eyes shifted to mine, but she looked right through me as she spoke.

"*I'm being selfish. For once, I want something for me.*"

"*Adara,*" *I cooed.* "*You're the least selfish person I know. You protected Eshne, and you saved Ashin. You've helped us all at Hestia's.*"

"*I loved him, and he didn't love me.*"

My hands slipped from her arms. Heph.

"*He loved you,*" *I choked.* "*But you didn't love him.*"

"*I was too late. He came back too late. Too late.*" *Her voice faltered.*

"*Do you...do you want him back?*" *I didn't know what I was offering, as if Heph were a thing instead of a being, but I'd give him up. If she needed him, I'd give him back.*

"*Everyone's falling in love. My sister. You.*" *She paused, not answering me.* "*My sister's getting married.*" *She said, the words in surprise, as if I didn't know.* "*She's having a baby.*" *Her voice lowered and she choked on the last word.*

"*A baby.*" *Her eyes drifted to her feet.* "*I'll never have those things.*"

"*Yes, you will, Adara. The right man. The right place.*"

"*It can't happen for me. I already tried, and I failed.*"

Did she wish to try again? Did she want a second chance with Heph?

"*Even Flame,*" *her head shot up,* "*Flame. Two boys. None for me.*" *Tears didn't leave her eyes, but she choked on a sob.* "*Everyone is getting what they want except for me.*"

"*Do you want Heph? Do you want him back?*"

"*I saw you with him.*"

I shook my head. She couldn't have, but then I thought back to the open window and all the flames. A girl of fire would be attracted to such a display. I should have hung my head in embarrassment, but my eyes didn't leave hers.

"I can't apologize." *But the moment the words left my lips, I was sorry. Had I broken her heart? Did she feel I stole her man? She was my sister. I could never do that. I owed Adara everything.*

"I'm sorry," *I added, lowering my lids to avoid the intensity of her gaze.*

"You're sorry?" *Her voice rose slightly above the wind.* *"You're sorry. For what? For sleeping with him? For flirting with him? For capturing his heart when it once wanted me?"* *Her voice irritated.* *"He wanted me first, Phyre. Me."* *She slapped at her chest. I'd never seen her so intense, so angered.* *"I'm always second best, Phyre, but for once I was first."*

I didn't know what she meant. Adara was the first born of her natural sisters.

"I wasn't good enough, and he took another girl."

My brow pinched. What was she talking about? Heph and me? Heph told me about his relationship. He would have given her everything but he wasn't enough for her.

"I'll never be good enough with these." *Adara raged on, raising her hands and staring at the palms before flipping them to the back.* *"All I'll ever be able to do is hurt a man. Not love him."* *She fisted her hands and raised them upward.* *"Why? Why couldn't he love me?"*

Tears streamed down my cheeks as the wind picked up around us. My heart broke at the desperation in my sister to want Heph's love.

"I'm sorry, Adara. I'm sorry. I'll give him up. I'll give him back."

Her eyes snapped to me, as if she forgot I stood there in her tirade.

"I don't want to be second anymore, Phyre. But just know you're second, too. You came after me. And I came after her. Do you think a man like that can commit? He made promises to more than one of us at a time. Are you certain he means what he says to you? He told me he loved me. Has he said that to you?"

Her words slapped me and my cheeks stung. No, actually, he hadn't said those words to me, but I didn't wish to tell that to Adara. I wanted to believe Heph and I had said those words through our intense connection, as he entered me and filled me, he showed me that he loved me. He trusted me.

Adara turned away from me at that moment, and all I could do was stare after her before I ran for my room, my heart clenching in my chest, the fire extinguished in me.

Tears filled my eyes once again before I fell asleep. It had been nearly three months, but I couldn't stop crying myself to sleep each night. My thoughts were so out of whack, and I couldn't recover from all that happened in California. I returned with Seraphine and Ember to tell Hestia of Adara's attempt to kill herself, thinking she would race to her aid, but in her typical, calm fashion, she listened to the explanation of who saved Adara, and who remained with her. She trusted Idon's son, Triton, and she believed Heph did what he thought best. She smiled slowly, patting my hand as she explained that Adara could take care of herself.

"The healing process is longer for some of us. Adara's been responsible for her sisters for a long time. Now it's time for her to take time for herself." Unconcerned, Hestia dismissed our panic, allowing Adara and Ashin to remain behind. My heart dropped. Anger followed me for days. I lit flaming arrows and flung them into targets, piercing them with my upset, damning bull's eyes and circles, centers and home. And then I got sick.

A rarity among us was to have the flu, but chills wracked my body. My breasts hung heavy and my back ached. I was so tired that all I could do was work and sleep. Our smaller household felt strangely empty without our additional sisters. Seraphine grew less sarcastic and Ember took over as second mother-hen in charge. She forced me to eat when I didn't feel like it and sleep when I needed it more. My heart hurt the most, but she couldn't do anything about that.

+ + +

As I crossed back through the woods one day, I heard the roar of a vehicle, ripping up the forest. Rocks scattered, clamoring down like a rain storm, pattering as gravel spun from the earth. I couldn't race the intruder, but I slipped through the thick brush, following the sound. My instincts taught me to listen; a protective measure when one grew up on the run. A snap of branches. The crush of smaller twigs. Another spiral of dirt. There was only one way to Hestia's Home: the arched branch over the two-tire drive led directly here, unless someone randomly four-wheeled it through the woods. Even then, the protection around the property prevented intruders. One would have to recognize the curve of the tree that marked the entrance to get this far by car. Temple's stable was the opposite entrance, but as our northern guardian, no one passed his inspection.

I trekked around thick trees and under budding foliage. Spring arrived, although winter still lingered. My jacket hung open and dangled off my shoulder as I'd spent the afternoon practicing archery. My quiver hung loosely over the other shoulder, reminding me of Heph, as it was his gift. I held each arrow lovingly in my hand before I flung the shaft angrily at the target. Angry at myself for leaving. Angry at Heph for not following. Angry at Adara for wanting him.

In the shadow of the trees, the air chilled me, but my heart raced as I paced toward the disturbing noise of a revving engine tearing through trees. The vehicle drew closer, and I cut right, a huntress on the search for big game predators. A thin space ahead marked where the drive led, filling in slowly with new, spring foliage but still sparse from the last vehicle driving this trail. Thoughts of Heph skipped into my head and then jumped out, as I forced them to do daily.

I reached the two-tire path and kept myself covered by heavy growth around me until the last second. A curve in the bend ahead led directly for me. Stepping on the trail, I straddled the divots in the dirt. I stood with arrow raised, the fletching level with my eye, the string pulled taut and ready to fire. The roaring beast spun on its back tires, rounding the curl in the forest, crashing through the thinner brush and firing its heated breath at me. Screeching to a new gear, the brakes slammed, but I remained frozen, rooted to the earth. The beast slid forward with the abrupt halt, tearing up the ground beneath the tires. The grill of the car headed straight for my knees, and I screamed.

"Hephaestus!"

HEPH

My Camaro sputtered and twisted through the thin brush before stilling at the sight of her in the path. Slamming on the brakes, the car propelled forward in the soft dirt. Her mouth opened to scream, but her body remained stationary, her arrow aimed at the windshield. When the car stopped, her body pressed against the grill of the car. I pushed open the door with enough force that it bounced back at me.

"Phyre!" I yelled, rounding the vehicle. She shifted her aim, pointing the arrow at my chest, and we glared at one another, my heart racing at the thought that I might have hit her.

"What are you doing in the road?" I shouted.

"What are you doing here?" She bit back.

Firing questions at one another wasn't going to lower the sudden tension between us. Thicker than the tree-covering canopy, the air around us filled like pressing fog. I walked toward her, hands raised in surrender, but she refused to lower her weapon. Her narrow-eyed-aim followed my motions. I rounded the front of the car, letting the arrow press to my chest.

"Well, this seems familiar," I mumbled, chewing at my lip. Her eyes met mine, smoky blue shining bright under her unusual, beautiful hair.

"I had it aimed lower," she snipped, not taking her eye from the fletching and flinging out sarcasm to correct my memory. Her hand shook, and the arrowhead poked at my T-shirt.

"Fire at me, Phyre." My voice softened. "I'm already dead without you."

"Don't say that." Her voice choked.

"What else can I say? I'm sorry again. I messed up. I keep doing it, even when I want to do better."

Her head nodded, bobbing up and down. I leaned forward letting the arrow pierce through cotton and break skin. A trickle of blood seeped through my T-shirt, swelling in the fabric, replicating my desire. I bled for her.

"Take aim, Phyre. You already know you've pierced my heart. Take my soul."

This time her head shook slowly, side to side.

"I love you." The words shot like her weapon, striking her hard. She blinked, and the arrow at my chest instantly fell with the bow onto the hood of my car. Her hands landed flat on the metal hood as her head hung, and her back shuddered with a sob. She exhaled to calm her breathing.

"Phyre." My voice softened as I reached out a hand for her. She briskly wiped her cheek and stood taller, facing me. A hand rose to stop my stretch. Her jacket hung off both her shoulders, trapped by her elbows at her side. My eyes roamed her body, and my head tilted. *Did her breasts look larger or was it the hunger in me to fill my starving mouth with her?* Her shirt fit snug over supple breasts and a typically flat stomach, held a semi-familiar bulge. *Where had I seen that shape before?* She was practically glowing, something I hadn't remembered. "You're so beautiful."

"I…I can't do this again, Heph. My heart." Her hand fisted and beat on her chest. "My heart beats for you, but I can't go back and forth like we have. Adara…Adara needs you."

"Adara?" I stepped closer, but still not close enough. Her hand on my chest stopped me, keeping the distance between us.

"My heart beats for you, Phyre, only you. I love you."

"I love you, too." Another sob escaped her lips, and this time I let nothing stop me. I gripped her arms and pressed her to me, tucking her head against my chest.

"Say it again," I begged, my throat catching on the tender command.

"I love you, Heph. I love you." Her hands fisted in my T-shirt and I pushed her back to take her lips. My hands jumped to her waist, slipping inside her open jacket, and roaming her body. Flat palms skimmed the curve of her sides and lowered to wrap around her hips. Pulling back abruptly, I stared at her.

"What happened? Why did you leave?"

"Adara. She loves you."

I blinked at her liquid-filled eyes.

"Adara doesn't love me!" I exclaimed, surprised at her words.

"She told me. That night. She told me she loved you too late. She needed you, and I...I gave you up so she could have you."

"Phyre." My heart slipped from my chest and pooled at my feet, like the drip of wax under a flame. "Phyre, Adara's attempted suicide had nothing to do with you. Or me." I sighed. How long I'd worked to get myself through those thoughts, but Adara's reassurance finally convinced me. It wasn't me. It was her. Her scars ran deep, deeper than I thought Hestia might know, and Adara had things to work out for herself.

"Phyre, it was never about you or even me."

Tears fell harder, and she shook her head.

"Then why didn't you follow me?" As soon as she spoke, she closed her eyes, willing away the question.

"You didn't want me to. You were gone when I woke. You left me."

I stared at her. How much we had misunderstood.

"I was on the balcony. I saw Adara in the yard. But I saw the way you looked at her, and she looked at you. She needed you."

"I need you." Hands on her shoulders shook her gently.

"I needed you, too." Her hands came to rest on her lower belly, rubbing at her waist. *What had happened to her? Was I too late?*

"Needed? Past tense?"

Her eyes shifted downward, and her hands splayed over the top of her jeans. My breath hitched.

"What happened?" My voice shook as I hated that question.

"I'm pregnant." Her words startled me, and I released her shoulders, stumbling back. My stomach felt sucker-punched. *She'd been with another man?*

"I knew you wouldn't be happy." Tears fell harder, and a shaky hand covered her eyes.

"Who is he?" I said through gritted teeth, the old feelings of betrayal filling me like a boiling pit.

Her eyes snapped to mine, liquid and leaking, and then she laughed. Hysteria hitting her with her guilt, I decided, as she laughed harder, and tears dripped from her eyes like a slow falling rain. She bent at the waist and laughed even harder, and then the tears returned to real tears, and body heaving sobs.

"It's yours." Her eyes avoided mine, as she bit her lip and a tear wrapped around the corner of her mouth. "I've only ever been yours." Suddenly, my lips were on hers, drinking in the salty splash, licking up the streams bordering on her curving mouth. I drank in her sorrow and replaced it with my astonishment and joy.

She was having my baby.

She was having my baby.

"Say it again," I muttered against her lips, slipping my tongue into her mouth before she could respond. Her tongue lapped over mine before dragging back.

"I'm pregnant. It's yours."

My arms wrapped around her, lifting her against me, and then immediately setting her down.

"Did I hurt you? Did I hurt her?" My hands covered her lower belly, and her hands covered mine with a tear-choked giggle.

"No, Heph. No, we aren't hurt any longer."

PHYRE

Heph wouldn't let me walk the remainder of the way to Hestia's Home. He carried me, and the irony wasn't lost on me that we walked this same trail the first day I met him. This was the path where I fell in love with him, before I could acknowledge the feeling. In his arms, again, I loved him more. So much misunderstanding, so much wasted time, but I would not waste another second.

We entered Hestia's breakfast room, the heat of the fire almost stifling in the spring afternoon. Heph's arms came around me from behind and his thick hands covered my lower belly.

"She's having my baby," he announced, his voice full of pride as he spoke to Hestia over my shoulder. Hestia stood and smiled slowly at her favored, adopted son.

"Yes, she is, young man, and you are late." She admonished without ire and smiled wider as Heph's chin came to rest on my head.

"I'm asking permission to marry her." The words rumbled over my head and poured over me. I stiffened in his arms and Hestia stared at him before her eyes drifted to mine.

"That's not really a proposal, Hephaestus." Her tone a bit stronger than the teasing from a moment before, Heph lifted his chin. A conversation through eyes ensued over me, and I watched only Hestia, as she nodded once, and then Heph tugged me tighter to his chest.

"She's coming out to the barn with me or I'm staying in her room." His commanding gruffness startled me. His demands of Hestia surprised me, considering she ruled this roost, not him.

"I leave that decision to Phyre," Hestia answered, nodding at me, meeting my eyes once again. Love filled those eyes, but so did hesitancy. She'd offer nothing that made me uncomfortable. The barn frightened me with its memories, but it would also give us privacy. Heph and I needed time.

"The loft, it is," I stated, and Hestia's smile grew. It gave me comfort that I'd made the decision she wanted for me.

"I'll go prepare the room," she offered.

+ + +

The first night was awkward. While Heph and I had had sex, obviously, we'd only been together once. We hadn't spent a full night, in a bed, together and my nerves, along with the pregnancy, rattled as we moved around one another in the loft. He'd been attentive all day, never letting me out of his sight and placing his hands on me each chance he could, but the idea of intimacy after such a stressful separation, unnerved me.

Hestia replaced the damaged mattress with what she called a marital bed. Raised on four posters, the queen size mattress offered more room for two. Still covered in the rich, red coverlet, fresh, new white sheets dressed the bed with four lush pillows. Heph had already showered and crawled under the covers. Feeling suddenly shy, I changed in the bathroom into a cotton tee that hung to my mid-thighs, hugging the growing bump of my stomach, and thick socks covered my feet. I slipped under the sheets and lay on my side for comfort. His feet found mine and swiped under the soft cotton.

"There's still much I need to learn about you." He reached under the covers and removed my socks, tugging them off slowly. My thighs clenched at the instant image of him between them. "But I have the rest of our existence to discover everything." His words surprised me, but I was distracted as he positioned my feet between his thighs, using his skin as a natural heater to my cold toes.

"What if you don't like what you learn?" I teased with a hint of serious concern. "How do you know I'll live forever like you? What if I grow old and you don't?"

He was pensive for a moment.

"Hestia told me, it's a strong possibility you'd live a lengthy time like us. Fire can extinguish, she warned me once, unless it's nurtured and tended to properly." His hands massaged my calves and moved up behind my thighs while my feet still rested between his. The pressure on my heavy skin felt amazing. Almost as amazing as him buried in me.

"I don't plan to let you blow out. I plan to nourish you all the days of my life." His voice lowered and he dove under the sheets. My T-shirt rose and he kissed the tiny swell at my abdomen, continuing to kiss in a circular manner, round and round until he hit the center.

"I love you, baby," he whispered to my stretching stomach.

"I love you," I replied. His eyes shot up to mine, his head haloed with a white sheet over his dark hair. I smiled as I brushed a hand over his stubbly cheek. Turning into my palm, he kissed me there, lingering in the curve of my hand.

"I have something for you." He rolled quickly from the bed and returned back under the covers like a flash of light. Resting on one elbow, he pressed me to lie on my back. He lifted my T-shirt to fully expose my belly.

"Nice underwear," he chuckled noting his red boxer briefs stretching over me. My eyes followed his as he placed something on the center of my belly.

"You center me." I stared at the circular item, made of pressed silver. A wide band with a glass bead in the middle. A cherry-rosebud-colored sea glass circle filled the center.

"I want to marry you. I want you to marry me."

I stared at him, watching my stomach rise and fall. He wasn't looking up at me. For half a second, I thought of his other proposals. I thought of his proposal for the baby and not me. And then the second passed when he looked up at me in question, deep eyes filled with longing. The fact Heph doubted my response spoke loudly to me.

"I want to marry you. I want you to marry me." I smiled broadly, not able to help the growing grin and the spread of my cheeks. His mouth covered mine as it had in the woods and he savored me. He took his time to caress over the bow and trace his tongue around the curve, before sucking deeply on my lower lip. Then covering them both, he drew my breath and slipped his tongue inside my mouth. I swallowed his love and returned it with flicking tongue and melting lips. Heat rose quickly between us. He pulled back and slipped the ring on my third finger, staring at its placement on my left hand.

"I don't want to hurt you." His hand covered my lower stomach. Then his eyes came to mine. "I'm sorry I've hurt you in the past."

"You won't hurt the baby," I reassured him. "And I forgive you, if you forgive me."

"Always, Little Spark." His mouth sought mine again. Heph's hands multi-tasked, removing his briefs from me and slipping off the tee, only releasing my lips for a second to disrobe me. His own boxers removed, he slipped two solid legs between mine, balancing on forearms at my sides.

"I love you," he whispered at my lips while he braced at my eager entrance, waiting for the words.

"I love you," I assured him, and he slid inside me rapidly. Tipping back my head and arching my back, I drew him deeper before looking up at chocolate swirls melting like my heart.

"Welcome home."

HEPH

I was actually getting married. And becoming a father. My palms sweat as I forged the ring I would place on Phyre's finger, sealing her to me forever. How long I waited, and I thought of how Solis promised me, one day, *she* would be there. How fortunate I felt that Phyre was that girl.

I spun the clamp slowly, tapping tenderly at the narrow slip of metal. The heat firing it to a blazing orange, but cooled, the silver metal would have an antique sheen, as if the ring was antiquated. It would be a reminder of me. I was ancient in many ways, and my love had been waiting centuries for her. Phyre loved me, and my insides warmed like the fiery flames at the oven before me.

"That's a pleasant smile," Hestia said behind me and I turned slowly, keeping one eye on the treasure before me. "Smiles look good on you, Hephaestus." Her teasing tone only widened the spread of my lips, and if I wasn't already sweating from the heat, I'm certain she'd see my face flush. It was a trifle embarrassing to know she understood what could prompt such a smile. She allowed Phyre to remain in the loft with me, but noted we'd have to do something about a living arrangement. The studio barn could not be a permanent residence.

"I wanted to talk to you about a place to live." Hestia's face fell a little from her glowing compliment. "I know you won't approve of us living here, on the property, but I don't want to take Phyre to Zeke's estate, and…"

"Why not?" Phyre's voice interrupted my thought, her stern tone concerning me. Of greater concern was the ring I forged. I didn't want her to see it yet.

"Phyre, you need to get out." The harshness of my words startled her, and her soft eyes opened wide. My shoulders fell at the hurt look on her face. "It's just…"

She stalked off before I could finish. I shook my head, not able to chase her or I'd ruin the precious metal.

"Women," I grumbled and Hestia chuckled.

"We can be a handful. Especially with the extra hormones." She patted my shoulder as I turned to look at her. How little my surrogate mother knew of the experience, and yet, she had more motherly elements than my own. My face fell at the thought. Weddings should be about family. My own would not be in attendance.

"You could ask them," Hestia offered softly, as if reading my mind. "Zeke would come. He'd support you. Hera…"

"I don't need Hera's approval. Or Zeke's. This is my decision. Phyre is mine. This will be our day and I won't let them spoil it for us. For me." My voice rose higher as I cursed the slow process of making Phyre's ring. I needed to find her and explain.

+ + +

When I finally caught my little spark, she sat inside Hestia's marble temple. The days were warming, and if I were in California, on Zeke's estate, the shelter of the structure would be refreshing. On this day, the marble held in the cooler temperature and the space remained chilly. The coolness might additionally be emitted from my future bride.

"You didn't let me explain." I stood behind her curled body. Her knees drawn upward, her arms stretching to surround them as the bulge of our child stood in the way. My heart swelled with the thought. We were having a baby.

"I know why you don't want to take me there." Her voice drifted forward as her back remained to me. "It's because of her, isn't it?"

My lips opened without sound. *How could she think of Lovie?* I certainly no longer did.

"It has nothing to do with Lovie." I stepped forward and attempted to fold my body to the ground next to her. With the fire pit center, only a thin cement circle rounded the empty space filled with ashes covered by sand. My feet pressed forward into the pit. "Why would you think that?"

"You don't want to bring me there, as the consolation wife."

"Phyre." Her name rumbled from deep within, and anger struck. "That is absolutely not true."

My thick fingers wrapped around one arm, forcing her to look at me. Dried tears still marked her face.

"I asked you to marry me last night. I'm making you a ring. I want to build a home with you."

Glass blue eyes stared at me, and I loosened my hold.

"It has nothing to do with Lovie and everything to do with my father. I don't want you to be subjected to his folly. His multitude of children and his flirtatious ways. He has no boundaries and I definitely do not wish to share you with him."

Phyre shuddered.

"I know my father. He won't be pleased, but it has nothing to do with you. He won't have his way with me, and that's the issue. I didn't conform to his desire to marry someone of his choice. I chose you. You are the one for me, Phyre. You." My hands cupped her face, and my eyes begged her to understand. She was who I needed in my life and no one else.

"But you said you didn't want to live on the estate with me." Her voice was small, innocent. "I promise to control the fire."

"That isn't it, either. I don't wish you to control anything. You're mine to protect, and I want to serve only you." I paused, taking a deep breath. "Look, there is a small town near here. I want to open a shop there. We can build our own home in the woods nearby. It will be private. A place just for us, but Hestia and your sisters will be close."

Her eyes roamed my face.

"I don't want to be afraid to leave, but I am." Her head hung, but my hands cupping her cheeks forced her to look up at me.

"That's why we stay. This will be good. The estate is too much…of everything. We will have everything we need, here."

"Wherever you are will be my home, Heph." A tear slipped from her eye.

"And wherever you are will be mine." My mouth came to hers, taking in her lips slowly, dragging out the kiss. I wanted her to feel the truth in what I said. She was my center, my home, and I only wanted to make her happy. Instantly, she straddled me and I thought of Hestia's warning of pregnancy hormones. The second her core hit the heavy length of me, I threw out my confusion over the changing mood and welcomed Phyre's eagerness.

PHYRE

"Is this too fast? Am I not thinking this through?" I huffed as I faced myself in the mirror of my old room. My hand rubbed over the swell at my belly, hidden by the fullness of the white skirt trailing down my hips and covering my legs. The dress seemed old-fashioned and archaic, considering who I was and who Heph was, but still, I felt pretty. The thought of a formal wedding was what scared me.

"Honey, you look lovely. This isn't too fast. This is love." Ember stood behind me, twirling a curl of hair and spraying it into spiral perfection.

"I just feel like a time bomb. The fuse lit and the cord flames, but the explosion is still coming."

"What could go wrong? Heph loves you."

He has loved so many, I thought, the concept haunting me. I didn't want him marrying me only because of the child, and as much as he reassured me, I still had my doubts. Nibbling, gnawing doubts that I didn't want to feel. Heph loved me. He told me daily and I responded to reassure him I loved him, completely. But the breath-holding sensation choked me as I smoothed my hands down the beaded dress. I felt constantly on edge of *something* imploding.

"What if it's the baby? What if I hurt it? What if something is wrong with the baby? Will he still love me?" My hands shook as I stared at them, palms upward facing me. I worked every second to keep my emotions in check, as fear filled me that somehow, I would harm our unborn child. Then other thoughts consumed me. What if the child were already deformed or harmed in some other way, because of who I was?

"Honey, it's happened before. The baby will be fine." My eyes leapt to hers, not taking her meaning, but she fussed further with my hair, her soft voice pleaded as she spoke to me in the reflection of the mirror. "Do you really think Heph is concerned about a disability?"

We'd actually discussed Heph's concerns, as he mentioned them before me. He worried the child would be slow, like he had been at birth, or too large, and harm me. He worried that something would be wrong as well at times, and his fears only frightened me more. I didn't believe I had motherly qualities. It was the reason I wanted to remain near Hestia. I knew if I failed, she would help me, but feeling weak again, stressed me out. It made the fire roar inside me, but I refused its release.

"Heph wouldn't be upset," I said weakly, knowing the truth. After his own history of rejection from his mother, he was determined to love any child no matter what. When he said even if it had two heads, I panicked. My imagination had gone into overload with the increase of hormones and the suppression of my gift. New concerns filled me daily, and I exhausted Heph with them.

"That's right. He won't. He loves you."

"I love him." My voice trembled and the tears threatened to spill. It seemed if fire couldn't escape me, water would. I was a mess, and I giggled with hysteria under the surface of my skin.

"It's going to be fine. You'll be fine." Ember's warm hands soothed me, rubbing up and down my covered arms. My dress was a replica of the one I wore the night I gave myself to Heph. The beading and raised embroidery was enhanced on this masterpiece, though. I sighed at the thought of that night, my mind running wayward. What I needed was Heph to fill me. That's when I felt complete, centered, and calm. Looking up at my sister with her swooning eyes, the suggestion to make love to Heph immediately would be considered crass, and so I suppressed that thought as well.

A knock came to the door and Seraphine entered.

"You are stunning," she breathed, her warm eyes opening wide. "He's going to combust when he sees you." Her hands clapped together, and then fingers spread apart, motioning the explosion. I caught Ember next to me, shaking her head, slicing a finger over her throat.

"It's okay," I giggled, this time with humor. "I don't think Heph is the explosion I'm worried about."

Seraphine looked at Ember, who shook her head again.

Crazy pregnant lady, I deemed in my head and took one final look at myself before being led to the yard.

+ + +

The gathering stood outside the temple. An extravagant canopy had been made with four tree trunks and thick mesh material in white. Flowers twisted and twirled up the bark and a fire blazed in the background, within the stone structure. It was an earthy altar, allowing our guests to be witness as we vowed under sky and before fire to join as one. The baby stirred inside me, reminding me that his or her life stood testament to the joining of Heph and me.

Solis and Veva joined us, along with my sisters. Persephone and Hades were noticeably absent. I walked alone, my eyes trained on Heph, a trickle of sweat gracing his brow. I worried that he was as nervous as me, but the gleam in his eyes told me otherwise. A forest fire of passion raged in those normally melting chocolate eyes. His slow smile spread like flames, and white teeth greeted me, extinguishing my momentary fears. This man wanted me, and the baby kicked inside me to remind me why we stood here.

Reaching out a hand, Heph nearly tugged me to his side. His hands over mine were constant and warm, keeping me grounded, holding me centered.

"With fire, we forge the melding of two items. We sear them together, forming one union. With these rings, we join Phyre and Hephaestus together, melting and molding them as one under the flickering candle of love and before the blazing bonfires of passion." Hestia tweaked an eyebrow before she continued her blessing. Heph's fingers squeezed mine.

"With the heaven as our witness and the flames of our hearth as our sponsor, I join these two in unity, to live as one, to love as one, to be one. Let your unique spirits guide you as individuals to form a blessed connection." Hestia's hand lowered and rested on my belly briefly. "Joining you not only as god and his wife, but as a family." Her voice softened, and her hand removed. One cupped the bottom of our joined fingers, while the other covered the top.

"Through the warmth of the hearth, let your home be happy, your bounty be great, and your love blaze." She winked at Heph, who chuckled. My eyes watched his face, filled with pleasure. At that moment, it all became real to me. He wanted this, he wanted me. Not just the baby, not because of his father, not after failed relationships, but because he wanted me. My shoulders relaxed and my eyes blinked away the tears. Heph's face fell a little, and a thick fingertip brushed under my eye to catch a tear. His eyes questioned mine as the forest fire within his softened.

"Fire has the power to build," Hestia said, turning to Heph, "and the power to destroy." She returned to me. Her fingers pressed into mine. "But fire enlightens, like knowledge. It brightens the clouded thoughts. It warms the tender heart." I looked at Hestia as she spoke to me. "It brings comfort of mind and spirit." Her hands released ours.

"May the power of fire forge you together, forming a bond that cannot be undone." Her head tipped once in blessing, her homily complete. Next came the official joining, where Heph placed a simple silver ring on my finger, nestling it against the larger band with the glass gem.

"With this ring, I mark my target, showing the world that you belong with me. Your finger centers the ring, as you center me, and I am happy to call your hands and your heart my home." Before Hestia, Heph's typically gruff voice cracked on his words, overwhelmed with emotion. He leaned forward and kissed the joining of the rings.

With shaky hands, I placed a similar ring on Heph's. His thick fingers, swollen in the heat, and my trembling attempt made us chuckle nervously. My voice squeaked.

"With this ring, I circle you, claiming your heart, which I plan to hold, your name, that I'm happy to bear, and with you, I call anyplace a home. I love you." I leaned forward and kissed his ring. Raising my head slowly, his hand covered my cheek, and his mouth lowered to mine. I'd shared all kinds of kisses with Heph, but this one was the most special. Soft and sweet, this kiss marked me as his—permanently.

Our audience clapped and whistled when the kiss lingered a bit too long, but one clap continued and drew our attention.

"Hephaestus," the booming voice covered our congregation like a thundering cloud.

"Zeke," Heph breathed. Stepping forward, the large presence of Heph's father towered over me. There was still something eerie about Zeke. I couldn't place the feeling or what it stemmed from, but his brooding look and jovial smile confused me. In his presence, I feared he had plans to extinguish me or possess me. Which sensation was stronger, I could not determine. Sensing my unease, Heph shielded me, tucking me into his side.

"Let me be the first to congratulate you, son." The comment surprised me. "Such a beautiful bride." Zeke's hand on my hair startled me. Heph slipped me behind him, and my fingers dug into his shirt.

"What do you want?" Heph's gruff voice returned.

"I wanted to say…I'm sorry." Without seeing Heph's face, I knew his brow rose, his forehead wrinkled. "I didn't understand the strength of your feelings." I relaxed behind Heph, but my hands didn't leave his shirt for fear I'd blow away in the wind. Heph's only response was a nod, and then he reached behind him for me. Pressing me forward, hands still at my side, he spoke to his father. A small spark of unease hissed inside me with Zeke's nearness.

"Let me present, my wife, Phyre." The pride in his tone strengthened me. While I still questioned Zeke's intention toward me, Heph's hand on my hips assured me nothing would happen to me with Heph present.

"How precious a gift, to possess fire." Zeke watched me, and Heph pulled me back to his chest. One hand slipped forward to cover my belly.

"I see," Zeke whispered, watching the possessive move of Heph. The baby rolled under Heph's fingers, but he didn't mention it.

"Thank you for coming, Zeke." Hestia stepped in, both softening the tension clouding our moment and dismissing Zeke at the same time. "Join us at the house for a feast."

Heph and I would not be part of the celebration that followed. We had our own night planned.

HEPH

A bonfire crackled, lighting a thin perimeter around it as we sat under a spring sky. The air remained chilly but I pulled Phyre close to me, a blanket wrapped around us collectively. My mouth nuzzled at her ear and she chuckled.

"Tell me you love me," I mumbled, the tip of my tongue traced the soft curve of her lobe.

"I love you," she groaned as my teeth nipped at her neck. My hand slipped to her belly under the blanket.

"I love you." The words were a hushed whisper and something inside Phyre moved. I sat back as I recalled the sensation from earlier. "What was that?"

Phyre laughed and the sound matched the brilliance of the flames before us. "The baby," she said, and my hands roamed over the swell, palm lying flat in attempts to capture the feeling a second time. The baby did not disappoint. A tiny roll to the left and her stomach came forward for a second. I spun to the front of her and knelt between her legs. Pressing her back, I laid her flat and hitched up the flannel shirt draped over her mid-section. My mouth reached for her soft skin and I kissed her waist, as the baby rolled again.

"I love you," I muttered to her belly and she giggled at the words addressed on her waist. My tongue came out and licked a small circle. Phyre responded with a sigh. Her hands came to my hair and my mouth watered for more of her. Tugging at her waist, I slipped her leggings lower, exposing a dark mound and pale skin to the starlit heavens. This was our wedding night. A private consummation under the sky, with flames at our side.

My mouth made contact, and Phyre's hips bucked upward, allowing my eager lips to separate her and ravish her with the eagerness I always felt when I was near her. I knew this girl: how she moved, how she'd ignite, and I treasured the thought that I sparked the love within her.

"I love you." Her voice heady with desire as my mouth continued to consume her. Her breath hitched and her hands on my head tightened their hold in my short hair. "Hephaestus," she breathed, and I liked the breathless, needy sound of my name on her lips. Another flick and Phyre lit, calling out to the heavens in her release. The warmth lingered, smoldering to bright embers. Removing my jeans, I knew how to ignite her again, and I slipped to her center where she welcomed me. Holding me locked within her raised knees, she sang out almost instantly as I climbed, longing for escape from the heat and relishing in it at the same time. Bursting within her, I grunted like the animal I could be when she was under me. My mouth sought hers and my kiss told her: "I love you."

+ + +

Months passed. Our life formed a rhythm of work and lovemaking between building a small house and watching Phyre's body grow. My girl could swing a hammer and nothing made me prouder. Well, almost nothing. The shape of her body pleased me as it ebbed and flowed into a new dimension that included life inside her. I'd never been happier.

Phyre was quiet at times. Having our child frightened her and she'd tell me her wayward thoughts. I tried to assure her that the images were normal, the fear understandable, but nothing would happen to her or our baby. After her slim appearance at our wedding date, her body changed rapidly, growing rather large with a few months remaining in her pregnancy. She walked slowly, the strain on her tiny frame taking its toll. We were days away from finishing our home, a place I was excessively proud of as we designed and built it together. Seated upon a small hill, the view of the forest from any room was glorious, and I treasured waking each day and ending each night inside the place we would call home.

One day, I found Phyre in the loft apartment, rocking on the floor near the bed. Her arms wrapped around her mid-section, she clenched her teeth in pain.

"What's wrong?"

She could only shake her head. Her hands clenched and unclenched at the T-shirt of mine she wore. I stroked over her hair, feeling the clammy skin of her forehead.

"Phyre, sweetheart, talk to me."

"The pain. Something's not right." Her body continued to rock and her eyes closed, her teeth gnashed together as a growl rumbled from deep within her. Wrapping an arm around her, she refused to unfurl from the protective hold over her midsection. I picked her up, struggling at first with the added weight, and awkward shape of her body. She didn't curl into me like she typically would, but tucked into herself within my cradling arms. I placed her on the bed, and she slipped to her side, drawing up her knees. Her teeth chattered. My hand brushed back her hair and her eyes closed. Panic seized me.

"I'm going to get Hestia." Racing for the main house, I found Ember and Seraphine in the breakfast room. Hestia had gone to visit Temple at the stables they told me.

"What's wrong?" Ember asked, rising slowly from a bench.

"I don't know. Phyre." Reaching for her elbow, I guided her to the door with Seraphine on our trail. Entering the room, Phyre was visibly shaking, her hands over her protruding stomach.

"Phyre, can you hear me?" Ember asked, struggling to keep the sweetness in her tone while panic rippled in her throat. A moan responded.

"What hurts?" Ember encouraged, running her hands over Phyre's belly, pressing gingerly and Phyre hissed. Her eyes shot open, but her gaze was dead. She had no focus, only fear in her typically gleaming blue eyes.

"What's happening?" I barked.

"I think the baby wants to come now," Ember said.

"It's too soon," Seraphine stated, ticking off her fingers to count down the months. "She needs longer to marinate." The joke was lost on us. Phyre's constant fear was that she'd cook the baby. She'd wake in a cold sweat at night, afraid her heat was too much and the baby wouldn't survive. I snarled in response to Seraphine.

"We need Hestia," Ember snapped, and Seraphine left the room instantly. Time ticked too slowly, and I paced the room while Ember sat next to her sister, stroking over her damp hair. Phyre's eyes closed and her breathing shallowed. Her fingers worked over her bulging stomach.

Finally, Hestia entered, like a breath of fresh air. Ember jumped up to allow Hestia room and she tenderly placed her hands over the large bump on my Phyre's body.

"Hephaestus, would you excuse us for a few moments?" Hestia asked, lifting the hem of my T-shirt on Phyre.

"No," I growled, not willing to let my eyes leave my wife.

"Go," groaned Phyre, the sound painful, clawing at me. With a huff, I stepped out of the room, settling only briefly on the couch before standing to pace the small living room. We hadn't taken Phyre to a traditional doctor. There wasn't a record of who she was, nor an explanation for what she could do, so modern conveniences such as hospitals were out of the question. I cursed our status and prayed briefly to any god or goddess willing to listen, and then I remembered the goddess of children was within my family. Reaching for the new cell phone Phyre demanded I learn to use, I made my first call.

"Veva, I need you."

+ + +

Arriving long after midnight, Veva leapt briefly for me with Solis on her heels before she entered my bedroom. Ember had given Phyre something to drink that relaxed the pain and allowed her to gain some restless sleep. I had only checked on her briefly, allowing Ember to sit as her nursemaid. I didn't wish to disturb Phyre, but I desperately wanted to lie behind her, holding her close to me, and assuring her things would be good. But my heart was losing faith. The groans and grunts stabbed me with each shallow breath and harsh sound from Phyre's clenched teeth.

Solis placed a hand on my shoulder.

"Let's take a walk," he encouraged, nodding toward the door.

"I don't want to leave."

"We'll just be outside," he offered, leading me by a heavy hand to give our crowded apartment some space. I trudged down the dark stairs of the loft with a weighted heart. Following Solis, we sat around the slow ember of campfire in the dark summer night. Solis let out a laugh.

"It's July," he said, as if the date should mean something to me. "Can you believe it's been a year?"

My thoughts raced. I didn't understand. Time moved at its own pace when you lived forever.

"This time last year, Veva hated me," he said, leaning forward to grab a stick and taunt the embers, hoping to spark a new flame. "And you were engaged to another girl at our father's annual festival."

My ankle crossed my knee and my chin came to rest on a closed fist. I snorted with the thought. July was the celebratory month of our father, Zeke, and his summer party a mandatory call for all relatives to return to the estate for a week-long festivity to celebrate *him*. During that week, he announced my forced engagement to Lovie. I chuckled bitterly with the thought. We obviously weren't attending this year.

"Did she marry him yet?"

"Who? Lovie?" Solis laughed and sat back with a thud, the fire refusing to respond to his prodding. "I think they will be perpetually at odds. Plus, Zeke won't approve of their marriage after what she did to you."

My eyebrows shot up. "Really?"

Solis sighed. "Despite his hard shell, he really does wish to believe in love. I think it's why he's always flirting, why he's constantly lusting. He loves the thrill of new attraction. The possibility of something. The problem is he has no commitment to sustaining it. He lacks the hard work of fidelity." Solis looked down at his hands, and I questioned his thoughts. He'd once been as wayward as our father, treasuring the kill but not the feast. Solis had left many women heartbroken in his wake, but he promised me one true love existed for him and me.

"You aren't sorry, right? You still love Veva." Panic took me, and I sat forward, ready to pummel my brother if he hinted that he'd thought otherwise of Vee.

"Are you kidding me? She's the greatest thing to ever happen to me. I don't plan on ever losing any feeling for her." I sat back in relief.

"What about you, Heph? Are you happy?"

"Happier than I've ever been," I replied unequivocally, confident in my answer.

"So you didn't marry her because she was pregnant?"

"What?" I sat forward again, my voice booming almost as deep as our father's.

"It's just, I worried you picked her for that reason. I mean, I can see that she loves you. She worships the space you occupy, but you were always getting engaged and trying to do the right thing. I just want to be certain you married her for her, not some obligation you felt."

Not even finding the strength to blink, incredulously frozen in place, I glared at my brother.

"Take it back," I bit. His honey-colored eyes shot up to mine. "Take. It. Back."

"What did I say?" he offered, narrowing his eyes at me.

"I love that girl with my whole being. I worship the air she breathes, the fire she produces, the heat she stirs in me. I did not marry her for the baby, but it's a bonus, to be certain. I married her for her, because I want her to be with me always. So, take. It. Back."

"I'm glad to hear that Heph." Veva's tender voice spoke behind me. "Because there may be a problem. I need to get her over to the main house where there is more space in her old room, and I can monitor her better. And as for you," Vee pointed at Solis. "Apologize for being an ass and then come help me."

I stood immediately as did Solis. "What's wrong?"

"She's gone into premature labor and we need it to stop. She'll need bed rest for a few weeks. No more hammering," Veva admonished. "No more standing on her feet. She needs to keep those babies in a bit longer."

I stared at her, my ears ringing at the sound of an -s at the end of one word.

"Babies?"

"You're having twins." Veva smiled slowly, but the sparkle didn't reach her blue eyes.

"Two?" I asked slowly, raising my hand with two fingers extended. I swallowed hard at the thought.

"Yes, two, but first, we need to worry about your wife."

My wife. The words rang in my head.

"What's wrong?"

"I think she was dehydrated, so we'll start with an IV. I'd like to monitor her heart so I'll need to get to the nearest city for a machine."

"Let's go," I said, reaching out for her arm and dragging her toward the stable where my car was parked.

"Dude, it's the middle of the night," Solis stood, blocking my path. "Let's start with moving Phyre first, and then we can go from there."

My mind was a whirl. Move Phyre. Have twins. Make way for more room in my heart. I nearly burst with excitement and fear.

"She's going to be all right, right?" I questioned, Veva's typically teasing eyes somber, and I didn't like Vee's answer.

"Let's hope so."

+ + +

Time passed too slowly. Phyre refused to let me touch her, bring her comfort in any way. She was shutting down from me, and I was going out of my mind. I wasn't a violent man by nature but I hated to be ignored. I was ready to remove those babies myself if it brought my wife back to me. The first week was hell. Monitors and tubes attached to her, checking her heart, which beat too fast, and feeding her veins, which needed more liquid. She complained of feeling a struggle. She needed to release the flames but feared letting go. She was a frustrated dragon.

One night, the tickle of a hand came over my wrist. My head rested on the edge of the bed, and I let her fingers crawl over the dark band covering my wrist. Her finger wiggled, struggling to get under the leather strap. Slowly, I lifted my head and undid the clasp. We didn't speak, her delicate digits still searching over my wrist, fumbling for something blindly in the darkness. Once her hand found the compass tattoo, her palm wrapped over it, and drew my arm up to her. My eyes shifted to her face. Her eyes closed, peaceful. In her sleep, she had reached for me, needing the instrument at my wrist for comfort to remind her of home.

Come home to me, Phyre, I whispered in my head. Awkwardly she angled my arm, placing a too-brief kiss on the sensitive skin before wrapping her arms around the thickness of my forearm.

"I love you," I said, my voice choking with the sound. I missed her.

"I love you," she mumbled sleepily. I shifted in my seat next to the mattress, and scooted upward to allow her to sleep with her head pressed to my arm, her hands securely holding onto me.

+ + +

A whimper followed by a blood curdling cry woke me. Veva rushed into our shared room in Hestia's house. Phyre panted, and Veva held her fingers on Phyre's wrist.

"Okay, beautiful," Veva began. "Let's end this torture." I stood abruptly, holding Phyre's limp hand in mine.

"Vee, what's happening?"

"This is it, Heph. She can't hold them in any longer, and I'm getting concerned for her." Veva had studied to be a midwife in college. I'd never seen her in action but I'd heard she worked miracles on a girl at the estate who was pregnant. I had faith in Veva, in my heart, but I doubted everything in my current state.

Phyre groaned.

"She's going to be okay, right?" I questioned for the millionth time. Veva had turned the room into a virtual hospital, complete with units for future babies and monitors of all types. Her concerned eyes searched mine. She understood that we could not risk taking Phyre to a modern hospital. We didn't know what would happen when she gave birth. Hestia had no history of birthing children, so there was no telling what could happen.

"Heph, I need you to be strong." Veva's hand came to my shoulder, and I took a deep breath.

"I can't lose her," I whispered.

"You won't," she tried to assure, but her normally tough tone was weak. Phyre groaned again, and Veva spun away from me.

I did what I was told. I held Phyre's hands. I whispered words of encouragement. I wasn't convinced she heard me. She gnashed her teeth and swore under her breath. She screamed out in pain, making me want to tear down the house, and uproot the whole forest, if it would soothe her. Veva sweated through her smock and Ember stood on the other side of Phyre, helplessly doing the same thing as me.

What seemed like a lifetime passed before one squiggling, messy baby boy appeared.

"Handsome like his father," Ember giggled in relief.

A minute or two later, another boy came shrieking into this world. They both looked large to me, and I marveled that my tiny Phyre had nurtured such amazing creatures.

I kissed over Phyre's forehead and stroked back her hair. Her eyes drifted closed in defeat and exhaustion.

"Let her sleep for now," Veva said, but I couldn't stop touching her, telling her how much I loved her, and thanking her for giving me so much joy.

Then a monitor beeped. A screeching, elongated sound ripped open my heart, and blood drained out of me.

"Heph, move," Veva yelled, pressing down on Phyre's chest. She counted as she worked and I was vaguely reminded of something. Adara on the beach, Triton trying to revive her. As if underwater, I heard Ember scream for Hestia, and commotion ensued. I had hardly moved, stepping back only enough to watch Veva work, and listen to the nails-on-a-chalkboard noise of a flatline monitor.

PHYRE

I'd been dreaming. The forest was in bloom, and I ran through a meadow. I was laughing as I chased two tiny beings, giggling with delight, and teasing me with their pleasing sound. I spun to find Heph walking in long strides behind us. He could have easily caught me, as I could have reached for these two stumbling babes running before me, but we keep up the ruse of one following the other, soaking up the sound of blossoming summer and bubbling laughter. Heph smiled at me, and the world stood still. I stopped chasing, and waited for him to approach me. His smile shyly grew, and his eyes gleamed. I anticipated the kiss he would give me when he neared me. He was constantly touching me, pampering me with tempting kisses and a tender embrace. I couldn't get enough of him, and my heart raced.

And then, he passed me. He didn't stop and wait, but followed the boys without a glance at me. Their laughter grew and their pace quickened. Heph broke into a run after them as I stood still, watching them get ahead of me, too far ahead of me to reach them even if I raced. My heartbeat slowed and I remained frozen to the forest floor, watching them continue off in the distance. Heph hadn't looked back. The babes led the chase. They climbed the hill for our house, our home, built together with hope for a future filled with love.

Heph didn't look back.

The boys didn't stop.

And I stood still.

Then the house burst into flames

HEPH

"Make her stop," Veva screamed, as flames fired from the hands of my wife. The sheet caught instantly and Ember flung it off Phyre. Hestia stood over Phyre, chanting in words I didn't understand, but the recess of my mind recognized as ancient Greek. Veva looked up at Hestia, her eyes questioning for a moment, before the words began to mumble from her lips. Surprised at her own recognition of the ancient sounds, she worked harder over Phyre's chest while Ember tried to extinguish flames at Phyre's finger tips.

I stood as if in a strange dream, women hustling and chanting around me. The door flung open and Seraphine entered with Ashen and Adara at her heels. Flame filed in last, and I was brushed aside. I stood in the corner of a too-crowded room.

"Why didn't anyone tell me?" Adara interjected into the chaos. The hurt in her voice spoke volumes as the others hung their heads, knowing they'd kept this secret from their sister. The thought was Adara had enough to focus on within herself; she didn't need to know that another of Hestia's girls was having a baby.

"We didn't want to worry you," Ember offered weakly.

"I could have helped," Adara replied. Hestia shook her head, suddenly knowing a truth she never shared with the others. Adara's eyes found her foster mother and Hestia smiled, encouraging whatever mystery to finally be shared.

"I had a child. I know how this is done." My heart dropped at the admission. Adara spun for the window seat. I didn't understand anything I witnessed, but under the cushion was a stash of candles and boxes of matches, collected from a variety of places according to their different color shades and sizes. Lighting one candle and then another, Adara passed the pillars of wax with flicking flames to each sister. Veva still worked at Phyre's chest but her pressing slowed, her mouth hanging open in wonder.

Each of Hestia's girls, including Hestia took a candle and stood around Phyre. I panicked that their chants were a séance of sorts, a calling of the fire, willing it to extinguish. Wetness covered my face, mixing with the perspiration of too many bodies in a tightly confined space. I stared at Veva, willing her to do something. Vee looked up at me and removed her hands from Phyre's chest. Tears trickled down her face as well. She shook her head once and stepped back from the bed, letting Phyre's sisters engulf the space instead. A circle formed around Phyre, and Veva came to me. She wrapped her arms around my waist, but I hardly felt her touch. I stood, staring at my wife's limp body, surrounded in a ring of smoky flame and soft chants.

"I'm so sorry, Heph," Veva muttered at my side, but I stared in disbelief. This couldn't be happening. I loved her, and she loved me. We'd been married. We built a home. She gave me two beautiful boys. Suddenly, my attention turned to two innocent babes, swaddled and laying within clear glass cradles. I walked methodically to their crib and scooped up one at a time in each arm. Veva held the door for me as I stepped into the hall, pressing my sons to my chest, and sobbed.

+ + +

"What the fuck is happening?" Solis barked at my side. He'd taken a baby from me, and paced the hall outside Phyre's room. Between the soft sound of singing inside the bedroom and the gentle cries of two hungry boys, I couldn't think. My own tears had subsided for the moment, and I found Solis staring at me.

"She's…" I choked on the word, not allowing myself to speak it. She couldn't be. "She's…"

Solis' honey-eyes questioned mine, softening as his expression fell. "No," he hissed under his breath, and I nodded to answer him. Veva remained outside the door, her forehead pressed to it. Guilt sat on her shoulders, though I knew she'd done what she could. The fire was engulfing my wife, and Veva wasn't a firefighter.

Another set of feet stomped up the stairs and my heart dropped. I felt his presence before I saw him. Death followed him, despite his quiet demeanor.

"Hades?" Veva sighed, looking up at our blue-faced cousin. Her body twisted and she braced herself like a giant X over the entrance to the bedroom. "You can't have her," she bit.

"I'm not here for her. You know that's not my thing." Hades' wasn't Death. That was another entity, but Hades represented the underworld, and my thoughts travelled to fiery pits and darkened heat. He'd come to take my wife underground, if it was best for her. I pressed baby one against me.

"What do you want?" Vee snapped, more aggressive than she should have been. Too startled still to believe all that was happening, it should have been me questioning our cousin. I should have been the one demanding an explanation, but my heart had stilled and my compass didn't balance. My inked wrist ached, as if the fire inside it had lost its flame. I was lost, with images of my magenta-haired girl lying limp in a bed of flames.

"Vee, it's time. Do your thing," Hades said. I looked at my sister, her face aghast as she stood wide-eyed staring back at Hades.

"What do you mean?" Veva questioned.

"I mean, it's time." His sapphire blue eyes narrowed, and Veva swallowed. She nodded as if she understood and turned for the door.

"What's happening?" I asked, completely puzzled at this display. The appearance of my cousin. The sudden confidence of my sister. Even Solis held a goofy grin. "What the…"

"Veva needs to realize her power," Solis answered.

I blinked.

"What power?"

"The one that protects women and children. Her midwife skills need a second chance." I stared at Solis a moment, still not comprehending.

"Is she using my wife as some kind of experiment?" I barked.

"She's going to bring your wife back." Solis' words empowered me and I handed the baby to Hades. An awkward transition occurred, but after a moment, Hades understood how to hold him. Two broad steps and I entered a room heavy with wisps of lingering smoke and choking fragrance.

"She's asking for you," Veva said, and I stared in wonder as my wife lounged upright on the bed. Her skin shone with sweat, but her smile was restored. She peered at her hands, but looked up instantly as I stood at the end of the bed. Like a phoenix rising up from the ashes, Phyre sat among fire scorched sheets and the remaining heat of flames.

"Hephaestus," she whispered from her magenta-cherry lips, and I took my first real breath in hours.

PHYRE

Heph's face looked ashen, streaks of sweat trickling down his cheeks. His expression remained passive as he stared back at me. I worried that my dream was reality. Our home had burned. I lost the boys, and I'd lost him. Dampness covered my skin. I shook with the effort of dying and rising again, something completely foreign to me. I heard them chanting, and Veva pressing on my chest. I smelled the fire and felt the flame, and all the while I raced after Heph in my nightmare while he ran away from me. But the call to the flickering flames and the sounds of my sisters turned me away from the retreating back of Heph. I struggled in the dream, especially when he didn't respond to me.

Don't you want me anymore? I thought in my head, but there was no answer to my call, and the songs of sisterhood carried on. Making a decision to follow the fiery sound of ladies chanting, I turned for my sisters and ran. A gulping breath seized my chest, and I swallowed the necessary oxygen to feed the spark within me.

My little spark, the words rang out, and a blaze of energy grew. I raced for the cry of my sisters and opened my eyes to see Veva standing over me, her smile refreshing as her eyes glistened.

"Thank the gods," she whispered.

"Thank a goddess," Hestia corrected, and she hugged me. Moments later, Heph entered the room and standing at the end of the bed was where he remained. I'd lost him for real, I thought, with all the magic of my rebirth, and…my head turned to the right, finding two cradles empty.

"No," I groaned, suddenly feeling the weight of a hammer slam into my chest. "No," I cried out, staring at the emptiness of two infant beds. The smell of burning fabric and the lingering heat suddenly suffocated me. My babies. My hands clutched to my chest as my heart, moments ago dead, raced with life, while staring at the loss.

I'd begun to rock and two arms embraced me, pulling me into a solid-wall of a chest. Breathing deep the scent of man and forest, I took gulping breaths of Heph to clear the visions in my head.

"What did I do?" I muttered into his chest, feeling unworthy of his tender hug. Thick hands stroked up and down my back, slowly fingering each vertebrae of my spine, as if counting the keys of a piano. The rhythm soothed me when I didn't deserve to be comforted.

"No," I pushed back on Heph. His expression instantly giving away his hurt. I didn't deserve his support after I'd killed our children. Weeks we'd been without each other. He was afraid to touch me, and I feared I'd hurt him. While I wanted him to hold me, and reassure me as he often did, I couldn't imagine intimacy with the weight in my belly and the pain in my back. Heph worried he'd hurt the babies and never initiated anything other than soft kisses and delicate brushes over my skin.

"What the...?" Heph growled, his expression shifting to anger. Tears fell immediately at the stern look on his face. He'd forgotten himself. For a moment, he forgave me, but reality set in and he remembered, I'd tarnished our children. No, I'd killed them. The salty liquid fell faster; fell too late, as it always did.

"I'm so sorry, Hephaestus. So sorry," I choked, stating his full name as I rarely did. My head shook back and forth, closing my eyes to block out the disappointment in his. "I didn't mean it. I never meant...I couldn't control it."

"What the..." Heph's voice softened and a thick hand covered my shoulder. "What are you sorry for?"

"I killed our babies," I sobbed, covering my face with my own searing, scarred palms. The salt from my eyes stung the open sores, but I deserved the pain. I'd heal all too quickly, while my heart would break, and my head would hurt for the rest of my days.

"You didn't kill our babies," he said, stroking his hand down my arm and cupping one hand in his. I looked up.

"I didn't?" Something in my face made him smile, slowly, hesitantly.

"No, the boys are in the hallway with Hades and Solis." My eyes flicked over his big shoulder for the partially opened door.

"But...I thought..." Drifting my attention to the empty cradles, I stared. My second hand was encircled with his and he pressed our fingers together. "I don't understand."

"We lost you," he said, his voice low and shaky. "You started to burn after giving birth, and I thought..." He choked on a sob and released one hand to cover his forehead.

"You aren't upset with me?" The question seemed unwarranted when the expression on his face stilled me.

"Upset. You died and came back. I don't know what to think, but *upset* is not the word for it."

I stared at the puzzled look in his chocolate eyes gone hollow and unfocused as he blinked back at me.

"But you were standing there...and you looked angry...and I thought..." His mouth covered mine and hands delved into my hair. He tugged at the strands as he pulled me toward him, pressing himself against me. God, I missed him, and just as eagerly I returned the kiss, hands circling his neck and forcing him to me. I couldn't get close enough in my relief. Relief that he wasn't upset. Relief that he hadn't left me behind. Relief that I hadn't killed our babies.

"The babies?" I pulled back, releasing his firm lips with a soft pop. "What did we have?"

A soft chuckle behind him broke the tension and Heph twisted to see Veva and Ember each holding a large bundle.

"You had two boys," Ember cooed, staring down at one dark head of hair. Veva turned to face the second child toward me.

"They look like their father," I laughed quietly, noting the dark features of each.

"Let's hope they have their mother's spirit," Heph said, lovingly staring at me, and forgetting our audience, I lunged for him again, breathing in the warmth of his mouth and the taste of his tongue. We had time to make up for, and thankfully, time to repeat all the things we'd missed out on over the last month.

"I love you," he mumbled against my closed lips. I swallowed his words and whispered them back before opening my lips and proving it more.

A cough broke our reconciliation, and I blushed, but not too deep. I was proud of Heph's love and my hands slipped around his arm, afraid to release him. He held out one arm, reaching for one child, and Ember crossed the room to bring me the other.

"What will you name them?" Veva asked, a smile in her question, along with curiosity.

I looked at Heph, as we had discussed this at great length. We didn't want something typical, and agreed that we wanted names worthy of courage, worthy of the journey we took to find love.

"Hammer," Heph announced, staring in wonder at one set of eyes matching his own.

"Anvil," I whispered, my eyes watering again at the set that peered up at me.

"Two symbols of strength," Hestia offered. "Excellent choice and strong names for two boys."

"The next one will be a fire symbol," Heph said, looking up at his adoptive mother.

"Who says there will a next time?" I laughed, completely dismayed and discouraged to ever repeat what just happened.

"There's going to be a next time," Heph assured as his mouth leaned for mine, and his lips told me we'd be repeating more than having babies, but practicing making them as well.

EPILOGUE

HEPH

"You should have seen your face," I teased, handing a glass of wine to Hades. The expression on his face still stern in remembrance.

"I don't know what to do with babies," he scoffed, shrugging a shoulder before taking a sip.

"Kids?" Solis shuddered, as if the word was dirty.

"You both lie," I laughed, looking from face to face of my two friends. Solis paced like a pro with Hammer in his arms. Holding a child was second nature to him, and with the experience of our father having so many, I worried if it might be in Solis' genes. Hades was a quandary. His father had produced him, but his mother had been another type of goddess, opposite his father. She was life to his death, similar to Hades and Persephone now. Yet, he looked just as natural holding a child, questioning the miracle in his arms.

"I wouldn't know what to do with a child," Solis replied.

"You'd love it. Him or her, actually," Veva said walking into my new living room. She'd been helping Phyre get used to all things female and mothering, and the smile on her face told my brother that he'd be a good father, or else. She crossed the room and wrapped an arm around his waist, and he drew her into him. Hades looked on longingly.

"I'm sorry Persephone couldn't make it. If she'd known you were going to be here, she would have joined us," Veva offered, softening the pained look in our cousin's face.

"It's fine," he waved her off, taking another sip of his wine. "It's better this way." His head hung forward and his too-long hair covered the sadness of his face. He lied again. It wasn't better. There wasn't anything better than being with the one you loved, who also loved you back. On that thought, a tired Phyre sauntered into the room. The boys safely tucked into their new nursery next door to our master suite, she smiled slowly as her eyes met mine. Phyre walked straight for me, and I opened my arms to encircle her. She wasn't shy in her displays of love for me, and her face nuzzled into my chest too briefly before she looked up at me.

"Asleep?" I questioned, knowing two hungry boys kept her awake most nights.

"Asleep," she whispered, a sultry hint in her voice. We used any spare minute we had between crying children and incessant feedings to rebuild the time we lost while she was on bedrest, and our heads got the best of us, thinking we'd lost one another.

"That's our cue," Solis said, turning Veva for the front door with Hades trailing behind. My heart pinched at the thought he may never have what I did, but the soft click of wood, closing out the world, returned my thoughts to my own little space. Lips hit my neck, and I bent to lift Phyre, her body instantly curling into mine.

I carried her to our new room, complete with a larger bed, crisp white sheets and a replica of the quilt she once set on fire. I wanted to take my time with her, but knowing time wasn't on our side with two infants, we rushed to remove clothes and climb between the downy coverings.

"I can't wait," she whispered, slipping her legs apart and wrapping one thigh over mine.

"I'm not going anywhere," I said against her lips, still lazily moving under mine.

I slipped into her, surrounded by warmth unknown by any fire. Heat coursed through us both as our passion ignited and a rhythm set faster than rolling flames took the lead. From the moment this girl shot my tire, she pierced my soul, and I wanted nothing more than to be right where I was, inside of her, filling her, while she filled me with love.

THANK YOU

My gratitude in this crazy writing life continues to grow. I'd like to thank Amy Queau for her amazing support as a cover designer and Kiezha Smith Ferrell for her editing expertise. Additional hugs to Karen Fischer for her eagle-eyes after the fact, and Ella, Tammi, Amy, and Sylvia for final reads. Much love to authors who support other authors as friends and colleagues: Michelle Mankin, Michelle Lynn, and Mia Kayla – my girls!

My family continuously needs my appreciation, too. They let me live in my fantasylands and write my little stories, ignoring dinner, laundry, and them, occasionally. Thank you for letting me carve a little slice of me into my life.

CONTEMPORARY ROMANCES

L.B. Dunbar

The Sensations Collection
Small town, sweet and sexy stories of family and love.
Sound Advice
Taste Test
Fragrance Free
Touch Screen
Sight Words

The Legendary Rock Star Series
Rock star mayhem in the tradition of King Arthur.
A classic tale with a modern twist of romance and suspense.
The Legend of Arturo King
The Story of Lansing Lotte
The Quest of Perkins Vale
The Truth of Tristan Lyons
The Trials of Guinevere DeGrance

Paradise Stories

MMA chaos of biblical proportion between two brothers and
the fight for love.
Paradise Tempted: The Beginning
Paradise Fought: Abel
Paradise Found: Cain

Stand Alone

A rom-com story for the over forty.

The Sex Education of M.E.

MORE BY ELDA LORE

Modern Descendants
Hades (#1)
Solis (#2)
Heph (#3)
Triton (#4) – coming Fall 2017

ABOUT THE AUTHOR

Meet elda lore, the alter ego of the contemporary romance author, L.B. Dunbar. As elda lore, the classic world of mythology is captured and retold in modern tales, rekindling stories of endless love. Her enjoyment of fantastical romance began the moment the Beast gave Beauty a library. Continue to join her on her journey through paranormal romance where love is timeless.

CONNECT WITH
elda lore

Stalk me: www.facebook.com/eldaloreauthor
Search me: www.eldalore.wordpress.com
Read me:
https://www.goodreads.com/author/show/15614540.Elda_Lore

Follow L.B. Dunbar
Search me: www.lbdunbar.com
Pin me: www.pinterest.com/lbdunbar/
Read me: www.goodreads.com/author/show/8195738.L_B_Dunbar
Follow me: https://app.mailerlite.com/webforms/landing/j7j2s0
Hang with me: www.facebook.com/groups/LovingLB/
Tweet me: @lbdunbarwrites
Insta- me: @lbdunbarwrites

20052436R00124

Printed in Great Britain
by Amazon